WON'T LET YOU GO

A SLAYING LOVE NOVEL
BOOK 1

AMANDA SIEGRIST

Short Stories

Paint By Murder

Follow Me, Sweet Darling

Sleighville Novel

Dashing Through the Fear

Here Comes Chaos

Standalone Novel

The Danger with Love

Conquering Fear Novel

Co-written with Jane Blythe

Drowning in You

Out of the Darkness

Closing In

A DETERMINED DETECTIVE. A WOMAN REFUSING TO BEND. A KILLER WHO WILL MAKE SURE THERE ARE NO SECOND CHANCES.

1

WHISPERS OF DOUBT FLOATED AROUND. Too late to turn back now. She was no quitter.

Zoe inhaled a deep breath and walked into the bar, spotting her two best friends right away. Sliding onto a chair at a high-top table, she pulled down on her dress a little. Talk about short. Yet, sometimes a woman had to do something drastic.

"I swore you said you had a date with Mark tonight. What are you doing here?" Dee's eyes grazed up and down. "I don't think I've ever seen you in anything like that before."

Zoe resisted the temptation to tug down on the bright-red dress that clung to her body and stuck to her like a glove two sizes too small. The back of the dress only reached to the lower half of her back where the fabric scooped in a graceful curve. The top of the dress hugged her firmly, her chest showing way too much cleavage, which was exactly the point she was trying to make tonight.

Sexy. This dress screamed nothing but sexiness.

"Mark who?" Zoe turned to Rina. "What is that? Looks yummy."

Rina started to speak when Dee rushed in, her brow raised. "What did the douche do now? I still can't believe you're dating him."

Rina offered Zoe a small smile. "What happened?"

"Yeah, Zoe, spill already. Don't make Rina jump down your throat." Dee primped her bushy red, curly hair as her other brow rose.

Dee was in high form tonight. Zoe almost slumped in her chair when a man walked by glancing at her appreciatively. The dress was doing its job.

Take that, Mark.

She redirected her attention to Dee, who she knew wouldn't let anything slide. Rina, on the other hand, would wait patiently.

"Mark dumped me."

"That low-down, dirty douchebag." Dee pursed her lips as she shook her head. "What's with the dress? You never wear things like this."

"He said I had no sex appeal. I sleep with him one time, and he says I have no sex appeal. That man just totally checked me out. He did, didn't he?" Zoe pointed nonchalantly toward the man sitting at the bar who had walked past them.

Rina nodded. "You're gorgeous. Why wouldn't he? I'm sorry about Mark."

"Forget that douche. I told you from the beginning he was one." Dee raised her hand to flag down a server.

"Is there any man who isn't a douche to you?" Rina chuckled, then took a sip of her drink.

Zoe laughed. "Do I look silly?"

"You look like a woman I'd take home. If I swung that way, that is." Dee looked her up and down once again. "Damn fine-looking tonight, Zoe. Screw Mark."

A young blonde woman with more cleavage than Zoe would ever have walked up to the table. "What can I get you?"

"I think I'll just have a glass of wine. White Zin. Thanks." Zoe turned back to her friends when the server walked away. "And to think I was passing on drinks tonight because of him."

They worked for an accounting company, Mills, Murphy, & Young Accountants, each one a secretary to one of the partners of the company. They became fast friends when they went out one night for drinks to complain about their bosses. Going out for drinks had become a weekly ritual, regardless of whether or not they wanted to complain about work. Until she started dating Mark.

"Never again will I pass on drinks with my two besties for a man. He showed up at my house for our date and said, 'Zoe, this isn't going to work for me. There's no spark here. No sex appeal.' Then he left. I wanted to have a pity party. I decided he wasn't worth it. Then I saw this dress in the back of my closet. It's a little tight, but I feel sexy."

"Girl, that thing is damn sexy. I'll let Mark know exactly what he is tomorrow morning," Dee said.

Zoe laughed, knowing quite well, no matter what she said, Dee would do exactly that. Who cared? Mark deserved every nasty word Dee would throw at him. He didn't hold back when he broke up with her.

"I'm glad you changed your mind. You look great. That dress isn't something you normally wear, but it looks wonderful on you," Rina said softly as she swiped a lock of her beautiful auburn hair behind her ear. Utterly perfect. Everything about Rina was always perfect.

"It's, like, three years old. I bought it on a whim. I never had any intention of wearing it because, you're right, it's not me." Zoe pushed a strand of her sandy-brown hair behind her shoulder.

Why couldn't her hair be perfectly straight like Rina's? Or even overly curly like Dee's? Instead, she felt cursed with slightly wavy hair that never straightened completely or curled flawlessly.

She managed to add a few curls tonight that had yet to flatten. Tonight would be her night. Already one man had given her a glance. Perhaps one would ask her to dance. Anything to make her feel like she was beautiful. Worthy. Not sexless.

God, she hated Mark.

"Here you go. Would you like me to start you a tab?" the perky blonde asked as she set the glass of wine in front of Zoe.

A tab? They normally didn't do tabs when they went out. A drink or two after a crappy day at work and then back home. "Yeah, that would be great. Thanks."

Dee leaned back, her brow raised again. "You're gonna set the town on fire tonight, aren't you?"

Zoe picked up her glass. "Hell, yeah. Screw Mark. I'm going to enjoy my time with you two and maybe with a guy or two. I feel like dancing, drinking, laughing, and having a grand time tonight."

Rina picked up her drink and reached out. "Cheers, Zoe. You're beautiful. Don't let any man tell you otherwise."

Zoe raised her glass to Rina's and waited for Dee to join in. "To a good night with great friends."

WHAT THE HELL was he doing, sitting outside Rockster's Bar when his bed was calling his name? Zeke had no idea how they'd suckered him into doing this when he worked homicide, not vice. One minute he had been working on his latest murder case, about to wrap it up, and the next minute, he was finagled into going undercover to find a prostitute.

"You're the prettiest boy here, Zeke. That's what we need," Detective Tray Smith had said.

"I work homicide, man. I don't do vice. Where's Trevor? Isn't he the normal pretty boy you use?" Zeke had asked, glancing around with hope in his eyes that Trevor would magically appear.

"He's out with the flu. We got a tip that Ray-Ray has some of his ladies going to Rockster's tonight. This is big. He's the biggest pimp in this town and is constantly changing his operations to throw us off. We need his girls to put pressure on them to get Ray-Ray himself. Narcotics are even getting involved. Not only is he pimping, he's getting into the drug scene. We need you to get one of his ladies. You have a natural suave with women," Tray had said with a smile. "Your captain already gave the okay."

"Geez, you went to my captain. You owe me big for this."

"Great. You have to go looking distinguished and available. Maybe a hint that you want sex. Got it?"

"Whatever. I got this."

But did he really have this? Sure, he was good with the ladies, but that didn't mean he wanted to use his skills to catch a prostitute. Talk about feeling dirty. He never understood why women would want to earn a living that way.

Stalling. Not usually a word that popped into his vocabulary.

A go-getter. Persuasive. Confident. Those were good words to describe him.

Yet, he sat immobile, unable to move from the car. Sitting in a crisp, button-down white shirt and black pants that screamed money didn't even help boost his confidence to get out of the car.

How did he get suckered into this again? A smooth talker. Words flowed freely and easily. He should've been able to weasel his way out of this. Now, he had to use the right words to nab a woman.

He normally never lacked female attention, but lately, he had been suffering a long dry spell. Recently turning thirty-five, he came to the realization that maybe it was time to settle down and quit sleeping around. His sister had already been married for the past ten years and had three kids, and his mother constantly bothered him to start a family as well.

His skin crawled just thinking about settling down. Marriage meant commitment. Commitment meant one woman. One woman meant sex with the same woman for the rest of his life. Was he ready for that?

As his hand glided over the smooth steering wheel, he jerked. Damn, maybe he was finally ready. Or more like, he should be.

A clear night, the stars in addition to the streetlights gave a perfect view of the entrance to Rockster's. People milled around outside waiting for cabs or deciding what bar to hit next. Compared to the other bars around town, Rockster's stood out as one of the classier ones. Located in the heart of downtown St. Cloud near the university, it beamed with sophistication. Some college students ventured inside, but mostly, it attracted business-type professionals looking for a little downtime after a long day at the office or companionship. Probably the reason Ray-Ray picked this spot for his ladies.

The plan was for him to find his mark and lure her to a hotel near the bar. They already had a room set up. Normally, they would follow him and have cameras set up in the room. This time, he would go in solo and camera free. Ray-Ray had gotten smarter, training his girls to recognize a setup. Most undercover operations failed because the women realized beforehand what was in store for them.

The clock on his dashboard beamed eleven o'clock. No more stalling. Do the job. His bed was still calling his name. His latest case had drained his energy. This current situation wasn't helping him either.

With a quick step out of the vehicle and a slight pause to inhale, he cleared his mind of everything but the task at hand. The night tasted clear, yet his insides gurgled with unease. He'd have to take a shower when he got home, just like the times he finished with a murder scene that left him feeling disgusted. He'd probably attract a gorgeous woman tonight, but he'd still feel dirty after it was all said and done. A prostitute. That's all that needed to be said.

As he walked into the bar, his feet itched to turn back around. Definitely not something he wanted to be doing on a Wednesday night. People lined the bar, some sitting enjoying their drinks, others waiting for one. A peek at the dance floor showed it half-full with people swaying to the music. The tables and chairs scattered around were filled with people as well. Not one table appeared available.

He hadn't gone out in a while, and if he did, Rockster's wasn't his normal hangout. Another reason Tray wanted him for the job.

Damn Tray for knowing so much about him.

He slid into a chair at the bar that just emptied, asked for a beer, and scanned his surroundings. A few women sparked his interest, and he glanced over them appreciatively. As he paid the bartender and then took a swig of his drink, he didn't know which woman was his prize until his eyes landed on her.

One look and she took his breath away. She sat precariously on a chair at a high-top table all by herself. The bright-red dress clung to her delicate body and screamed, "I'm ready for sex!" Her legs, long and tan, asked to be felt up with a slow caress. His hands started to tingle with the urge to walk over there. The coldness from his beer seeped in, wiping that urge away.

Do the job. Getting hard as a rock over one woman with a simple glance wouldn't accomplish his goal tonight. Only make it harder.

Pinching the bridge of his nose, he shifted in his seat to relieve the pressure in his pants.

He couldn't help it. Just one more quick look.

Her creamy breasts gave a wonderful view, enticing a man to touch. To suck on a nipple and see the delight etch across her exquisite face. The way her hair fell upon her shoulders in waves undid him. Or the way her smile lit up the room, as if bright sunlight was beating down on him, heating his body up from the intense rays.

He started to throb painfully below his belt. Such a gorgeous woman within his reach.

Holy shit. Feeling this way about a woman, who in all likelihood was a prostitute. No way any normal woman would come in here all by herself looking like that.

Damn. He would have to arrest her. Could he be wrong? Could he turn this night into a successful operation nabbing another woman and get the number of *that* beautiful woman who made his blood sizzle?

He needed to eliminate her and find a new possible target. Glancing around, he eyed several other women who fit the perfect bill of a prostitute. But, unable to control it, his eyes kept gliding toward the woman he considered forbidden fruit.

Perhaps this was his libido telling him he had gone way too long without a woman. Tray had been wrong. He wasn't the perfect guy for this.

Sitting at the bar, nursing this beer wasn't going to get him anywhere. He needed to snag a prostitute. Officially eliminating the woman of his desire would be a good place to start. He could cross her off his list and continue to seek his target. Once the job was complete, he could come back and ask her for her number.

Get the job done first. Get personal second. And then his libido could quit complaining.

This shouldn't be any different from working homicide. Work with the evidence and start putting the pieces of the puzzle together to solve the mystery.

Taking another sip of beer, his eyes never wavered from her. She would look his way. One sultry glance usually did the trick. When she finally looked, if she didn't get the message, he'd lost his touch.

Zoe pushed a strand of hair behind her ear as a sigh escaped. What had she been thinking? When Dee and Rina left an hour ago, she should've left, too. After three glasses of wine, her mind hadn't been thinking. But her body had. She wanted a little more attention before the night ended.

The number of looks she'd already received, even a few dances with two different guys, meant the night had been a success. Thoughts of Mark had scattered into the never-gonna-care-again box. She proved tonight that she was sexy. That's all that mattered.

She didn't need a man. Of course not. She just needed to know she was sexy enough for a man. No need to sit here any longer. As she grabbed for her purse, her hands stalled on the strap.

Whoa. Talk about getting checked out by a man.

No words could describe the piercing stare that undressed her with ease. He had short, cropped black hair, slightly spiked in the front, enough to make her want to run her hands through the rest of his hair to make those ends stand up as well. He had a strong chiseled jaw, a smile that lit up her heart without effort, and deep-blue eyes. Even halfway across the room, his eyes mesmerized her. Pierced her right to the soul.

She'd never reacted to a man's simple gaze like this. Yet, as she stared back, his invitation was obvious. The way he looked her up and down, begged her to come to him. His eyes roamed her body from head to toe, stripping her clothes until she was completely naked.

That one look almost made her instantly wet. If she had panties on, her wetness would've probably pooled on them. Except, in one moment of insanity, she had decided to go commando. "You don't want your panty line to show, do you?" she had asked herself.

No, no, she didn't. She wanted him to have easy access.

Whoa. Where had that crazy, insane thought come from?

Sexy.

He made her feel utterly sexy.

The previous men who had approached her hadn't even come close to accomplishing her goal. She had obviously been waiting for him.

Without thinking about anything but his eyes reeling her in, she stood up from her chair with her purse and drink and sauntered over to him.

Since when did she know how to saunter?

Being brazen, something absolutely foreign to her, she

stepped right between his legs. Leaning into his lap, her lips curled with delight as his touch sent her body into flames of desire. The heat of his body was almost as exhilarating as his eyes.

"Hi."

He grabbed her by the waist, gently pulling her closer. The tingles of pleasure increased. "Hi."

She wanted to strip right there in the middle of the bar. What was wrong with her? She never acted like this. His eyes still held her transfixed. His warm hand soaked into her skin, heating her up beyond coherency. Words stalled. Hell, she didn't even know his name.

"Nice night."

"Nicer now that you've come to me," he replied in a silky tone.

Her heart melted right then, seeping to the ground in a heap of pleasure. His face was pure heaven, but when he spoke, his voice slid over her like honey. She drained the last sip left in her drink, then leaned closer as she set it on the bar. "Mmm. You smell good."

"You smell delicious yourself. What I wouldn't do for a taste of you."

Leaning away, she couldn't do anything but stare into his deep-blue eyes. Nothing needed to be said. She saw what he wanted. The same thing her body ached to have. How could one man make her want him so easily with one simple glance?

Those eyes. She couldn't explain it any other way. Acting like this—well, she didn't act like this.

"What I wouldn't do for you to taste me..." Did she actually say that? Utterly insane.

The lack of his touch would bring her back down to the

real world. Her heel rose to take a step back when his smooth, honey-silk voice slid over her—again.

"Then let's have a taste." He pulled her closer and nibbled at her neck. "I have a room not too far from here."

No question asked. She didn't need to be asked. The only thing she needed was the delightful nibbles caressing her neck not to stop. She pushed away, her body already missing his touch, and grabbed his hand. "Lead the way."

ZEKE PULLED her out of the bar, maintaining a firm grip on her hand. Soft. Smooth. Delicious. He imagined her skin felt the same all over. Letting her hand go would take a dozen men to rip him away. Ridiculous. Where was his control?

He had a job to do. He couldn't open his pants to a prostitute, and yet, he wanted to so badly. No doubt she was what he came for. The way she brazenly stepped up to him and spoke to him were clear giveaways. The evidence spoke for itself.

Damn Tray.

Never again. No one at the precinct would talk him into doing this again. His body couldn't handle it. Once he got her to talk money, he'd have to pull the cuffs out and take the worst cold shower of his life when he got home. This night just went from tiresome to unbearable.

The silky touch of her hand had him shoving her against the wall as soon as they stepped into the elevator, kissing her with an intense passion as they went up. Just one taste. Definitely against normal protocol when it came to a working girl, but her simple smiles directed his way couldn't keep him away any longer.

Suddenly, the door opened. He instantly let go, snatching her hand again, and made his way down the hall.

Allowing her to enter the room first was a bad idea. She sashayed inside, increasing the excitement coursing throughout. Even from behind, she made him weak in the knees. Her back was openly bare, revealing more creamy, smooth skin. Her ass could make a man die of happiness. The urge to grab it and squeeze compelled him to follow her.

As he walked farther into the room, the hotel essence screamed at him. Plain bed with a taupe comforter. Uninspiring paintings on the wall. Fake flowers in an off-white vase that wasn't centered on the table. The look of the room snapped him back into the ruse.

Talk price for services. Not ravish her body until they were both sated with pleasure.

His mouth started to open to begin the game when she dropped her purse to the ground and whipped around. Her delicate arms wrapped around his neck as her lips met his. Their tongues swirled together in unison. A moment of insanity hit him in the elevator, not resisting the urge to kiss her. This kiss ranked as sweet and delicious as the first one. Her hands brushed his neck with tiny tickles, then snaked their way through his hair.

Passion and excitement ran together like heavy waves. The sweet taste of wine she drank intoxicated him even further. Kissing her didn't seem like enough. He needed more.

Something subtle pricked his senses that a normal prostitute wouldn't act this way. Why weren't they talking prices? Or perhaps this was how Ray-Ray's girls performed. Tray had given him a breakdown of the operation beforehand. Ray-Ray's women were more sophisticated and high-end.

They gave their mark what they wanted, recognizing right away what the man's needs were.

He pulled away from her mouth. Conversation first. She obviously read his needs very well, but they needed to talk prices. Instead, she yanked his mouth back down, her movements forcing him to take a few steps back where he hit the wall. Her body instantly molded to his.

Grasping her body, wanting her more and more as each minute passed, he knew he had to stop this. He was a cop. The only reason he held this beautiful woman in his arms was because he was a cop. He would've never been out tonight if not for this damn assignment. He couldn't cross the line no matter how much desire, need, and want flowed through his veins.

Foolish. His behavior was completely foolish.

But his aching heat told him maybe he could help her get out of this life. She could do so much better than selling herself to men. His hands tightened around her waist at the thought of other men having their filthy hands on her, the jealousy strong and clear. The kiss turned hotter as the image wouldn't dissipate. No hands would touch her body unless they were his.

Just one little taste underneath her dress and then he would stop. He'd finish the job and work on piecing her life back to a better path. One that involved him.

His hands slid down her back to her ass, slowly sliding to the edge of her dress. His fingers brushed back and forth before reaching underneath and gliding his hands back up. The moment he felt nothing but pure skin, he lost all thought. Nothing else mattered.

He led her gradually to the bed as he pulled the dress up, barely losing connection with her mouth. By the time he reached the bed, he had peeled the dress off. One gentle push and she lay on the bed ready for the taking. Pure delight in every sense. Bare-naked—not even a silky, lacy bra needed to be removed by his skillful hands. His pants became tighter by the delicate picture lying in front of him.

He quickly removed his clothes and slid over her body, connecting them, skin to skin. Dying to do this the minute he'd laid eyes on her, he took her breasts and caressed them as he sucked on a hard nipple. She cried out in delight, arching into his body, pleading with him to take her already.

Her wet moisture clung to his tip. He could explode into oblivion at any moment. Slowly, he entered her inch by sweet, delicious inch, staring into her eyes the entire time. No words were necessary. Communication with a simple gaze. Rocking into her, he swiftly felt a deep intimacy he had never experienced before. Sex normally was a release, a fun way to connect with a woman. Not this overwhelming sense that he never wanted to let her go. He wanted to explore her body and find every spot that made her cry out with pleasure.

Moving closer, kissing her neck as they moved as one, they clung to each other as if this would be the last time they ever shared a moment. The intensity, the magic swirled around them, creating a beautiful scene he would never forget.

The moment would end soon. He knew it, sensed it by the tiny noises she made. The way she became louder and louder. Thrusting harder, she met him each time. Suddenly, she cried out, squeezing delightful pleasure out of him. He came with her to the height of oblivion, pushing one last time and spilling his seed deep inside her.

Without moving, Zeke lay on top of her, absorbing her beauty. The connection between them made his heart beat faster, made his mind into putty, made him realize he never truly knew what sex meant—until her. How in the hell had he lost control? He didn't even put a condom on.

Shit.

Just like that, glorious bliss turned into sheer panic.

He had sex with a prostitute. Not simple sex, but the best sex of his life. And they didn't use protection.

Shit, what did he just do? How in the hell did he forget he had a job to do? Clearly, she was better than he imagined.

Without a word, he quickly rolled off her, refusing to meet her eyes. He yanked his pants from the floor with a jerk and started to shove them on. How would he explain his actions back at the precinct?

Simple. He wouldn't. This never happened.

He couldn't arrest her now. His heart couldn't take it. Not to mention, his job would be over. Finished. Unemployed.

Sleeping with a damn prostitute. For the first time in his life, he had been thinking with the wrong head. He had to pay for her services rendered. She had to make a living somehow. The thought of pulling his wallet out had his fingers itching like he was swathed in poison ivy.

How did he help her out of this life and ask her out? How pathetic did that make him? He could lose his job over this and all he could think about was when he could see her next. His hand clenched around his wallet as he wrenched it out of his pocket. No other man would ever put his hands on her body again. Only him.

He turned toward her to see her dress back on. The sight of her made him salivate all over again. But he had no choice.

The wad of money hung in the air. "I'm not sure how much you charge, but this should be more than enough."

Her eyes darted to the money, then back at him. No

expression filtered anywhere. Not delight. No satisfaction. Nothing but hollow emptiness.

Without a chance to react, she slapped him in the face and walked out of the room.

His cheek stung from the blow, tiny pinpricks radiating down his jaw as he stared at the door.

Shit. The best thing to walk into his life had just walked out. And not as a prostitute as he'd originally thought.

2

_____

DEE SAT PERCHED on Zoe's desk while Rina stood to her side. Every day, all three of them converged to one of their desks for gossip. Except this time, Zoe didn't want to gossip that much. Her pride had taken a huge blow. She was still reeling from it.

"That skirt isn't short. It goes over your knees. You're crazy," Dee said as she rolled her eyes.

"It goes to my knees, not over them. I want to make sure it's appropriate for work, that's all," Zoe replied, tugging on the hem to try to lower the skirt below her knees.

Her self-confidence had dipped to the lowest it had ever been since the disastrous night with her mystery man a month ago. She still couldn't believe he had taken her for a hooker. When she told Dee and Rina about it, they couldn't either.

"Quit worrying about that other jerk. I know that's what you're doing. I saw Mark give you a few glances of regret. He's noticing the new you and is jealous," Dee said.

"Has Mark said anything to you lately?" Rina asked as she glanced around in case Mark happened to be near.

"No. Thank goodness. I want to forget him and sex man," Zoe said.

"Yeah, but best sex of your life. A little worth it?" Dee offered.

Zoe raised an eyebrow. "New subject. I have some good gossip. I had to work late last night because I didn't have enough time to finish some reports for Mr. Mills. I know he left earlier. I thought I was the only one here, until I saw him walk back in and head straight to Mr. Murphy's office."

Zoe waited patiently, knowing they would take the bait. For the past few weeks, Mr. Mills and Mr. Murphy hadn't been getting along. They were, in fact, avoiding each other like the plague.

"What was he doing in there?" Dee asked, the intrigue flashing within her eyes as she leaned forward.

"I have no clue, but he went on his computer. I even saw him remove a flash drive. He didn't realize anyone was still in the building until he saw me at my desk. He didn't say anything other than good night. It was all very strange."

"If Mr. Murphy knew he was in his office, he'd have a conniption," Rina said. "Where is Mr. Mills? I haven't seen him yet."

"I know. He was here late last night and never once told me he wouldn't be in today. It's almost lunchtime and he's never forgotten to tell me he wouldn't be in." Zoe glanced at his office as her brows dipped with worry.

"I want to know what he was on the computer for," Dee piped in.

"Ladies. We should be working, not gossiping. If Mills, Murphy, or Young were in, they wouldn't like it. Have any of you seen those three? There are some detectives here looking for Murphy or Young," Mark asked as his eyes slid over Zoe with an appreciative glance.

Zoe uncrossed her legs, trying to scoot them under her desk more as Dee said, "No. Goodbye, Mark."

Mark glared at her and walked away.

"Why are the police here? Maybe you should tell them about Mr. Mills," Rina said.

"And say what? It was weird, but not police worthy weird. Why are they looking for Mr. Murphy and Mr. Young? Why not Mr. Mills? Do you think everything is okay with him?" Zoe asked.

"I'm gonna go see what I can find out," Dee said as she slid off the desk and scurried away.

"I know Mr. Young was here earlier, but I haven't seen Mr. Murphy yet this morning either. Like you, I hope he's okay," Rina said.

Zoe gave her a knowing look as Rina walked back to her desk. The police might want to talk to her. Nerves suddenly flooded her bones. She had the urge to pee. Or perhaps the urge to escape. If she went to the bathroom, maybe her anxiety would lessen if the police came to talk to her. It wasn't as if she had done anything wrong.

She scrambled to the bathroom before anyone could stop her.

ZEKE AND HIS PARTNER, Detective Ben Stoyer, followed the office manager, Tori Black, to Mr. Mills's office. She informed them that Mr. Young arrived earlier this morning, but abruptly left an hour ago. Mr. Murphy had yet to show up.

They already knew where Mr. Mills was.

At home—dead.

His neighbor had called the police when he noticed

Mills's back door open. When the responding officers arrived, they found his body. The phone call from his boss had roused Zeke from a deep sleep, instantly putting him in an ornery mood, especially when he'd been having the same delicious, torturous dream he had every night.

Two gunshot wounds to the chest. No reports of gunfire the night before or early in the morning. Hard to pinpoint the exact time of death until they had the results of the autopsy, but Dr. Everly, the coroner, had approximated the time of death around ten or eleven last night. The neighbor had informed them he saw Mr. Murphy leave the house around eight last night. He also stated Mr. Mills hadn't been home yet, but Mr. Murphy banged on the door a few minutes before he finally gave up. It had been impossible not to notice with all the noise coming from next door.

Mills wasn't married and his parents were deceased, according to his neighbor. He was fairly positive Mills had no girlfriend or any other problems, except the recent fighting with Mr. Murphy.

"Here's Mr. Mills's office. His secretary, Zoe Sullivan, appears to have stepped away from her desk. She can help you with any of his work when she returns. I can go find her," Ms. Black said.

"We appreciate that. We would also like to talk to Mr. Murphy's secretary," Zeke said with a thousand-watt smile.

"Of course," she replied, smiling extra wide as she walked away.

"Really, man? Do you have to flirt with every woman that you talk to?" Ben said with a chuckle.

Since that failed prostitution night, Ben had assumed he was coming on to any female within a hundred yard radius. He told Tray and his team the night was a bust, but Ben had known better. They had been partners for seven years. Zeke couldn't lie to him. He eventually forced out of Zeke what had transpired and couldn't believe what he heard.

A straight-laced cop. One of a kind. Nobody could describe him any other way.

He would never jeopardize his job for a woman, and yet, he had.

Ben had agreed when he said maybe he had been wrong in his assessment of the situation. She probably hadn't been a prostitute. Knowing how he treated her was like a brutal punch to the gut. Screwed up the best thing that ever walked into his path. He had botched it from the beginning, even failed to get her name to try to fix his mistake.

"I would call that being friendly," Zeke retorted without making eye contact. Thinking about his mystery woman, or what Ben thought of him, wouldn't solve this murder.

"Whatever you say, man. You need to move on."

Zeke walked by him without a response as he stepped into Mills's office. Acknowledging what his partner was saying, or admitting the difficulty in moving on from what happened, would only make the pain worse.

Before, when he saw an attractive woman, he would glance over her appreciatively. Now, his eyes only saw his mystery woman. She had ruined him for life. Could the pain get any worse?

With their warrant, they hoped for better luck in finding some useful evidence in Mr. Mills's office. His home hadn't issued any clues, except the neighbor's description of Mr. Murphy. They desperately wanted to speak to him, coming up empty everywhere they looked. His wife had been unhelpful, informing them he hadn't come home last night. She even attempted to call him with no luck.

Her worry had been obvious to Ben and Zeke. Worry surrounded them as well. The difference: she was concerned for his well-being, while they were concerned he was their killer. They couldn't locate him or his car. All signs pointed to him running.

Zeke walked over to Mills's desk as Ben went to tackle the filing cabinets. As he shuffled through the papers lying around the desk, he wished for anything to jump out at him. Something to get his mind off the woman he needed to forget. He wanted to blame his partner for bringing her up, but he could only blame himself. She invaded his mind all the time. Normally, he could switch his emotions off until he arrived home where no one else could witness his torture.

"You can't be in here."

Zeke's hand froze on a piece of paper as the familiar voice slid over his body, igniting the one delicious memory he could never forget.

Impossible.

He slowly glanced up, grabbing a hold of the chair next to him as his knees threatened to buckle. The smooth leather of the chair did nothing to anchor him to the ground.

Smooth, silky skin. Sweet, delightful murmurs of pleasure as he had caressed, nibbled, and devoured her body. Pure beauty stood before him.

Dressed in an elegant white blouse and a black pencil skirt close to her knees, he wanted her as instantly as he had the last time. Her outfit wasn't as sexy as the red dress, but it didn't matter. Nothing would ever take the luscious craving he held for her away. His pants grew tight as he stared into her eyes.

"You! What the hell are you doing here?"

"I didn't know you worked—"

"Why would you? You thought I was a hooker."

"Hold on a minute. Is this the woman you slept with that night?" Ben interjected, glancing between them.

Zeke's face heated with embarrassment as his lips dipped into a painful frown.

Her mouth fell open as her eyes darted back and forth. "You're more despicable than I thought. Get out...or...or I'll call the police," she hollered again, pointing to the door.

"I am the police!"

Silence enveloped the room as they stared at one another. His stomach ached as his feet itched to move closer to her. The hurt in her eyes. Just as suddenly, they went round with shock as if a sudden realization came over her.

"You thought I was a hooker and then you were going to arrest me, weren't you?"

His hand released the chair from the death-like grip he had been exerting and averted his eyes. That's exactly what he had planned to do. How could he explain he'd read her wrong? That he regretted insulting her. He wanted a second chance.

"I can explain—"

"No need to explain. You were doing your job. Of course, perhaps you need more training to realize who is a hooker and who isn't and how far you should really go in that kind of situation."

"Would you quit interrupting me? Can we please talk about this privately?" He took a step forward, pleading with his eyes as best as he could.

She backed up and crossed her arms. "Why are you in Mr. Mills's office?"

His stomach twirled with disgust as her bottom lip trembled. Damn, she was on the verge of tears because of him.

"Great question. And let's all lower our voices. People are starting to stare." Ben gestured toward the office window where the blinds hung halfway down. "We need to look into Mr. Mills's files and ask you some questions about him. I'm assuming you're his secretary Zoe Sullivan?"

"Assuming is a very dangerous thing, sir. Look what happened the last time an officer of the law assumed something." Her voice sounded in control, yet the glistening in the corner of her eyes couldn't be mistaken. Tears were coming.

"You're right. Zeke's an asshole. Nobody's denying that. Please, what's your name?" Ben asked calmly, glancing at Zeke. His lips were pressed together, clearly showing his annoyance at being called an asshole. He couldn't deny the title, but damn if it didn't hurt his pride to hear it from his partner.

"Well, I am his secretary. He hasn't been in today, and I'm not quite sure when he will be," she replied, sucking in a small breath as the tears still lingered in her eyes.

"Why in the hell wouldn't you just say you were his secretary from the beginning? Clearly, my partner was right in his assumption," Zeke snapped.

Damn the sadness filtering in her eyes. Nobody to blame but himself. His heart would break if tears started to fall. And yelling at her wouldn't help his case any. Why was he yelling at her?

Fear could make a person do ugly things. Such a coward.

"Not my fault when people assume things," Zoe said with a shrug.

"When was the last time you saw Mr. Mills?" Ben asked.

"Why are you asking about him? Don't you work hookers or something? Is he involved in the sex trade of some kind?"

"Are you serious?" Zeke growled. What else did he expect her to think after the night they shared?

Zoe's lips tightened as her arms stayed curled together. At least the tears didn't look close to falling anymore.

Ben shook his head at Zeke and walked up to Zoe, blocking her view of him. "Let me clarify a few things so we can get back on track. I'm Detective Ben Stoyer, and that idiot over there is my partner, Detective Zeke Chance. He was helping that night on a prostitution sting. He obviously made an error in judgment. We don't work vice, but homicide. Mr. Mills was found dead this morning."

Zoe would've lost her balance if Ben hadn't been standing so close to her. He wrapped his arms around her waist and guided her to the chair in front of the desk. Zeke clenched his fists at the sight. No man should be touching her. Not even his partner.

The jealousy hit him like waves crashing against the shoreline. Only his hands belonged on her. And yet, he lost his chance. He had insulted her, degraded her, and cheapened what they'd shared. The feeling in his stomach reached new heights, making him search for the nearest trash can, which sat next to the desk.

"Take deep breaths, Ms. Sullivan," Ben said, glancing at Zeke.

Zeke couldn't help but glare daggers. The silent glint in Ben's eyes communicated how badly he'd screwed up. *Deal with the consequences.*

A knock on the doorframe made him avert his eyes.

"Ms. Black said you wanted to speak to me about Mr. Murphy. I'm Rina Chastain, his secretary." She walked inside the office and approached Zoe. "What happened, Zoe?"

Zeke crossed his arms like a petulant child. If Ben wanted to take over, he'd let him.

Ben looked away from him, shaking his head. He

looked at Rina and rocked back on his feet before finding his voice. "I'm Detective Ben Stoyer, and that's my partner, Zeke Chance. Mr. Mills was found murdered this morning."

"Oh, my. Zoe, are you all right?" Rina said as she rubbed Zoe's back, glancing between Ben and Zeke, her expression blank until her eyes landed back on Zoe.

Zeke wanted to shove everyone aside and embrace her in the fiercest hug imaginable. Rejection would be inevitable, possibly even more anger and tears directed his way, but anything would be better than the paleness covering her skin.

"Where's Murphy? Where is he?" Zoe clutched Rina's arm, the panic falling out in waves as she focused on Ben. "He's not dead, too, is he?"

"We were hoping you would know where he is, Ms. Chastain. His wife hasn't heard from him since last night. We can't say if he's dead," Ben replied, looking back and forth between Zoe and Rina.

"The last time I spoke to him was yesterday around five, right before I left," Rina responded softly, her eyes avoiding his gaze as she clasped her hand over Zoe's.

Ben crouched down to Zoe's level. Zeke wanted to growl for him to back off. "When did you last speak to Mr. Mills? Did he mention any problems he was having?"

Zoe looked at him, glancing briefly at Rina as well. She bit her lip, hesitating. "I worked late last night. I thought I was alone, but then I noticed him in Mr. Murphy's office. Maybe around eight thirty."

Zeke didn't think he could feel any worse until those words left her mouth. Shivers of fear wracked his body. Mr. Mills was likely killed shortly afterwards. Zoe may have been the last to see him alive.

"Did he say anything?" Zeke finally spoke, his arms falling to his sides.

She refused to lift her eyes his way. "He said good night. The entire encounter was strange. I'm pretty sure I saw him take a flash drive from Mr. Murphy's computer. They haven't been getting along lately. The tension's been very thick in the office."

"Do you know what was on the flash drive?" Her skin still held the pale hue. How could he focus on the facts when she looked like that?

"If I did, I would've said so," Zoe snapped as she dared a glance, glaring as she did.

"Can't we get along?" Zeke asked.

"You're a jerk," Zoe declared as she looked away.

"Whose ass do I have to kick for you?" a woman with crazy curly hair asked as she walked into the office without invitation. Her head instantly snapped between him and Ben.

"It's nothing," Zoe muttered.

"Oh, it's something. You rarely call anyone a jerk."

Rina ignored the question. "They're both detectives with homicide. Mr. Mills was murdered."

Her jaw dropped, then she composed herself just as quickly. "When was he murdered? And my instincts say it's the dark-haired one behind the desk. Why is he a jerk?"

"I'm not a jerk—" Zeke started to say.

"Yes, you are," Zoe yelled.

"Time out. Who are you?" Ben asked the woman as he stood up and gave Zeke a look to knock it off.

"Deena O'Malley, secretary for Mr. Young. Cop or not, I'll kick his ass for hurting my friend," Dee said with a death glare pointed directly at him.

"Did Mr. Young happen to mention where he was going?" Ben inquired.

"No. He left about an hour ago, quite quickly, actually. He received a phone call right before he left and it wasn't a happy one, that I know," Dee replied, refusing to remove her eyes from Zeke. Not much got to him, but he had to admit, the look she was giving him was somewhat unnerving.

Ben looked back at Zoe. "Are you sure it was around eight thirty that he was here, Ms. Sullivan?"

Zoe nodded.

"I still wanna know why he's a jerk," Dee said, the glare intensifying.

"Mystery man right in front of you, Dee. That's why he's a jerk. You called him one, too, and some other choice words," Zoe blurted as she tossed a shaky hand toward him. She jerked unsteadily from the chair and ran out of the room.

The pain that bled from her mouth had him taking a step to follow her when his partner put a hand out to stop him. "She needs some space, man."

"A cop, huh? Come on, Rina. We need to follow her before she does something rash, like cry over this jerk," Dee exclaimed as she turned to leave the room.

Rina slowly followed her, then suddenly turned back around. Her voice didn't rise once in volume. "She won't be back until you leave. I think it's best if you have any questions pertaining to Mr. Mills you ask me, Dee, or Ms. Black. She went out that night to heal from another man treating her unkindly. Instead of going home feeling better, she felt even worse. You have no idea what that did to her. Please leave her alone."

Rina didn't wait for a response. She walked out of the

room as if she'd hollered at the top of her lungs instead of speaking softly.

Her words resonated around Zeke. He had treated her like a prostitute, diminishing the beauty they had created. He'd give anything to turn back the clock and change his actions.

The best thing to walk into his life and he had royally screwed it up. He hadn't known her name until five minutes ago. Yet, he couldn't ignore the connection he felt that night. Something he had never experienced before.

It had felt right. Perfect. And he wanted more.

Zeke stared at the doorway, willing Zoe to come back even as he did, knowing that she wouldn't.

"She's right, you know. I don't think it's best to talk to her," Ben said, intruding on his thoughts.

"I know. We both need to cool down and then—"

"Maybe you need to let this one go."

"Why does everyone insist on interrupting me? I'm not letting her go. I was a jerk. I'll admit it. I made a mistake. A huge one. But she's special and I have to fix this. I can fix this." He said the last words as if they were true, but they didn't come out very strong. Defeat filled his bones as the seconds ticked by. How could he fix this?

"Let's search through his office and continue to track down Murphy. We have a murder to solve first. Unlikely relationship last."

"Thanks for the vote of confidence, partner."

"Hey, man, you dug yourself a deep hole. It's gonna take a lot of digging to get out of that one."

Ben was right. He hoped he wouldn't be buried alive by attempting to dig himself out. His heart throbbed painfully at the thought of losing. He had already spent an entire month without her. Complete torture. Living another day without her seemed impossible.

They searched Mills's office but didn't find anything suspicious. They took his laptop as evidence, eager for the crime lab to get their hands on it. Any tiny lead would make them happy.

As he walked out, he slipped his card onto Zoe's desk. He wrote his cell number on the back with, *please call. I want to explain*. His optimism had dropped when she fled the office, but he could still dream she might call him. He'd give her a few days and then drop in on her.

The word *quitter* wasn't in his vocabulary. A little time and space might help the situation. He had to explain what happened, his reasons for everything. Or at least let her know she wasn't cheap or dirty, but beautiful and sexy.

Revulsion swarmed around as he thought about what he did to her and the pained look in her eyes as she ran away.

How did he expect her to forgive him when he couldn't even forgive himself?

3

"I'M FINE, Rina. I promise. I'll be in tomorrow," Zoe said, ending the call with her before she could argue in her sweet, gentle way that always made Zoe cave.

If anyone would dare to come over, they would see how truly miserable she was. Her hair, tossed in a messy bun, didn't even see the shower today. Her grungy pajama pants hung low on her waist and the rattiest shirt she owned clung to her chest. Perhaps dressing better would've improved her mood, but she couldn't find the energy.

Three long days had passed since hearing about Mills's murder, Murphy not surfacing, and learning the name of her mystery man. She should be shocked about her boss's death and the other one missing, but she couldn't get beyond the surprise of running into Zeke.

Even his name was sexy. Damn him.

Every day she woke up determined to forget him. Yet, every night she went to bed dreaming of him. Her treacherous mind refused to flush him clean out of her system. She had found his card on her desk. Her initial reaction had her hand hovering over the trash can, but she never opened her fist.

No matter how horrible she felt, the disastrous emotions swirling constantly in her mind, she couldn't seem to toss his memory away. She still wanted him. Why?

And why hadn't he called her yet? Or dropped by the office? He said he wanted to talk. He couldn't possibly expect her to reach out to him first. It'd be a cold day in hell before that happened.

She went to work the first two days, but the effort to get out of bed today never came. Every time she glanced at Mr. Mills's empty office, her skin prickled with unease. Mr. Young had returned to the office the next day, never explaining why he had disappeared. He had told everyone he was cooperating fully with the police, as should they. When he learned more information about his two partners, he would let everyone know.

Dee, of course, yearning for suspense, insisted he was hiding something. Zoe had tried to drown out her voice, not wanting to think about it, and Rina had no opinion on the matter. What would it accomplish to contemplate what happened? Nothing. Except drive the fear further into her veins.

She still couldn't get the image of Mr. Mills walking away from her desk that night. The last time she ever saw him alive.

And the phone calls. They wouldn't stop. Two days ago, someone called her cell asking, "Where is it?" She had no idea what the person was talking about and hung up. Since then, she had received several hang-ups.

Today the person asked again, "Where is it? I won't keep asking." She had declared as confidently as possible, "I have no idea what you're talking about. Stop bothering me." She didn't wait for a response and hung up immediately.

She needed to voice it to someone. Telling Dee would create over-exaggerated suspense she didn't want. Telling Rina would cause concern she probably couldn't handle.

Earlier in the day, it had crossed her mind to tell Zeke. He was a cop, after all. He could point her in the right direction.

Then the image of him holding out a wad of money slapped her in the face. She never wanted to see him again. The image would then morph into the vision of his beautiful blue eyes as they undressed her with slow, deliberate strokes. She wanted to see him again.

Complete insanity. Back and forth, her turbulent thoughts went all day.

She threw her phone to the side and crashed against the couch cushion. Perhaps she should've told Rina about the calls. A quick glance at the clock told her it was nine o'clock. She should just go to bed. Of course, the minute her head hit the pillow and she closed her eyes, Zeke's handsome face would appear without effort. She would replay the night like a movie on a projector. Why had she acted the way she had when her eyes landed on him?

She stood up from the couch, determined to go to bed without thinking about him. Positive thinking. She would wipe him from her mind sooner or later. She merely preferred sooner.

The doorbell rang. The sound tripped up her feet, almost making her tumble to the floor. Could it be the person who had called her? Should she hide or check it out?

Exhaling a deep breath, she took a few steps toward the door. One quick glance. Flight-or-fight mode could kick in after that.

Two feet from the door, the doorbell went off again. She twisted her body to bolt, but froze. Nobody had ever called her a coward. Tentatively, she peered through the hole and jumped back as if the door had shot up in flames.

Running away seemed like a very good option.

Zeke.

Why was he here? How did he find out where she lived? No phone call from her should've been an obvious answer. Or was he here concerning Mr. Mills and Mr. Murphy? Either way, she didn't want him here.

He should've shown up sooner. Maybe she would've opened the door three days ago, but he had to take his time to find her.

Back and forth once more. Wobbling in her resolve.

She glanced through the peephole again, his bright-blue eyes glowing in the night air. The intensity. The magnetic pull they had. Why was he standing on her doorstep? For her? And if so, what took him so long?

She backed away from the door. No. She didn't care what he wanted.

She turned to walk away when he rang the doorbell again.

Screw it. Maybe another slap to his face would get the point across.

Flipping the lock, she swung the door open. "Go away."

Zeke put his foot in the doorframe as she tried to slam the door on his face. "Five minutes, please. If you still don't want me here, I'll leave. I won't bother you again."

So he wasn't here about her work. He had no right to be standing at her doorstep invading her space, her home, or her heart.

His beautiful blue eyes sucked her in. She jerked her gaze away. Always his eyes reeling her in.

"Fine. The clock starts now." She walked away toward the living room. He wouldn't be receiving any manners tonight. Not to mention, distance. Lots and lots of distance.

Because her body was already begging him to take her.

ZEKE HADN'T REALIZED his heart was pounding until she gave the okay to enter. One chance. That's all he had to make her see reason. To show her the connection they had, the power between them, and become a permanent fixture in her life. Any other result was unacceptable.

He followed her inside, her décor filling his soul with happiness. Sweet and beautiful, just like her. Why had he ever thought she was a prostitute? If he could kick his own ass, he would. Maybe he'd have Ben do it.

Soft colors painted the walls, matching the cream furniture perfectly. Knickknacks adorned the walls, shelves, scattered even along the floor. One might say random things, but it fit well within the surroundings.

Homey. Commitment. Those things punctured his heart, as he couldn't stop looking around.

Shit. He was ready for it all.

But only with her. No other woman would do. She had ruined him for any other woman.

"I like your place. It's—"

"You came here to talk about my home." She raised a brow and glanced at the clock behind the couch.

A ticking time bomb. Evidently, she was going to time him right down to the last minute.

He sighed. "Why do you always insist on interrupting me?"

"You never have anything to say that I want to hear."

"If you would quit interrupting me, maybe I would say what you want to hear."

"You haven't said anything worthwhile yet," she pointed out with a sweet grin. But there was nothing sweet in her eyes.

"This isn't why I came here." He sighed, running a hand through his hair.

"Shocker. Doing the opposite of what you originally meant to do," she replied, her voice cracking slightly. "I think you said enough. Please leave."

"Wait." He held his hand up and gestured at the clock. "I still have four minutes left."

Tears settled in the corners of her eyes. Her gaze shifted between him and the clock before she crossed her arms and nodded.

"I never meant to hurt you. I got suckered into working vice that night. I wish I never did."

His fingers itched to touch her. To swipe a tender hand across her cheek and prevent any tears from falling.

"I did go into that bar looking for a prostitute to bust. I can't describe why I thought you were one. All I know is that when I saw you, everything else left my mind. I forgot I was a cop. I also knew it almost didn't matter you were...that I thought you were...a prostitute."

Zeke paused. She still stood with her arms crossed and with no discernible expression. Damn. Was that a good or bad sign? The tears swimming within her eyes hadn't dissipated, and that was definitely a bad sign.

"I had planned to talk money before it went as far as it did. I obviously wasn't supposed to touch you like that. I made a mistake. Shit. Not a mistake sleeping with you. I don't regret that. I made an error in judgment, assuming you were a prostitute." He ran a hand through his hair, squeezing his eyes closed before opening them again. Where were his smooth words when he needed them? "Can we start over?"

Zoe stared at him with the same blank expression since the moment he started speaking.

"Please say something. Even saying that you want to go to my captain about what I did. I accept full responsibility for my actions. They were unacceptable. I never once thought you were cheap or beneath me. In fact, I kept rolling through my mind how I could save you from that life and ask you out on a real date. That's how strongly I felt about you. You're so damn beautiful."

Her silence singed the hair on his arms. Her frequent interruptions were much better than her silence. And he really disliked when she interrupted him. But damn it, silence was ten times worse.

His time was up. For now.

He'd simply make a new plan of attack. He wouldn't walk away this easily.

"So damn beautiful, Zoe. Even when you're interrupting me." He waited a few more seconds before sighing quietly and turning to leave.

"I won't go to your captain," she whispered. She let him walk away until he was halfway to the front door. Maybe he didn't hear her. That would be best.

He turned around. "You can. I didn't mean to insult you. I—"

"But you did. You cheapened something special to me and...it's embarrassing. I've never slept with a man without even knowing his name. Obviously, you're good at your job to make me want you like you did."

"My job was nowhere front and center in my mind. Not like it should've been," he said with a slow grin.

"Get that grin off your face. You threw money in my face as soon as we were finished," she yelled.

"And I regret that. You have no idea how special you are. I've never felt that close to a woman in my life. Trust me, I've had a lot."

"Not something a woman wants to hear—how many other women you've had." Why didn't she let him walk out?

"Shit. Okay, I don't do words well. What do you want me to say for you to believe me?" He took a step toward her as the pain etched into his features.

"How about 'I'm sorry.'"

"I said I was sorry." The confusion that fell across his face was almost laughable.

"You never once said those words."

He took quick, long strides toward her. The indecision of whether to flee or not pierced her heart. His touch did things to her that she couldn't control. When he gently grabbed her hands, the potency of his touch scorched her, sending the desire to her very core.

Damn him. How could she back away now?

"I'm sorry for not saying I'm sorry right away. I'm sorry for insulting you. I'm sorry if any of it made you cry. I'm not sure I could bear to see that. Most importantly, I'm so sorry if I ruined what I think is the best thing to ever walk into my life."

His eyes, as usual, pulled her in. His hands anchored him firmly to her. But his silky sweet honey voice with his endearing words was what undid her the most. How could she not forgive that?

Yet, he could hurt her like no other man ever had. He already had once. She shivered. From desire? From fear? Maybe a little of both.

The absurdity of the problem she faced. They were fighting like a couple in a deep relationship when, in reality, they hardly knew each other. That made it more confusing.

Perhaps he saw her uncertainty because he pulled her closer, holding her hands securely to his chest. The connection she felt that night seeped back into her body, urging her to get even closer. But the hint of doubt kept her from moving an inch.

"Can't you feel what you do to me? I have no control when it comes to you. You're sweet, sexy, and on my mind constantly. There hasn't been a day that goes by that I don't think of you. I want a second chance. Please take a chance on me."

Her heart melted again by his honey-silk voice. He said he didn't have a way with words, but he did. He had to know it. But did he mean what he said? Could she trust him not to hurt her again?

Pure bliss sucked out the rational part of her mind as his hardness pressed against her, urging her body to take him.

"I like it better when you interrupt me, not ignore me," he whispered.

"You always yell at me for doing it."

"Silence is worse. Do I get a second chance?"

"Detective Chance wants a second chance," Zoe said with a small smile.

His lips curled into a delicious grin. "I'll grovel if I have to. We might've met in unusual circumstances, but I don't regret it for one minute."

Standing so close and holding hands didn't help her concentrate and make a responsible decision. In spite of that, she didn't want to move away; she wanted to inch closer. Very bad idea.

"I have no sex appeal. Perhaps you're still trying to trap me."

"Don't ever say that again." Zeke let go of her hands and grabbed her around the waist. He pulled her as close as he could where his heat throbbed delightfully against her. "You have sex appeal. Feel me. Who hurt you?"

"You did." Her words barely left in a whisper.

He cupped her face. "My actions in that bed never once said you had no sex appeal. Who hurt you?"

"It doesn't matter."

His eyes became hard, yet his hands stayed gentle on her face. "Your friend Rina said a man treated you unkindly. Please don't tell me he said you had no sex appeal."

She bit her lip and tried to avert her eyes. Mark had no place in this conversation. Her own damn fault for bringing it up.

"He was wrong. Maybe you didn't hear me earlier. You're beautiful, Zoe," he whispered as he bent his head close to her ear, nibbling softly.

"I need to step back. I can't think straight."

"I think you should stay right where you are." He lifted his eyes back to hers as a devilish smile lit up his face. His hands slid down her back to her ass and pulled her closer yet.

She shivered at the contact, memories flooding her as she leaned closer. A soft buzzing sound interrupted the moment between them.

Her phone.

She stiffened briefly before moving away from his embrace and grabbed her phone from the couch.

"Hello." Her hands started to shake as the words filtered

down her spine. "Stop calling me." She hung up the phone and tossed it onto the couch.

"Who was that?"

She needed a drink. A strong one. Like whiskey or scotch or tequila. Too bad she didn't have any of those. She took a step toward the kitchen when he grabbed her arm.

"Who was that? Stop ignoring me."

His warm touch erased the fear that had swarmed her senses. She wanted nothing more than to fling herself into his arms and disappear into his warmth. She slowly turned around. "Which is it? Don't interrupt you, or stop ignoring you?"

"Both, damn it. Now answer me. You're shaking like a leaf. You think I can't feel that."

She glanced to where his hand still held her arm, then looked lower to her hand that was slightly twitching. Perhaps he hadn't removed every bit of fear. She probably needed his entire body wrapped around her for that.

"I don't recognize the voice. I need a drink. Do you want one?"

He nodded and let go. She would've preferred that he kept holding her, but distance would be better. Too bad her mind and body still couldn't agree.

Zoe pulled a beer out of the fridge for him and poured herself a glass of wine. Manners usually dictated she ask what he would've liked, but she lost that when the phone went off.

"What did they say? Why do I get the feeling this isn't the first time?"

She leaned against the counter as Zeke fidgeted from across the kitchen. The action was so unlike him. Seduction, anger, irritation, regret. Those were normal emotions she recognized from him. But this nervousness struck her as odd. Was he unsure whether to approach her or not? She wished he would. She needed someone else's strength. Hers seemed to be dwindling down as the night wore on.

Distance. Remember? Distance was better. Just because sweet words poured out of his mouth didn't mean he deserved her forgiveness yet.

"Two days ago I got a call with someone asking, *where is it*? Today, I had a second call repeating the same question and adding in, *I won't ask again*. Same thing just now. A few hang-up calls as well."

"Why didn't you call me? What do they want?"

"Why would I call you? I hate you."

He moved swiftly, almost like a blur. His beer slammed onto the counter as he anchored himself to her. A sigh of relief almost escaped when his body met hers. He pushed away her fear once again.

"You want me. Say it with me."

She squeezed her lips together to stop herself from laughing. The audacity. So damn cocky. "You're really full of yourself."

He grinned. "Your eyes glow when I touch you. I can see the desire." His smile dimmed as his hands tightened around her. "You need to tell me about any future calls. In fact, we should have all your calls traced from now on."

"It's probably nothing."

"Ignoring me. Ignoring problems. Is that something you enjoy doing?"

She slapped his chest. "You're a jerk."

"And you've already slapped me. Once was enough." He brushed a tender hand across her cheek. "Don't hate me, Zoe. Anything but that."

"You know it's difficult to think when you're this close to me."

"Which is why I'm this close to you. I'll do whatever it takes to get back into your good graces."

"You're despicable."

To distract herself, or perhaps she couldn't help herself, she started to lightly trace his chest. That should make him happier than the slap she delivered.

"I don't know what this person wants. Despite my better judgment, I debated calling you about it. I can't promise anything, or that I don't have reservations trusting you. You hurt me."

Zeke slowly grabbed her face and kissed her gently on the lips. "I will never hurt you again."

"I can't promise anything."

Zeke grabbed his beer and her hand. "Come on. We need to talk about these calls."

He led her back into the living room where she listened intently as he pointed out things she should pay attention to the next time the person called and answered questions as he tried to figure out her mystery.

His presence made the phone calls appear not as scary as she originally thought. But letting him stay the night couldn't happen. Her heart still needed mending. When she walked him to the door, the unasked question settled in his eyes. No matter how much her body craved to let him stay, her mind knew better.

Forgiving him was one thing. Forgetting what happened was another.

4

Zeke rubbed his eyes and tried to focus on the papers in front of him. He didn't sleep much the night before, wishing all night he was in Zoe's bed, not his—alone. Right before she kicked him out last night, temptation burned on his tongue to ask if he could stay. He couldn't rush her, though.

Baby steps. It was going to kill him.

He already tormented himself by giving her space, waiting three days to knock on her door. Torturous, but necessary. Continuing to take his time was just as crucial. But knowing how her delectable body tasted, knowing what he was missing, the agony couldn't possibly get any worse.

"So, what are these phone calls?" Ben asked as he leaned back in his chair.

The precinct was hustling and bustling. As usual. They worked for the St. Cloud Police Department—a nice average-sized town that Zeke and Ben both liked. They had enough murders and death to keep them busy, but not excessively so. They weren't going out of their minds with caseloads upon caseloads.

"I have no idea. Neither does she. I could tell she was scared. I don't like it."

Zeke brushed a hand over his face. Talking about it made it more real. Ignoring it made him irresponsible. He had acted like that last month. He'd never fail Zoe again.

"Just a thought. And listen to me before you cut in. She was there that night when Mills came into the office and took a flash drive from Murphy's computer. Maybe someone knows that. Maybe Murphy knows that. We still haven't located him. His wife hasn't heard from him. Maybe this person wants the flash drive."

Zeke jerked back in his chair as if Ben had punched him in the gut. They hadn't found any flash drive in Mills's house, car, or office yet. Knowing Zoe was the last to see him alive and doing something suspicious didn't sit well with him.

Shit. She couldn't be connected to this case. He refused to believe it.

"Okay. You can cut in now," Ben said.

Words failed him. What could he possibly say that would make it not true? Nothing, that's what.

"Your words suck."

Ben chuckled. "Not what I was looking for, but all right."

He sat back up and shrugged. "I helped her put a trace feature on her phone. She sent me a copy of her phone records. Of course, the number comes up blocked. I tried calling her cell phone provider hoping they could help identify the number somehow. That angle doesn't sound promising. Plus, they asked for a warrant."

"I know how much you like this woman. We'll figure it out. I'm glad it went well last night with her. You've been a mess."

"No, I haven't."

"Geez. Yes, you have."

"No, I haven't."

"Why are you arguing with me? You have. A huge mess."

"Define huge mess."

Ben arched a brow. "When are you seeing her again?"

Zeke shrugged. Since finding her again, his confidence had taken a leave of absence. They didn't make plans. He had no idea when he would see her again.

"She doesn't fully trust me." He had to earn her trust. He left last night with the worry still swarming his stomach like bees hovering around a hive.

"You have a way with women. You got her to give you a chance. That's more than I thought possible," Ben said with a teasing laugh.

Before Zeke could respond, Captain Ganderson poked his head out of his office and hollered, "Chance. Stoyer. My office, now."

"You talk. I'll play it cool in the background," Zeke said as they made their way to his office. "And could you give me a little more confidence boost concerning Zoe?"

"Ha! You don't know the meaning of playing it cool. I do seem to recall you flying off the handle constantly back in Mills's office with Zoe," Ben said, laughing. "That was me giving you a confidence boost."

Zeke glared at him. "You have a funny way of showing it. I can't help my reaction with her. It was the shock of seeing her again."

Ben gave him a smirk as they walked into the captain's office. The captain sat behind his desk, looking annoyed. "Close the door."

"What's up, Cap?" Zeke said with his best smile as Ben closed the door.

"Hmm, let's see. How about a prominent businessman in

our community was killed. Or how about another prominent businessman is missing. What do you have for me? Anything? You two are sitting at your desks talking like a bunch of girls," Captain Ganderson said with a strained breath.

"I wouldn't say we were talking like girls. We weren't getting that detailed about things. I—"

"Shut up, Chance. I don't care what you were yapping about. What I care about is solving this murder. What do you have for me?"

"Dr. Everly confirmed time of death between ten and eleven o'clock that night, but he was unsure of the proximity of the victim from the shooter because there was limited gunpowder residue on the wounds. Suggests the shooter was far away when they fired the weapon, or used a silencer. No reports of any gunfire that night. So, we're leaning towards a silencer. Ballistics came back with bullets from a .40 caliber handgun. No matches yet tying the weapon to any other crimes. Feels kinda like a professional job."

Zeke paused, waiting for the captain to interrupt him. People seemed to enjoy doing that lately. When he didn't, he continued.

"Nothing strange in his finances so far. He wasn't dating anyone. The only problem we found is the mysterious issue between Murphy and him. Murphy was last seen leaving Mills's home before Mills came home. Murphy's wife hasn't been very helpful. Although, she did say he had been acting strange lately and refused to talk about the issues at work. We got a search warrant for both of their computers at home and work—still going through all that. Waiting for forensics to get back to us. Also checked Murphy's finances. Nothing strange popped up. Young, the other partner in the company, has been somewhat cooperative giving us full access to the business, but we're still looking into every-thing. We think he's hiding something. His secretary reported him abruptly leaving the morning Mills was found after receiving a phone call. He was quite evasive about it and wouldn't divulge who called or where he went when we asked. So far we haven't—"

"You're not telling me anything I don't already know. What new information do you have?" Ganderson finally interrupted him as he leaned forward, resting his elbows on the desk.

Zeke shrugged. "That's all we got, Cap. We're not any closer to finding Murphy. We—"

"That's not what I want to hear, Chance," Ganderson said, glancing at Ben to see if he had anything to add.

Ben shared a look with Zeke, then kept his mouth shut when Zeke subtly shook his head. "Mills's secretary might be connected to this case. She, as far as we know, was the last person to see him alive when he stopped at the office late that night. He took a flash drive from Murphy's office. She's been getting phone calls from someone asking, 'Where is it?' We think it could be related to the case, sir."

As soon as that slipped out, it felt real. Too damn real.

That's what the phone calls were about. Why didn't he see that last night when she told him? Because he'd been too busy groveling and attempting to feel her up, that's why. Put him in the same room as Zoe and he lost all train of thought, including the fact he was a cop and should be acting like one.

"Keep me posted. Get out and get to work. No more dallying around," Ganderson said as he pointed for them to get out of his office.

Ben walked out first with Zeke following. As soon as they were out of earshot range, Zeke muttered, "Thanks for the back up there, buddy. You made me talk the entire time."

"Hey, man. You said you were gonna play it cool in the background, and when you didn't, I decided to follow your lead. I wanted to mention the part about Zoe, but you told me no. You seemed to be handling it well," Ben said as he laughed.

"Really? He kept hollering at me and interrupting me. What is it with people interrupting me lately? I—"

"It's just so easy to do. I mean, look at your face. It's a classic look. I'm sure it turns Zoe on like nothing else," Ben snickered.

"Shut up. Don't talk about her that way. I'll deck you," Zeke said with a mock fist in the air.

"So you're saying it does turn her on." Ben laughed and held up his hands as Zeke took a step toward him. "Come on. Let's get lunch and work on her phone records. I know you hate hearing it, but the calls have to be related to our case. We should also head down to the lab. See if anything popped up from the computers yet."

Zeke plopped down at his desk. "I hate to think the calls are related to this case. I don't think I can handle it if she's in any sort of danger. Knowing someone's bothering her, regardless of the reason, makes me want to beat the living shit out of them."

"I can help you if you'd like. You have a lousy right hook."

Zeke aimed a glare at him, although it wasn't as strong as it could've been. He knew what Ben was doing: trying to distract him. Trying to make him feel better. Trying to make light of a situation that could possibly turn deadly for Zoe.

Coincidence? It couldn't be.

Ben sat down at his desk and leaned back. His eyes softened. "We'll figure it out before anything else happens. She'll be fine."

Zeke nodded. She had to be fine. He had just found her again.

He reached for his phone, then froze. Damn it. He forgot to get her cell number last night. Would she even talk to him if he called her office line? He wanted to hear her voice to know she was safe.

He continued to reach, but instead of grabbing the phone, he grabbed the papers he had been looking at earlier. He was still on shaky ground with her. Slow and easy. Upsetting her now could be very disastrous.

They hadn't made any plans last night, but nothing would stop him from seeing her tonight. She didn't know it yet, but he'd be knocking on her door again.

"ARE you sure you don't want to go out for a drink? I know I could use one. We can talk murder, intrigue, and suspense about the office," Dee said dramatically, feigning as if she were smoking a cigarette like an old-time detective.

Zoe gave Dee a weary look. Going home and curling up in bed with Zeke sounded like a much better plan.

No, it didn't.

Yes, it did.

Ugh, her rebellious mind still couldn't agree with her body. She wanted him and she shouldn't.

Take it slow. Even though they had already devoured each other with complete abandon, they had to take it slow.

Without notice, she saw perfectly before her his beautiful blue eyes and sweet voice. Oh, to actually see it for real in front of her. She'd probably pull him into a closet and have her wicked way with him.

Her treacherous body was so bad. Thank goodness her mind was still intact.

Good thing they hadn't made any plans. Some space to clear her mind of the situation would be good. She couldn't think straight when he was near. And when he touched her. Forget it. All coherency went kaput.

"Yo, earth to Zoe," Dee said, waving a hand in front of her face. "Girl, I know where your thoughts were. Remove that douche from your mind."

Zoe's cheeks flamed with heat as she inched away from Dee. "I'm not into the whole intrigue thing. Dealing with it at the office is enough for me."

Dee raised a brow as if she couldn't believe Zoe was ignoring the douche comment. Zoe didn't want to talk about Zeke, especially when she was so confused over what to do about him.

"You have it easy. Your boss is still around. My job has become stressful with Mills gone. Rina doesn't have it easy either, with Murphy still missing."

Rina nodded. "I'm worried about you. Those phone calls. Are you sure that trace feature will work?"

Zoe avoided eye contact with Dee as she replied to Rina, "Zeke said it would. I wish that part would disappear."

"Oh, so we agree." Dee puckered her lips as she propped a hand to her hip.

"The calls have been driving me insane," Zoe said as the hair on her arms prickled with unease. More like driving her into fear.

"I was talking about that jerk."

"Let's go for a drink, Dee, but I don't want to talk about

work. Zoe's right. It's been stressful. I'm worried about Mr. Murphy. He's a nice man," Rina said to Dee.

Dee whipped her head at Rina. Zoe let out a soft breath. When Dee felt strongly about something, she refused to let it go.

"He's a little douchey to me," Dee said with a smirk.

"You think most men are douches," Rina said as she laughed lightly.

"You're so right, Rina. I also think Zeke what's-his-name is a douche. Why are you giving him a chance? You do remember how he treated you, right?" Dee snapped at her.

Zoe winced. "You can't just let this go."

Dee shook her head and waited for Zoe to tell her something she couldn't. She wasn't ready to slam the door on his face. She should, but she wasn't ready.

"I know what you're saying, but you weren't there last night. I don't know what comes over me. My mind tells me I'm crazy for even giving him a chance and my body says do me now. If he hurts me again, I'll never forgive him. That I know."

"You're crazy. I'm telling you," Dee exclaimed, then paused slightly as her eyes glittered. "Was he that good?"

Zoe averted her eyes, staring at her desk for a moment. She looked back at Dee with a quick glance to Rina and smiled. "You have no idea. All he has to do is look at me for a quick minute and my body screams for him to take me. Then when he actually touches me, I lose it altogether. How can I pass up a chance like that? I know better than to completely trust him yet."

Rina gave her a sweet smile. "If that's what makes you happy, then you should. You have to admit, Dee, what Zoe told us earlier about what he said. It was romantic."

"Yeah, romantic all right. He's good with words. Not a

good sign. Player written all over that. I'll kick his ass if he hurts you again," Dee said, refusing to remove the hard glint from her eyes as she stared at Zoe.

Zoe rolled her eyes. "Trust me, Dee. I still have reservations. Don't think I don't."

Before Dee could reply, Mark appeared around the corner, approaching them without hesitation. "Can I have a word with you, Zoe?"

"Where have you been this afternoon, Mark?" Dee demanded.

"Last time I checked, I didn't answer to you, Dee—a mere secretary," he retorted with disgust.

"You think you're a big bad accountant and above me, do you? Maybe you killed Mills to get his office," Dee snapped back.

Mark looked taken aback by the comment and muttered to Zoe, "Forget it, Zoe. I don't appreciate the company surrounding you right now. That was rude and uncalled for."

Mark didn't wait for an answer as he turned back around and walked away, stomping his feet like a petulant child.

"What was that about?" Rina asked.

"What did I do?" Dee asked innocently.

"You don't think Mark really killed Mr. Mills, do you?" Zoe asked, shocked.

"Of course not. But he came in here charging like a bull and I didn't like his attitude. He pretended like Rina and I didn't exist and basically demanded your attention. You have one douche to deal with already. You don't need two of them," Dee replied matter-of-factly.

"You had me worried there for a second that he could have," Rina said.

"Please, Rina. He doesn't have it in him to kill another

person. He's a wimp." Dee scrunched her hair, puffing it out more, even though it didn't need it. "I'm getting a drink. Who's joining me?"

"I'm going to take a nice bath or read a book or dream about a sexy man I shouldn't," Zoe said, refusing to make eye contact with either of them.

"One drink and no office talk," Rina replied.

"Let's go. This day was over, like, an hour ago." Dee took the lead as the other two followed her.

Zoe daydreamed the entire drive home. How delightful would her night be if Zeke came over? Too delightful. Too tempting. And oh so wrong. She had to maintain her strength.

Curling up on the couch sounded nice. Alone. That would be the safer option.

When she finally got home twenty minutes later, she couldn't seem to remove the silly grin from her face. It may be wrong to think about him, but it made her feel good inside. She'd feel even better if he came over. Maybe she didn't need to keep her distance that much.

He asked for a chance, and she would make him work for it. He had to prove to her that he meant what he said. No way would she make it easy. He deserved that for making her feel the way he had.

Could she stay strong? It was so hard to resist him.

Zoe slammed her car door shut and walked quickly up the pathway to her front door. Her steps wobbled as she neared it. The door stood slightly ajar. It wasn't noticeable from the street, but very obvious as she got closer.

Who would break into her house? Was the person still inside?

She certainly wasn't going to find out for herself. Taking a deep breath, she backed up a few steps and then raced for her car. The clicking of the locks boomed loudly in the small confines of the car.

Stay calm. What should she do?

Call Zeke—duh. He's a cop.

She opened her purse she had been clutching to her chest and started to dig through it. Where in the hell did his card go? She had resisted the permanent feeling of adding his number in her phone. No more. That damn number would be inputted into her phone immediately. After she called him, of course.

Deep breaths.

Too much crap. She opened her purse wide and dumped everything out on the passenger seat. Raking her hands over everything, she finally found the card tucked between an old grocery list and a receipt.

She started to dial his number and paused. Her fingers weren't hitting the correct numbers. The tremors were consuming her. After three attempts, she managed to hit the right numbers.

Stay calm. Zeke would fix this.

What happened to not trusting him?

Perhaps she didn't with her heart, but she did with her life. That made no sense. But it all felt right as the ringing echoed in her ear.

"WANNA GET A BEER TONIGHT?" Ben asked as they cleaned up their desks to call it a day.

They never liked to leave clutter, enjoying the satisfying feeling of coming in each morning to a clean desk. A clean desk meant they were making progress, even when they were nowhere near solving a case sometimes. Weird how they both thought that. One of the many reasons that made them perfect partners.

"I'm heading to Zoe's." Zeke didn't glance at Ben. He didn't want him to see the anticipation of seeing her, or the fear she changed her mind about him.

"I didn't think you had any plans with her."

"What made you think that?"

"Your silence earlier today was a good indicator. Maybe a day or two to think things through would be good for her."

"Are you crazy? I can't give her time to think I'm not good enough for her. I gotta stay strong and in her face." Zeke stood up as he shoved a pencil into his desk drawer.

"I don't know, man, she—"

"That's right, you don't know shit. Don't like being interrupted, do you?" Zeke asked as Ben frowned at the interruption.

His phone started to ring. Pulling it off his belt, he waved it in Ben's face. "Hold your wonderful response I'm sure you have. Phone's ringing."

"Gee, is that what that device does?" Ben rolled his eyes as Zeke answered his phone.

Zeke froze as the terrifying words slid down his spine. He glanced at Ben, who had stopped what he was doing when he noticed Zeke's pained expression.

"Calm down, Zoe. I'll be right there, honey." Zeke grabbed his car keys and motioned for Ben to follow him out of the building.

"Drive down the block and wait for me to get there," Zeke answered her. "I'll be there in a few minutes. I promise."

Zeke practically ran out of the building with Ben on his heels. As they got into Zeke's car, Ben noticed he hung up with her, asking, "What happened?"

"Someone broke into her house," Zeke said as he turned his lights and sirens on and stepped on the gas hard.

"The flash drive. You know it as well as I do," Ben replied.

Zeke glanced at Ben. Why did they have to think alike so much? Damn this case. And damn the person who dared to try to hurt Zoe. Over his dead body. She would hate him by the end of the night.

Because he didn't know how he would be able to leave her alone. He'd argue with her this time about kicking him out.

Zeke made it to her house in under ten minutes instead of the normal twenty. Before pulling into the driveway, he noticed her car about a block down. She didn't wait for a signal from him because she started her car and made her way to them as they exited his car.

"Stay in your car. We'll check the house out," Zeke said, ignoring the fright in her eyes. This was one time he needed his complete focus.

"You could get hurt."

"Zoe, honey, this is my job. Go to your car, please."

Zoe nodded and turned around. He waited until she got back in her car and locked the doors, then looked at Ben as he removed his handgun. "I'll take the front. You take the back."

Ben nodded and proceeded around back.

Zeke walked up the front steps, stepping carefully toward the door, and eased it open with his foot. He entered, his heart pounding. He had walked into many different types of situations. Crime scenes. Traffic stops. Responding to calls without knowing whether the suspect was armed. Hell, a bank robbery one time.

His heart never pounded like it did now.

He jerked at the sight in front of him. Unlike the night before where sweetness and beauty met his eye, now hatred and destruction glared at him. To his right, the living room sat shattered into pieces, her couch torn up, knickknacks scattered and broken, pictures on the wall thrown to the ground. The intruder left nothing untouched.

He continued his sweep of the house, meeting Ben near the kitchen. Ben signaled his area was clear. They made their way to the stairs, moving stealthily, and met the same treatment of destruction as they reached the top. Room by room, they searched for an intruder, coming up empty.

Ben met Zeke in the hallway, holstering his weapon. "She's going to freak when she sees this. It looks like whoever did this destroyed everything."

"They were definitely looking for something. It feels personal as well," Zeke said, as he clenched and unclenched his hands. He couldn't wait to get his hands on this person and rip them apart. No one would touch her. Not in harm. And definitely not intimately. That was his job.

"Can you call in a forensics team? I need to check on Zoe," Zeke asked.

Ben nodded and pulled out his phone.

Zeke walked back outside. Zoe still sat in her car, staring at the house. The moment she saw him exit, she darted out of the car before he stepped one foot off the porch. He didn't hesitate the moment she was within arm's reach. He pulled her tightly into his embrace.

He breathed in her delicate scent, a mixture of vanilla and lavender. Holding her felt perfect. Meant to be. Could she feel it as well?

He didn't want to do anything but hold her. Ignore everything around them. Of course, he couldn't do that. He pulled her back slightly.

"No one's in the house. We have a forensics team on the way." Zeke paused, waiting for her to look at him. When she didn't, he put his fingers under her chin. The fear still lingered in the depths of her eyes.

"You can't go in there. It's going to need a lot of cleaning and...whatnot. I'm positive they were trying to find whatever they think you have."

Zoe gasped. "So it's the same person who's been calling me? I don't have anything."

Zeke cradled her cheeks and kissed her lightly. To comfort her, but also to calm himself down. "I don't know that for sure, but I'd bet on it. I'm generally not wrong." Zoe gave him a smirk at that comment. "I said generally, not never."

"You can't stay here tonight. I'm not even sure I'm comfortable with you staying here alone until I figure it out," Zeke said, asking his unspoken question with his eyes that he was afraid to say with words.

"Where am I supposed to go?" Zoe said with a frazzled tone as she brushed a strand of hair behind her ear.

Clearly, he didn't plead with his eyes well enough. Or she refused to acknowledge what he wanted. Probably the latter. She didn't trust him.

"Zoe, I want—"

"Hey, Zeke. What do we have?" Susan asked, smiling brightly as she walked up the pathway holding her crime scene kit.

Zeke frowned. This had to stop. Now everyone seemed to cut him off. Did a memo go out around work to dig it in? He could actually see Ben doing something like that simply to annoy him. It wouldn't be his fault when he exploded.

He stepped away from Zoe, but still stood close enough to reach out to her. "Break-in. Anything destroyed or appears to have been touched, fingerprint it. I want to know immediately when, or if, you find anything useful for me."

"Is this related to your murder case you're working on?" Susan asked, as she started up the porch, obviously oblivious to his annoyance.

Zeke couldn't look at Zoe. He'd probably see the fear increase. "Probably. ASAP, like I said."

"You got it," Susan said with a thumbs up and proceeded inside.

Zeke took his time turning back toward Zoe. Instead of fear, as he expected, nothing but raw anger poured from her features.

"When were you going to tell me this was related to Mr. Mills's murder? That's what she was referring to, wasn't it?"

"I was going to tell you. I—"

"When were you going to tell me? Next week," Zoe snapped.

"Quit interrupting me."

"Quit assuming things about me."

"What did I assume this time?" He brushed a hand through his hair, grabbing on the ends slightly.

"You think I can't handle it. That I'm scared or something."

Zeke laughed. Her eyes lit up with flames. He'd screwed up again by laughing. But damn if she hadn't read his mind.

"You are scared. You're actually going to deny it. I think—"

"I think you're still a jerk."

Zeke's brows dipped as his lips became tight. "You never listen to me."

Zoe shrugged as if she didn't care, yet she couldn't hide her fear. The anger displayed well in her face, but the shaking in her hand told him everything.

"They most likely want that flash drive you saw Mills take."

"Well, I don't have it."

"I know that. Can we please talk about—"

"You two seriously need to learn how to communicate better. I could hear you both hollering from inside the house," Ben said, walking out of the house, smiling. His smile grew as Zeke let him know with one look exactly what he thought about him interrupting.

Oh, yeah. He could definitely see Ben telling people to mess with him for the fun of it.

Deciding not to pay attention to him, Zeke turned to Zoe. "Look, I see Officer Spencer pulling up. Stay with him, by your car, whatever. Just don't leave the area. Ben and I have to canvas the neighborhood. We can finish this conversation later."

"Not sure we have much left to discuss." Zoe turned around and walked back to her car.

What did she mean by that comment? He hoped it wasn't what he thought it meant.

"You're never gonna stay in her good graces yelling at her," Ben said.

"Is that all the wonderful advice you have?"

"You want more? I have plenty up my sleeve," Ben said with a chuckle.

Zeke shook his head and walked away to relay what was happening to Officer Spencer.

They started knocking on doors, hoping for a lead of some sort. It took about thirty minutes to walk up and down the block, interviewing the few people who were home. Nothing panned out. Nobody saw or heard anything.

"We need something. This case has given us nothing but

aggravation." Zeke walked with long, quick strides, eager to get back to Zoe.

"Something will pan out soon. It always does, usually," Ben said.

"It's either always or it's usually. It can't be both." He jerked his hand toward her house as his strides became faster. "Why is she laughing? What is Spencer saying to her?"

"You need to get laid. Your disposition is seriously lacking. Oh, right, you can't seem to control your temper with her. What are you to do?" Ben said, laughing.

"You can't control yourself with the jokes, can you? He better not be hitting on her. Is he hitting on her?" He groaned when he saw a car pull up with Dee and Rina exiting. "Great, just what I need. Two people who hate me."

"Temper. Don't use it. That quiet one scared me more than the loud one," Ben reminded him as he walked in a completely different direction. Zeke glared at Ben's back. Now he had to face them alone.

Deep breath. He could do this.

"What did you find?" Dee demanded.

"Nice to see you again, too," Zeke said.

"You didn't answer my question because..." Dee waited for him to answer.

He cocked a brow. Why couldn't he be nice? The best way into Zoe's good graces could possibly be through her friends.

"I have no answer yet. We're still working on it."

"Can she go get her clothes?" Dee asked.

"Why?"

"Because, Einstein, you told her she couldn't stay here tonight, and she needs clothes to wear tomorrow," Dee snapped.

"Where are you staying, Zoe?" He turned toward her. Not much was written on her face. Not anger, nor fear.

Before Zoe could respond, Dee blurted, "With me. You honestly don't think she's staying with you, douche man. Do you?"

"I don't think she should be staying with you either," Zeke said, grinding his teeth as he tried not to yell.

"I certainly won't hurt her like you have. I don't think you should be given the chance she's giving you. I want you to stay away from her," Dee said firmly, shoving her finger against his chest to make him move back.

Zeke barely budged an inch, although, his hand flinched. Sure, he could arrest her for pushing a cop, but she was only protecting her friend. He could respect that. Not that he wanted to. And while he might deserve every word she said, he refused to back down.

"Yeah, and how are you going to protect her when they come for her at your place?"

Silence filled the circle. Even Dee became speechless, as her lips froze in place to look like a fish blowing bubbles.

"Do you think they will follow me wherever I go?" Zoe asked, finally breaking the silence.

Zeke could act like a devil and knew what worked for him. He stepped closer and grabbed her hands. "Yes. I don't want to think about what could've happened if you had been home. They want something that they think you have. Just because they couldn't find it in your house doesn't mean they'll stop. I keep saying *they*, but it could be Murphy. He's our prime suspect right now."

Zeke pulled her even closer and bent his head toward her ear. "Stay with me, Zoe. This...whatever is between us... you're important to me, even if I have a hard time showing it sometimes."

He kissed her neck, hoping to erase the tiny tremors consuming her body. The longer he held her, the more he could feel them slowly diminishing. Keeping physical contact always seemed to be the trick to calm her down and make her see things his way.

Yeah, that did make him kind of despicable. But he had to use what worked to get his way. Losing her was not an option.

She pushed away, but not entirely out of his arms, for which he was grateful. "How long should I stay with you if I choose that option?"

"I knew it." Dee shook her head as if the idea was ludicrous.

"I don't want to fight with you, Dee. I only want what's best for Zoe at the moment. Do you want to see her hurt? Because I don't." He clutched Zoe's waist as he turned toward Dee.

Dee poked him again in the chest. "I have seen her hurt. By you."

Rina laid a hand on Dee's shoulder as if she could tell how much he hated when she touched him. He was so close to slapping handcuffs on her for it.

Or maybe he deserved it.

Yeah, he deserved it. He hurt her.

"Zoe, you're probably safer with a cop until things are figured out. I don't know what they know, but I have to disagree about Murphy. I can't imagine he'd murder someone let alone burglarize someone's home," Rina said softly.

"Trader," Dee muttered under her breath as she shared a look with him. "Rina has a very small, minuscule point. Not about Murphy. He's a douche. I don't like it, but you better keep your paws off her while she's there."

"Do you mind if Zoe speaks for herself? I'm pretty sure she's quite capable of it." Zeke looked back at Zoe, squeezing his hand around her waist as a tremble rippled throughout her body.

"Okay. A day or two," Zoe whispered, sharing a look with her two friends. What that look meant, he wasn't exactly sure. Hopefully, one in his favor.

"I'll go grab you some clothes. It's still a crime scene." Zeke let her go as she nodded in acceptance. She didn't need to know how bad it looked. That could come later. One problem at a time.

Mission accomplished. That's all that mattered. He now had her in his domain. He could see complete forgiveness on the horizon.

Or maybe that was wishful thinking on his part.

5

"DEE, you have to lay off a bit," Zoe said as she turned away from watching Zeke walk inside her house.

"Not a chance. If you're not going to protect yourself, I'll do it for you."

Zoe shook her head, knowing Dee meant well, but she couldn't possibly understand the way he calmed her down with one simple touch. She'd been scared when she called him. She'd been scared when he arrived and walked into the house. She had finally felt safe the minute her arms wrapped around his strong frame. When she had to let go, a small amount of fear had crept back in. The more she learned about the situation, the stronger the fear became. Then he'd touch her gently and it would all melt away.

And she tried to pretend with him that she wasn't scared. He knew. He also knew his touch helped.

What happened to taking it slow?

At the moment, she didn't care. She just wanted him to come back, hold her, and call her honey again. Each time his silky voice uttered that word, she loved it. It made her feel special and wanted. Like he cared. She wanted to believe he cared.

About ten minutes later, Zeke came back out of the house with a suitcase. She said good-bye to her friends, telling them she would be at work tomorrow and not to worry about a thing.

Zeke had expressed his concern about her driving, but she insisted she was fine and proceeded to follow him to his house. As she drove, her mind went wild. What would happen once they reached his house?

She could ignore his sexual power. She could jump his bones the minute they entered the house. She could continue to pretend she wasn't scared and didn't need his touch.

Why did she have to resist him? He was either going to break her heart or be the best thing to enter her life.

As she pulled behind his car in the driveway, a huge breath escaped. No more fighting him. No more fighting the intense emotions that flowed through her when he was near. She couldn't place all the blame at his feet. It was certainly his fault for insulting her the way he had, but she didn't have to throw herself at him in the bar. She played a part in the situation as well. She had to remember that.

Zeke helped her with her luggage, barely speaking as they entered his house. She stood in the foyer as he went down the hallway. What bedroom was he putting her stuff in? Since she came to her momentous decision, she wanted it to be his bedroom.

Her crazy, wired nerves wouldn't allow her to voice that decision. She would wait for his signal. It probably wouldn't take that long. His eyes sparkled with desire every time he glanced her way.

After dropping off her suitcase, he found her in the same spot he left her. "Are you hungry?"

"I guess I could eat. I want to change, though."

"I put your stuff in the spare bedroom. Second door on the left. I'll scrounge in the kitchen for something to eat."

Zoe nodded and went down the hallway. So, he hadn't put her stuff in his room. How could she change that without coming right out and saying it?

Talk about being ready to move forward with him, and for once, he didn't maintain his usual cockiness by putting her stuff in his room. Her making the first move wouldn't happen. The need for him to do it was too strong. She honestly didn't believe it would take him very long. At least she hoped it didn't.

Her suitcase lounged on the bed, sitting lonely, clearly asking to be moved to another room. His room.

"Knock it off, Zoe." She shook her head and opened up the suitcase. He had packed it well—all nicely folded. Her work clothes sat on top. She started removing them carefully, setting them on the bed.

Noticing he'd grabbed mostly skirts, her mood dipped at the thought of wearing them all week. She rarely wore skirts to work, feeling self-conscious with her body ever since that disastrous night.

Did he pack the skirts on purpose? She could picture the disastrous night as if it happened yesterday. His hands smoothing down her back, then inching slowly until he reached the edge of her dress, scooping underneath and—

Not going to think about it.

She picked up a black skirt. The same one she wore the day he appeared back in her life. He had stood by the desk, taking his time to look her over appreciatively. The way his eyes slid up her legs to her blouse, removing each button with his penetrating gaze.

Stop it! These images didn't help besides offering her the brutal reminder that she had given him the impression she wanted her space. And right now, any sort of space was the furthest thing from her mind.

The room suddenly filled with a stifling heat. Her cheeks flushed as she pulled her shirt away from her stomach. Fresh air would be nice. Shaking her head quickly to dispel the erotic visions, she continued unpacking.

It wouldn't kill her to wear skirts the rest of the week. And it gave Zeke opportunities to take advantage of her if the sudden feeling came over him. Again, she wondered if he'd packed them deliberately.

He also packed lounging pants, jeans, T-shirts, and a few tank tops. When her eyes landed on her panties and bras, her cheeks burned hotly again. She could only imagine him combing through her lingerie drawer. She owned a few sexy lingerie pieces. Thankfully, he packed none of them. But what if he had?

She could've put one on and sauntered out to the kitchen. She'd enjoyed sauntering up to him the first time they met. So brazen, so bold...so hot! But he didn't.

Sauntering? What was she thinking?

He sure packed a lot of clothes for more than one or two days. Was he trying to tell her something?

She grabbed a pair of sweat pants and a T-shirt, laying them over all the other clothes. He said she was beautiful. Did that mean she was beautiful in absolutely anything she wore? Now was the time to put it to the test. Her hand hesitated to grab the shirt. Maybe it was too plain and boring. If she wanted him to want her, she should be putting more effort into gaining his attention.

Her eyes started to scan the other clothes lying around when a piece of red caught her attention. Her hands whipped through everything, making a complete mess.

The red dress.

The same one that made him think she was a hooker. Why did he pack this?

With trembling fingers, she picked it up. What did this mean?

She had put the dress on several times, trying to see the hooker look he saw. It held to her skin tightly. Skimpy even, revealing in too many spots for her comfort. But she had felt sexy in it that night. Definitely not like a hooker. Each time after that, she felt like a hooker.

She stared, mesmerized by the dress. A subtle scent drifted toward her, breaking the spell. His aftershave. The will to confront him became impossible as she couldn't tear her eyes away from the dress.

"You okay? I threw a pizza in the oven and it should be done in about five minutes."

The sound of his voice suddenly gave her strength. Swiveling slowly, clutching the dress to her chest, she didn't say a word as she looked at him. She honestly didn't know where to start.

ZEKE STARED BACK. The red dress pierced his eyes brutally. He didn't think she would unpack the whole suitcase right away. He didn't even now why he had packed it. When he saw it hanging in the closet, he couldn't resist. Images of her delectable body went off like a bolt of lightning. His body ached to redo that night. Make it up to her somehow for hurting her.

That disastrous, glorious night replayed in his dreams nightly, making him wish for redemption. He realized he might have thought on the surface she was a prostitute, but deep down he knew she hadn't been one. He would've never slept with her otherwise. He knew he wouldn't have.

They stared at each other, silence surrounding them. He'd screwed up again by impulsively packing that dress. Screwing up repeatedly with her seemed to be his thing.

The silence. He hated the silence from her. Why couldn't she yell at him already? The silence made it worse. Words, yet again, failed to come to his rescue.

Zeke knew he should say something. Words were his forte with women. With life. They normally rolled off his tongue with ease. They had gotten him out of some sticky situations before. Yet, he had no clue what to say.

"I love that dress." Zeke winced when her eyes went round with shock. "You're gorgeous, Zoe. That dress on you turns me on. I don't know why I packed it. Call it a moment of insanity. I didn't mean to upset you. I saw it hanging there and then I saw you wearing it. And... What are you thinking?" He couldn't keep talking when she stared at him with a blank expression.

"That this dress makes me look like a hooker," she whispered.

He took a step toward her. "That dress makes you look delicious. My job was to find a hooker that night. The moment I saw you, my job went out the door. I would've never slept with you if I had truly thought you were a hooker. I know that with complete certainty."

She looked away.

"You don't look like a hooker. You look like a sexy, confident woman. I want to peel it off you, taste every loving inch of you, and make sweet love each time I see you in it." He inched closer, his heart pounding to the floor.

Her hands shook a little as she still refused to look at him.

He could fix this. She would never shiver in disgust, fear, and hatred again because of him. He'd make her see precisely what that dress meant. He'd go with what always worked for him.

His touch.

He closed the distance, taking the dress from her hands. Tossing it onto the bed, he grabbed a button on her blouse.

She finally looked at him, confusion marring her face. He paused for a moment to stare back.

When she made no move to shove him away, he continued his quest. Unhooking the last button, he gently took the shirt off and unbuttoned her dress pants. He let them fall to the ground, grabbing her hands to help her step out of them. She still maintained eye contact, not uttering one protest.

His touch always calmed her down. That had to explain her silence.

She stood lovingly, half-naked in front of him, and he wanted her so badly. Of course, he wanted it to be exactly like that night. Removing her bra and panties would be the most difficult part of this task.

Closing his eyes, he unsnapped her bra and slid her panties off by feeling her body as he went. The silky smooth skin that moved within his hands brought his tortured pain to the hilt. So many nights he dreamed of her, he felt as if he had each delicious part of her body memorized already. Finally feeling her in his hands again—surreal, magical even. He wanted to smooth his hands over every inch, discover and possess each part of her. And he would. Later. Slowly and deliciously.

He reached down to the bed, eyes still tightly shut, and picked up the illustrious red dress. His fingertips brushed her skin as he tenderly glided it down her sweet body. When he felt the edge of the dress slip from his fingers, he opened his eyes.

Gorgeous. Delicious. Exactly like that night.

He smiled inside and out when she took control. Leaning into his body, she moved closer to his ear and whispered, "You smell good."

Finally, he didn't screw up. As soon as she spoke, he knew this was what they needed to do to move on. To forget what happened that night. Make new memories.

"You smell delicious yourself. What I wouldn't do for a taste of you," he replied, pulling her even closer, overwhelmed with the need to have her.

"What I wouldn't do for you to taste me."

Shuddering in her arms as she spoke those words, he caressed her back as he inhaled her sweet scent. His lips ached to taste her everywhere.

"Take me now. I need you, Zeke," she whispered delicately into his ear as she nibbled.

That sounded like the best invitation ever. He swept her into his arms and carried her to his bedroom at the end of the hall. It seemed like miles as he walked there. Screw the spare bedroom. She would be in his room as long as she was in his house.

Laying her gently on the bed, he quickly removed his clothes. She was about to take her dress off when he stopped her. "No. I love that dress. I mostly love taking it off."

He pulled her to a standing position, his body begging to

dive into her. Because he loved the feeling, he pulled her close and stroked his hands down her back, over her ass and to the edge of her dress. Little by little, he slid his hands underneath the dress, moving back up her body, caressing her ass as he went, and gently removed her dress. He loved that part. If he had the willpower, he would continue to do it over and over until she writhed in his arms, begging him to stop. But he didn't have the willpower.

"You are so beautiful. I don't regret meeting you. I only regret how I ended the night. I swear never to be that idiotic again. Let me show you how I truly feel." Zeke eased her onto the bed, sliding over her body. He positioned himself so he rested on her mound, her wetness teasing him.

He lowered his mouth to her breast, taking in her delicate nipple, sucking hard. She moaned his name, arching into him.

"Please take me," Zoe pleaded as she attempted to grab for him.

"I want to taste you," he whispered as he took the other breast that demanded his attention.

"You can taste me later," she cried as he sucked and lightly bit her. "Please. I need—"

Zeke cut off her words as he devoured her mouth. He demanded entrance, his tongue not waiting for permission. His tongue touched hers, sliding over it, playing with it, dancing in unison. Pure deliciousness. He could never get enough of her sweet taste.

He kissed her as he pressed into her center, teasing her, feeling her wetness touch him. That instant contact had him dying for more. He really wanted to taste her, but he would finish that later. They had all night.

Without breaking the sweet kiss, he slid into her with ease. The moment he was deep inside, she wrapped her legs around him and pulled him in even farther. Immediately, he felt where he belonged. Completion and a sense of rightness calmed his soul. He slowly moved in and out, wanting to savor every moment. She wasn't having any of that as she clung to him, increasing the pace.

Moving as one, he matched her pace as they rocked together. Already attuned to her body from that one glorious night, sensing her getting close, he thrust harder and faster as she made delightful noises in his ear. She grabbed his back, scratching down as she hit her crescendo. The intense pleasure had him exploding with her. He rocked into her two more times, never wanting it to end.

LIKE THE LAST TIME, he laid on top of her as they came down from the high. Tiny sizzling tingles still exploded throughout her body as he lay on her. Of course, this was where it all went wrong last time.

Waiting for the stiffening posture and rejection, the flashback drove the pleasure away. She wanted to feel cleansed from that disastrous night. When he started to undress her and put on the dress, she knew they could move on. Yet, as she lay underneath him, the old feelings of insecurity sweeping in, she wasn't sure this was the best idea.

A light kiss touched her neck. "Not even a minute gone by and I want you again. I just might."

Her momentary flashback disappeared and the pleasure flowed back in. Crisis averted. Warning bells disarmed. She could lay here and enjoy the moment.

"Do you know what you do to me? I have to admit, I was afraid of commitment before I met you. Not anymore. I want a real relationship with dates, long phone calls, and silly inside jokes only we know about," he whispered into her ear.

Zoe moved her head so she could look into his eyes. He stared back with passion and sincerity.

"I made a decision to follow you to that room, so I can't lay all the blame at your feet." She bit her lip. "Anything you do from this point on is fair game."

"Fair enough." He kissed her lips, lingering a bit. "You're only going to stay a day or two?"

"How long do you expect me to stay?" Zoe countered. He said he wanted commitment. Did he mean the forever kind right away?

He kissed her again. Fiercely. Deeply. She shuffled her hands through his hair as the kiss turned tender.

"Your phone records are useless. Most of the numbers were unknown or blocked, but there was one number that wasn't blocked. It indicated it came from a pay phone not far from your office downtown. We tried pulling video surveillance surrounding the pay phone with negative results. I'm concerned about your safety."

"One day at a time."

He smiled and brushed a hand across her hair. "You're hard to negotiate with."

"We've barely begun," she said as she swatted his ass.

"You keep touching me like that and I'm liable to start making love to you again," he said as he slowly rocked back and forth inside her.

"Seems to me that's what you're already doing. Maybe I touched you like that because I was sick of waiting for you to start again," she said with a devilish smile.

"My sweet Zoe. Don't say things like that to me." He started to pick up the pace. Zoe grabbed his ass to get him deeper.

They were enjoying the pleasure, the fun, when a loud, piercing sound erupted throughout the house.

"What's that?" she shrieked as she loosened her grip.

He grabbed her hand, putting it back on his ass as he continued to thrust inside her. "I can't stop now. I think it's the damn fire alarm. We forgot about the pizza."

Zoe laughed as she gripped him firmly, meeting his thrusts as the alarm echoed throughout the house.

Although deafening and annoying, the noise couldn't damage the glorious lovemaking between them. He shifted his position slightly, instantly hitting her sweet spot as she screamed out, climaxing. He let himself go as well, spilling his seed into her for the second time that night. He collapsed onto her luscious body again.

"Don't you think we should get the pizza?"

He lifted his head. "The only thing I'm hungry for right now is you. I'll clean the mess up. And then, my darling Zoe, I'm going to explore every inch of this beautiful body."

She smiled. "I like the sound of that. I'm a little hungry, though. Do you have any chocolate syrup?"

"I sure hope I do. I would hate for you to go hungry. Keep the bed warm."

"Don't forget the syrup," Zoe hollered as he ran out of the room.

Still the best sex of her life. Forgiveness was a very beautiful thing. The magic they created. She couldn't wait for him to get back to bed.

Oh, the fun they would have.

6

_____

"So, it's been two days. Is she going back to her house tonight, or still staying with you? You haven't dished out any good details either," Ben asked as he picked up the report from the lab that recently landed on his desk.

"First of all, I won't be dishing out any details with you. I'm not going to gossip about our sex life like that. And second—"

"Whoa, wait a minute. There is a sex life going on? I knew you finally got laid. You've been much better to work with." Ben laughed as Zeke glowered at him. Ben started to laugh even harder when he refused to break the stare.

"I might go back to my horrible disposition with you. What's it to you anyway, whether I'm getting any?"

"Hey, I have to live vicariously through someone else as I'm not getting any lately." Ben shrugged.

Zeke laughed, but still wouldn't divulge any information. His time spent with her between the sheets was for his knowledge only. He craved her every day, every hour, every minute, right up to the last second. And when that craving peaked to the point of pain, he indulged it until they were both sated with undying bliss. That feeling of desire, the beautiful magic they created, well, he would never share that with Ben—or anyone else who dared to ask.

The last two days could arguably be the best two days of his life. Surprisingly, they hadn't fought over anything. But he couldn't say he didn't enjoy their tiny battles, the angry demeanor she developed. The way her face flushed a bright red, her body slightly shivering with outrage, and scrunching her face with fury, made him instantly hard. Thinking about that glorious look had him hard sitting at his desk. As long as he could always get her to forgive him, he enjoyed their angry repertoire back and forth.

He had even mentioned protection finally, considering he lost his senses three separate times and forgot to use a condom. She had assured him she was—and had been—on the pill. After he grabbed the chocolate syrup he thankfully had stocked, he snatched his half-empty box of condoms lying in wait on the bottom of his bathroom drawer. They put good use to that box. So much use that he had to swing by the store tonight before he headed home to buy a new box.

The anticipation of how he would use them had him itching for the door. He adjusted his position in his chair unobtrusively, anticipating the ecstasy that waited for him at home. Three more hours. He could do it.

"Sorry, buddy, I won't be sharing my sex life with you. Go find your own woman. Why don't you ask out Zoe's friend—Rina, I think it is. She's cute and sassy. In a quiet way," Zeke said with a grin.

"Are you nuts? I told you she's scarier than that loud one. The quiet way she warned you off Zoe scared me. I guarantee you she's a whole lotta woman under that quiet demeanor. No, thank you." Ben shuddered, yet his eyes displayed an entirely different emotion.

"We could double date."

"This report is useless. The lab found nothing suspicious in Mills's computer at home or work. Just work-related crap. This case is frustrating as hell. Why was he murdered? Where is Murphy?"

Zeke put his hand out for the report, deciding to let the Rina conversation slide. Although, he had a feeling his partner might actually like her. He never skirted a chance for some fun teasing back and forth as he just had.

Ben handed it over as Zeke said, "Well, we have two possible scenarios. He killed Mills and ran. Or he's dead as well. Which one you like better?"

Ben shrugged. "He killed Mills and ran. Otherwise, we have to find a new suspect. He's the best we got right now."

Zeke combed through the report, getting equally as discouraged as Ben. He wanted to solve this. For his sake and for Zoe's. "Did the lab find any discrepancy with these numbers? It has to be related to the company why he was killed."

"Lab found nothing odd. Although, they have an enormous amount of clients at that company. We can have them dig deeper into it. They're still working on Murphy's computer. They noticed some files had been deleted. They're trying to retrieve them with however they do that digital retrieval shit. I guarantee that flash drive Zoe saw with Mills is the key to this case. I know you don't wanna hear that, man, but it's true. You know it."

He didn't want it to be true. He'd have to cover his ears next time Ben wanted to say that. Hearing it caused his stomach to twist with pain.

A pencil hit him square in the chest and fell to his lap.

"You listening to me?" Ben asked.

"I should arrest you for assault," Zeke said as he picked up the pencil and twirled it in his hand. "I know it's the most likely scenario. I don't like it. She doesn't have it. Whoever's bothering her just doesn't believe that. I almost wish she did so we could move on with this case."

"We should head back to the office and talk with Young again. He said he was going to look into the company with a fine-tooth comb for us. Although, he's hiding something. I don't trust him."

"Yeah, me either." Zeke paused as he saw Tray walk into their area. He averted his eyes, hoping he wasn't headed his way.

"Hey, boys. How's the murder life treating you?" Tray asked.

"Like it always does," Zeke said without giving eye contact, even though he could feel his presence right next to him.

"You up for another undercover sting for us? Trevor's going, too. But we thought two undercover would be better. We need to get this guy. His shenanigans are increasing, especially with the drug running. We think he's been having his girls sell after they do the deed with their mark. We got two dead Johns that OD'd after sex. The girls called them in, but obviously, they didn't stick around for the cops to arrive. It's cocaine. Pure shit, too. I need to get this guy. It's not about the sex. It's dead guys popping up now."

Zeke finally looked at him and rubbed his hand over his face to stifle a groan. "Look, man, I hear ya. I'm sorry, though. I'm knee-deep in shit over here with a murder I got going on. Not my only case either. I'm pretty sure the dead Johns got handed to Newman and Sauer. Why don't you ask them? Sauer's kinda pretty for a guy."

"Sauer's also nervous as hell around women. Can you imagine him talking to a prostitute?" Tray countered.

Zeke chuckled. "Yeah, I could, actually. It would be funny as hell. Okay, Newman's not that bad with the ladies. His crooked nose gives off the *I was a football player* vibe, if you know what I mean. You suckered me in last time against my better judgment. Not happening again. Ben and I are swamped. Sorry."

"Thanks anyway. I'll check ya guys later." Tray walked away and headed toward Newman's desk. Zeke guessed he wasn't even willing to give Sauer a chance. He wouldn't either, except to laugh at his attempt to talk to a woman.

"If he only knew," Ben jested.

"Shut up. That doesn't deserve a response," Zeke muttered, as he threw the pencil he'd been twirling around back.

"Yet, you responded." Ben laughed as he stood up. "Come on. Let's run by Young's office and catch up with him. You can even see Zoe."

Zeke liked the sound of that. He grabbed his jacket from behind his chair, shrugging into it. "I never miss an opportunity to see her."

Zoe paced inside Zeke's bathroom. What a small, confined area. There wasn't enough room to pace comfortably.

Two days ago, she had the best sex of her life—again. Two days ago, Zeke brought up the fact they hadn't used protection either time—a month and two days ago. She casually told him it wasn't a big deal because she's on the pill. They did, however, start using condoms.

What she didn't tell him was after that fateful night, she

was so stressed and over men that she stopped taking her pills. In fact, she couldn't even remember the last time she had her period. Did she miss it? She had been stressed, depressed, and so out of it until he walked back into her life that she hadn't paid attention. That was, until he brought up the subject of protection. Then she freaked. It took her two days to say something to Dee and Rina. Their reaction to her worries had scared her—and rightly so. Especially Dee's.

"What? That son of a bitch got you pregnant," Dee had shouted.

"What happened to him just being a douche? I said I wasn't sure. I can't remember when my last period was," Zoe had said with a frown.

"Well, he upgraded himself to a son of a bitch. I'll kill him."

"Why are you upset? Zoe is rather calm right now. If anyone should be upset, it should be her. I thought you were on the pill," Rina had interjected.

"I am—or I was that night. I don't know what to do. I can't even tell him. What happens if he decides a baby isn't what he wants? What if what we have is only sex?" Zoe had finally voiced her real concern.

She didn't deny they had a connection, but was it purely a sexual one? Or more than that? She didn't even know if he wanted kids or marriage or a happily ever after. He only ever mentioned commitment. She didn't know what that entailed exactly. A monogamous relationship until they decided to call it quits, or a fairytale future together?

"Talk to him. You will never know until you do. A pregnancy test wouldn't hurt either. That would relieve a lot of worry and wonder," Rina had said as she sent a small warning to Dee to settle down.

Dee had raised her eyebrows at Rina in a get real look, then turned back to Zoe in a non-shouting voice, "Maybe Rina has a small point...again. It's rather annoying when she's the voice of reason all the time. If he doesn't step up if you're pregnant, then I'll kill him."

After their tension-filled talk, she left work right away, stopping at the local pharmacy store for a pregnancy test. She went straight to Zeke's house. During the entire drive home she had glanced worriedly at her phone, the temptation to call him hammering in her chest like a stake to the heart.

But she never made the call. If she wasn't pregnant, she could forget the whole thing and pretend it never happened. He'd never be the wiser. Unless, of course, she still got pregnant down the road from having sex two days ago when they hadn't used a condom. She immediately started taking her birth control again the next day. She hated to deceive him, but fear won that battle.

It had taken over an hour to finally pee on the stick. Her nerves had been raw and the urge to pee wouldn't come. It was like her body refused to help her out, trying to tell her, *you don't wanna know.*

Now, pacing in the bathroom, waiting the torturous three minutes the instructions told her it took to tell if she was pregnant or not, rattled her nerves to the point of exhaustion. She had decided to go with the digital kind, worried that she wouldn't be able to read two pink lines or not. It would be impossible to misinterpret, pregnant or not pregnant flashing in her face.

She stopped pacing and looked at the stick. Nothing glared back except the hourglass timer blinking away. Who in the hell created this? Who thought three minutes was a good amount of time to find out if your world was changing?

It wasn't. Time suddenly became her enemy. Her horrible, horrible enemy. What was wrong with one minute, or even thirty seconds? She could only take so much torture.

She glanced at her watch. Only a minute had passed. It felt like an hour already.

Ugh! She couldn't take it.

She walked out of the bathroom with wobbly legs and headed for the kitchen. Pulling a glass from the cabinet, she turned on the faucet and let the water flow for a while until it turned as cold as it could get. The urge to pee again came full force. Why couldn't her impulses have been kind to her an hour ago? Her misery would be over.

She ignored the pressure and filled up her glass. Taking a long, slow sip, she savored the cool liquid running down her throat. Suddenly, eyeing the glass with irritation, she took a gulp, emptying the contents swiftly. There. That task should've taken at least two minutes to complete.

She walked back to the bathroom, then rushed to the counter as the urge to pee instantly vanished. The hourglass symbol flashed. She couldn't take it. How had three minutes not gone by already?

Then she remembered what the instructions said. Sometimes, the devices were faulty. If her stupid stick was faulty, then she'd have to pee on another stick. Wait another three minutes. She only bought one package. One package contained two sticks. What happened if both sticks were faulty?

She slapped the counter. A stinging sensation traveled from her hand down to the tips of her toes. She wouldn't be able to handle the frustration of driving back to the store and buying another package.

She couldn't take it. Her boiling point had tipped the scale, the stress engulfing her.

A loud scream erupted.

Zeke unlocked the front door and sighed in relief. He had stressed the entire drive from Zoe's office. He'd been surprised when Rina told him she'd left early. When he asked why, she refused to look at him and said Zoe hadn't been feeling well. She wouldn't explain further. His anxiety ratcheted up a notch, knowing quite well she was leaving something out.

They had talked with Young, who provided no additional information. Zeke knew deep down he was lying and hiding something, but he hadn't cared. His worry for Zoe took front and center. He told Ben he was calling it a day and rushed home.

He closed the door and flipped the lock when he heard a scream. "Zoe!"

He pulled his weapon out of his holster and rushed to his bedroom where he heard the scream. Zoe stood outside the doorway to the master bathroom.

She jumped, putting her hand to her chest. "Why do you have your gun out? What's wrong?"

"What's wrong? What the hell do you think is wrong? I heard you scream and thought you were in trouble. What's wrong with you?" Zeke shouted.

"I didn't mean to scream. Please put the gun away," she said calmly.

Zeke holstered his weapon. His hand shook as he did. She stood so calmly. Too calmly for his tastes. He shouted at her and she didn't shout back. She always shouted back.

"Clearly, it's something or you wouldn't have screamed.

You left work early. Rina said you weren't feeling well. What's wrong?"

"Why were you at my work?"

"Does it matter? I want to know what's wrong. What aren't you telling me?"

"Why were you there?"

He shifted on his feet as he raised a brow. Ignoring his questions. Something was obviously very wrong here.

"We were talking to Young. Mills's murder has to do with the company somehow. Ben and I have no solid proof, but we know he's hiding something. Be careful around him. There. I answered your question, now you answer mine."

"I'm pregnant. I just took the test and it was pissing me off," Zoe finally mumbled.

The floor shifted. His knees almost buckled as the words *I'm pregnant* echoed around the room. She couldn't possibly have said that. She was on the pill.

He wasn't ready for that. Or was he? What did she mean she was pissed? She didn't want a baby—or she didn't want a baby with him.

Damn. And he thought his anxiety when Rina told him she wasn't feeling well was bad. Upgrade that feeling to catastrophic.

When he rushed home to find her, he never expected this. "Are you sure?"

"If you don't believe me, look for yourself. The stick's in the bathroom," Zoe said sharply as she pointed to the open door.

Without a word, Zeke walked past her into the bathroom and stared at the stick.

Pregnant.

Well, shit. Now what did he do?

Correction. What did they do?

He walked out of the bathroom. "How did this happen?"

"Gee, how do you think? Insert long pointy thing into waiting hole," Zoe snapped.

"Thank you, captain obvious. Not what I meant. You said you were on the pill," Zeke snapped back.

"Yeah, the pill isn't one hundred percent effective. Ask any doctor. I didn't ask for this, you know. And it could've happened from two days ago."

"Why do you say that? You've been on the pill. They may not be one hundred percent effective, but pretty damn close to it."

"Because I haven't been on the pill since that disastrous night."

His lips formed a tight line as his entire body went rigid. "You said you were on it. You lied to me."

"I didn't mean to. You mentioned protection and I suddenly couldn't remember when I had my last period. I panicked," Zoe said as her voice broke. "I'm sorry."

"You panicked. That makes it okay?" He shook his head. Anger. Frustration. Fear. It all consumed him.

Her hand wiped her cheek with a swift motion. "Like you've never panicked in your life.

Panic. Hell, yeah, he had panicked in his life. He could remember it all so clearly. The exact moment he realized when he thought he slept with a hooker and couldn't seem to regret it. That a woman came before his job. That he wanted to do it all over again. That he thought he had to pay her for her services. That he had been completely wrong in his assumptions. And how he let her walk out of that room.

He knew panic well.

"We'll figure this out." Zeke paused, unsure of what else to say. "I'll start making supper. We can talk about...baby stuff later."

———

JUST LIKE THAT. He walked out of the room. No hesitation. No waiting to see if she wanted to say something else. Nothing. He simply walked out.

That wasn't what she wanted to hear. Or what she wanted him to do. She wanted him to shout with joy and pull her into his arms. Tell her everything would be all right. What did *we'll figure this out* mean?

Her house had been cleaned, cleared of all destruction. Zeke had hired a cleaning crew for her, informing her it was best if she didn't see her house that way. She immediately agreed. His simple look and hesitant words told her it wouldn't be a pretty sight.

Perhaps she should go back home now. His reaction indicated he wanted space. She would give it to him. Not that she wanted to.

She wanted to stay right here—with him. She hadn't had much time to accept the truth since he busted into the room with his weapon out. But she had plenty of time while waiting to pee and pace during the three long torturous minutes.

Overwhelmed, confused, a little frightened, no doubt about that. But excitement overruled all those other harrowing emotions. She could already imagine a tiny bundle of joy just like him.

Two days of bliss. Two days of learning, of talking, of exploring their lives together, but not enough time to truly understand a person. Their tumultuous relationship happened so quickly. And yet, none of that mattered to her. She could picture him holding their beautiful creation and knew he'd be a wonderful father. She wanted that family with him. The question remained. Did he want it, too? It wasn't looking good in her favor.

She cleaned up the mess in the bathroom as the tears finally found release. Holding them back in front of him had taken an amount of strength she hadn't realized she possessed. One tear had escaped, and she wiped it away quickly. He obviously hadn't noticed because he didn't comment or do a thing about it. Like wrapping her up in his warm embrace. Or maybe he saw it and simply didn't care.

She sat down on the toilet, letting out all the emotions she had locked inside. There was no holding back this time. They came out like a rushing waterfall. Nothing would stop them. Or maybe one thing could.

His touch.

She wanted him to magically appear in front of her and tame her tears. She wanted him to be happy about this. And accept her apology. She didn't mean to lie. Nothing but panic.

She figured it was very fitting the roles had been reversed. He hadn't meant to treat her the way he had that lone night. She knew that now. He had apologized. And what did she do? She had given him a hard time. Took her time to let him back into her good graces. So how long would it take him to forgive her?

After marring her cheeks with tear stains, creating a headache of great proportions, she calmed down. Washing her face as best she could, the bed called her name, until Zeke came in an hour later telling her it was time to eat.

She refused to look at him when he stepped into the room. She had to look like a complete mess. When she stepped into the bathroom, the mirror confirmed it. Washing her face again, it did nothing to erase the marks of her tears from earlier. Her eyes were still puffy and red-rimmed. She looked pathetic and downright scary.

What would he think? No sex appeal here. Wait until she was fat and round. His disgust of her would increase. His lack of acceptance and encouragement with the situation brought her self-consciousness front and center. She tried to stop it and failed.

She walked out of the bedroom, determined to keep her composure. She wouldn't cry in front of him. If he ignored it again, she'd never survive the rejection.

ZEKE STOLE glances at Zoe as she ate, taking nibbling bites as she went. His worry increased each time she moved her fork around but made no move to take a bite. Was it the pregnancy? Did her anger over the situation make her not hungry?

The evidence couldn't be mistaken. It was written all over her face. She had cried. That quick swipe of her cheek right before he walked out had been a tear falling. He hadn't been positive if that was the case, but clearly, it was. Why had he walked out?

Anytime he needed the perfect words to leave his mouth he seemed to freeze instead. What could he possibly say to change her mind? He knew she cried over regret and disappointment that they were pregnant.

He wanted this baby. So badly.

As he prepared supper, a simple spaghetti meal, calmness swept through him. He couldn't imagine anyone else as the mother of his children. He stood at the counter for a few minutes, letting it sink in. The longer he stood there with the picture of her sweet face, holding their baby, the more excited he became.

He couldn't wait to tell his mom. Her excitement would probably overshadow his. She'd been waiting years for him to join the baby making in the family. He needed to catch up to his sister.

Imagine all the fun they could have. Trying to make another baby after this one would be nothing less than glorious. Just like her. Even as she sat at the table, red eyes and all, she was beautiful. He wanted her. He knew he always would.

He cleared his throat to gather courage to talk about the baby when she quietly said, "I think I should go back home now."

Zeke almost dropped his fork. "Why?"

Zoe looked up. "Because we both need some space to think about the future. It's not just about us anymore. We have to make the right decisions."

"What decisions?" Zeke demanded.

"I don't know. That's why I said we needed some space," Zoe snapped.

"I know this threw us for a loop, but we have to be smart here. Someone still wants that flash drive from you. What are you going to do if they come at you when you're home alone? You just said you have more than yourself to think about now."

He gripped the fork handle as panic rushed to his heart. He did not, for one minute, want her leaving his house. Because of the murder. Because of the baby. Most importantly, because of her. He could tell by the way her face fell into fear that the murder case never entered her mind.

"Fine. I'll stay for a bit longer. You'll solve this case soon, right?"

"I sure hope so. For both our sakes."

THEY FINISHED their meal in silence. Zoe barely touched her food. She pleaded a headache afterward and went to lie down. She went to his room, not having the energy to move to the spare bedroom. Did he still want her in his bed? She had no clue. But she knew she wanted to be in his arms. Not fighting. Not feeling this distance.

She didn't think it would happen, but she fell asleep. Later that evening, the bed dipped a little when Zeke joined her, rousing her out of a pleasant dream. Yet, he didn't say anything.

She stiffened, waiting for rejection. For him to fall right to sleep. Or maybe even kick her out of the bed. They hadn't gone to bed one night without taking each other.

Out of nowhere, an arm snaked around her waist and pulled her closer. For the first time that night, contentment washed over her. He made no move to caress her body or start a bout of lovemaking, but it was okay. She didn't need that. All she needed was his arms wrapped tightly around her. That said enough. The morning may show a different story, but at the moment, everything felt good.

Sleep came easily again. She drifted awake when a loud ring reverberated around the room. A glance at the clock said it was only three thirty.

The bed shifted as Zeke rolled to his side of the bed. "Hello." A few more pauses and then she heard, "Shit. I'll be right there."

She finally turned toward him. He twisted the switch from the lamp on his nightstand. Light filled the room. He looked at her, then scooted closer and pulled her into his arms. "I have to go. There's been a murder."

She snuggled closer. She didn't want him to leave. Hated the thought of it. Hated that they hadn't settled anything to her liking. "Can't someone else take it?"

The minute she asked, she knew it was selfish and unreasonable. She didn't want him to leave, but perhaps he wanted to leave.

She buried her face into his chest before she could see the truth in his eyes.

Closure. That's all she wanted before he left.

"I have to. I'll always get calls at this hour because murder doesn't sleep. That's part of the package when you're with me. It sucks, but it's my life." He paused and kissed the top of her head, his hot breath flowing down her neck. Soothing her. Comforting her.

"The body's been identified already. I need to be there. It's...it's Murphy." He kissed her head again and rubbed her back when shivers wracked her body. "I don't want to leave. I can send an officer here. I don't—"

"No, that's not necessary. I'll be fine."

He pulled her away and cupped her face. "Do you have to interrupt me?"

She couldn't help but offer a sweet smile. He smiled back, then kissed her briefly. "I think you should be fine. No one should know you're with me. I won't have an officer sit with you, but I'll have them drive by a few times. Okay?"

"Okay. You're right. Besides Dee and Rina, no one knows I'm dating you."

He must not have minded the word dating as it fell from her lips because he pulled her in for another kiss, grabbed her tightly into his embrace, and pushed her into his hard erection.

"What I wouldn't do to finish what I just started. Go back to bed." Zeke lightly kissed her forehead and hopped out of bed.

Zoe watched as he quickly changed, kissed her again on the lips, and ran out the door. Nothing was said about the baby. She felt foolish thinking they would when he needed to leave. She touched her lips, treasuring the memory of his last kiss, taking it as a good sign everything would work out between them. She hoped so, anyway.

She went back to sleep, or at least tried to. Worry plagued her mind, making it difficult to fall back into a decent sleep. Worry about the baby. Worry about the relationship. Worry about Zeke working a murder she was tied to.

7

ZEKE PULLED up to the crime scene already full of commotion. Patrol cars lined the street as the flashing lights illuminated the night. Yellow crime scene tape was strung up in a wallowing loop preventing entry to the small crowd lined up dying to see what the body looked like.

Vultures.

It never failed to amaze him how fascinated people were with murder. He slammed his door, ignoring the imploring looks and questions directed at him as he made his way to the barrier, ducking under as another officer held it up for him. Zeke nodded a thank you, then made his way down the slight hill to the embankment where the body had washed to shore.

Ben stood at the bottom of the hill. Normally, Zeke always managed to arrive before Ben, enjoying the immense pleasure of giving him shit for being so slow. Like him, Ben hated to be awakened out of a good comfortable bed. The difference, though, was that Zeke could shake off the sleepiness quicker than Ben. It was quite a statement that Zeke had arrived last.

Ben looked up from the body near his feet as Zeke approached. "You had to have a quickie before you left, I see."

Zeke grimaced, wishing that were actually true. Her kiss had tasted like heaven. As usual. He had also felt the uncertainty in the air as he kissed her. It scared him being away from her and losing ground.

"No. But I found it difficult to leave the side of a beautiful woman." Zeke wasn't willing to share anything more. "What do we have?"

"See for yourself. Gunshot wound to the back of the head. Looks executioner style. Coroner's on his way, but I'm guessing he was killed around the same time as Mills. I was hoping Murphy was our man. No wonder we couldn't find his car. Whoever killed him wanted to make it look like he killed Mills and ran. Maybe we were never supposed to find his body."

Zeke neared the body, noticing the wound on the back of the head, as well as numerous abrasions covering his body. "Looks like he floated awhile with the other injuries. Who found him?"

Ben looked at his notepad. "A Neal Holl. He was walking along the bank, picking up garbage. It's particularly dirty down this way."

"Picking up garbage at this time of night?"

"Hey, man, that's what he told me. I don't think he's our guy. If that's the excuse he wants to use, then so be it."

Zeke sighed. He looked at the river. Garbage littered everywhere, up and down the stretch. Susan was bent down near the edge of the water, putting anything she saw into an evidence bag.

Murphy had washed ashore on the Sauk River, on the west side of St. Cloud. Zeke wasn't positive where the river started, but he recalled a few memories of tubing down this very river starting in Rockville and jumping off a mile before this area. It was disturbing to think about a body floating down the river. Soiled his memories a bit, especially seeing the garbage. What happened to the good days when you could enjoy nature without society polluting it?

"So he came down the river, suggesting he wasn't killed in St. Cloud. Unless the killer dumped him farther upstream hoping he wouldn't be found," Zeke said as he looked back over at Ben.

"I'm going with body dumping. He never came home that night after knocking on Mills's door. Where did he go and who did he run into?" Ben countered.

"Good questions. Let's find out. First, we have to notify his wife. I hate this part."

"Yeah, me, too." Ben frowned and then hollered at Susan. "Find anything useful yet? The murder weapon, perhaps?"

Susan walked toward them, shaking her head. "You wish. It's never that simple. I'm collecting most of what's down there. First, for evidence purposes, and second, because it's disgusting how dirty it is. I'll let you guys know what I have, if anything, when I do."

"Thanks, Susan." Zeke patted Ben on the shoulder as he guided him back up the hill. "Let's get the hard part over."

They headed to their separate vehicles, briefly stopping at the precinct to take one car to Murphy's house. They arrived twenty minutes later to break the bad news to Carly Murphy.

As Zeke got out of the passenger side, he looked at Ben. "You take the lead. I'll follow you."

"Man, you say that all the time and you always take it from me." Ben shut his door and followed Zeke as they made their way to the front door. "See. You're even walking first."

Zeke abruptly stopped at the steps, moved to the side, and gestured with his hands for Ben to walk first. Ben raised his eyebrows with a smirk and proceeded ahead of him. Ben took a deep breath and rang the doorbell. They waited patiently, not hearing any noise from inside. Ben rang the doorbell again.

"No car in the driveway, but it could be in the garage. Maybe she's not home," Zeke whispered in Ben's ear.

"Dude. Personal space. Do you need to whisper like that in my ear?"

Zeke laughed. "Yeah. It's fun to annoy you."

"I'll keep that in mind for later. How's Zoe?" Ben grinned.

Zeke's smile dipped. "Not funny. I'll have you—"

Zeke zipped his lips shut when the door opened. Mrs. Murphy was wrapped in a terry robe, eyes half shut, with her hair haphazardly in a ponytail.

The moment she saw them, her eyes opened wide, alertness front and center. "He's dead, isn't he? Why else would you be at my home at five thirty in the morning?"

For once Zeke waited for Ben to speak. "I'm sorry, Mrs. Murphy. His body was found a few hours ago. May we come in and speak with you? We're terribly sorry for your loss, but in order for us to find his killer, we need to ask you a few more questions."

Instead of responding with words, she opened the door farther, gesturing for them to enter. She headed for the kitchen. "I need coffee. Would you like some?"

Ben glanced at Zeke, who shrugged. "Sure, Mrs. Murphy. That would be nice."

As they followed her, both of them took stock of everything as they passed it. Nothing seemed amiss. When they entered the kitchen, Mrs. Murphy pointed at the table. "Have a seat. I'll be right with you."

She busied herself preparing the coffee as they took a seat at the table. Zeke leaned over to Ben and whispered, "Does it seem odd she isn't breaking down? She didn't seem that surprised either."

"Two reasons. She knows how he died. Or it hasn't hit her yet. Some people don't break down in front of others. It's strange, though."

A few minutes later, Mrs. Murphy came to the table holding three cups of coffee. She handed them their coffee and took a seat. She took a sip before speaking. "I'm sure you're wondering why I'm not in tears. I won't say I'm not sad because I am. George was a good man, but we lost touch a few months ago. Our marriage wasn't doing so well. I was actually contemplating divorce. I even contacted a lawyer two weeks ago."

Carly paused, taking another sip of coffee. "I was very concerned when he disappeared a week ago. I actually thought he killed Mills. This is terrible."

"Mrs. Murphy, you do realize withholding the fact you filed for divorce is quite suspicious," Ben said.

"You'll look at the spouse first anyway in a murder. I didn't think it was important nor part of the reason he disappeared. I said I talked to a lawyer. I never fully filed for a divorce. He hadn't been served any papers."

"Is there anyone else you can think of that your husband had an issue with? Maybe someone he and Mills had a problem with," Zeke asked.

"No. Just Mills. We had our problems, but he was a good man. I didn't kill my husband. I won't be answering any more questions unless a lawyer is present. You two know how to find the front door," Carly said as she got up from the table and walked back into the kitchen.

Ben and Zeke shared a look before standing up from the table. "Thank you for your time, Mrs. Murphy. If you think of something important that you're willing to share, here's my card," Zeke said as he laid it on the table.

They exited the house, getting into the car before speaking. Ben started the vehicle. "Okay, that was weird. She acted guilty, yet got insulted when we acted like she was guilty."

"Maybe she killed them both. But why kill Mills? They have to be related. Coincidence that two people who work together are murdered and it's not connected? I don't do coincidences," Zeke said.

"Well, maybe Murphy killed Mills and Carly found out. She sees a way out without divorce and kills him. Let's dig deeper into their finances and life. Maybe it is all coincidental."

"Highly doubtful, but worth a try. What judge do we bother for a warrant? I know one that I'm not going to call," Zeke said with a laugh.

"I don't know why not. He'd give us what we want if you only asked nicely. But I guess let's go find one who doesn't mind working so early," Ben said as he drove back to the precinct.

———

ZOE STOOD by the garbage can in the break room, throwing away the rest of her lunch she had no appetite for.

"Hey, I was hoping to catch you by yourself. Dee seems to be your new hound dog."

"Is there a point to this conversation, Mark?"

The last person she wanted to speak to was Mark. Since

she took the test, it was as if her body had decided to show the signs of pregnancy. She'd been nauseated all morning. The sight of the bathroom was enough to make her nauseated. She already made several trips to the bathroom twice as much as she normally did.

"I'm sorry, Zoe. Please don't be mad at me." Mark took a step closer to her.

She backed up a step. "Mad at you? I'm over you. What is it with you suddenly wanting to speak to me all the time? I understood your words loud and clear the last time we spoke."

Mark sighed. "I was wrong. I miss you. I was going through a rough patch in my personal life and I took it out on you. I'm sorry."

Zoe frowned at him. "Sorry? You made me feel disgusting. And a rough patch in your personal life—I thought being your girlfriend would make me part of your personal life. What was so rough you couldn't share it with me?"

He averted his eyes. "I don't—can't talk about it. I want another chance. I can make it right between us."

She had the sudden urge to throw up. She couldn't decipher if it was Mark's insane request or being pregnant. Maybe a bit of both. "We're done, Mark. There is no chance."

He walked up to her, grabbing her arm before she could back away again. "Please, Zoe. I deserve another chance. I need another chance."

"You don't deserve anything. You hurt me. It's over," she said calmly, even as tiny shivers rushed up her arm at his touch.

"I didn't mean what I said a month ago. I was a jerk. I want to try again. Make it up to you," Mark pleaded, increasing the pressure on her arm slightly.

"There is no trying again," Zoe said, glancing at her arm. "Let me go, please. I'm seeing someone else."

Mark suddenly squeezed her tighter. Zoe grimaced in pain as he said through gritted teeth, "Who the hell are you seeing? Since when?"

"It's none of your damn business. Let me go. You're hurting my arm," she cried, pulling at his hand.

He let her go, taking a few deep breaths. "I can't lose you, Zoe. I want to know who you're seeing."

Zoe rubbed her arm as she took a few steps back. The glint in his eyes looked savage. She could still feel the strength, the repulsive feeling of his hand on her even as he stood a few feet away.

"Leave me alone, Mark. I'll call the police."

"You'll regret ever picking up the phone if you do that. You'll regret ever leaving me," Mark sneered at her.

"Leaving you? You broke up with me. Are you delusional?" Zoe said, suddenly terrified by the glimmer in his eyes.

"I remember the hot, cold attitude you dished at me. I remember just now trying to make it up to you. You'll regret this," he snapped, clenching his fists.

"You need to calm down." Zoe slowly backed up toward the door.

He almost rushed at her when Rina walked into the room. "Mark, there's a client on line two for you. I tried to take a message, but they weren't having it," Rina said calmly, as if she were unaware of the tension filling the room.

Mark unclenched his fists and glanced at Zoe with a smile. "We'll continue this conversation another time, Zoe, perhaps over dinner. I miss you." He smiled politely at Rina. "Thank you."

Zoe started shaking as soon as he walked out of the

room. Rina rushed to her side. "What happened?" Rina then glanced at her arm, lifting it up. "Did he do this to you?"

Tears started to flow freely as she wrapped her arm to her chest. "He scared me, Rina. He said I would regret not getting back with him. Is it okay to feel like your heart could explode? Could that hurt the baby?"

Rina's eyes got round, yet she maintained her composure. "I'm sure the baby is fine. Does Zeke know? You should tell him what Mark just did. I've never known him to be violent, but he left a bruise on your arm. He threatened you."

"He knows. He didn't seem too happy about it last night. We sort of fought, like we always do." Zoe sighed as she wiped her tears away as best she could. "I'm scared. I don't know if I should tell him. He wants me to stay with him until he solves these murders. I'm not sure I should go back there."

Zoe gestured at the doorway. "Now I have a crazy ex-boyfriend on my heels. Zeke probably doesn't want anything to do with me. A baby he doesn't want, a psycho ex-boyfriend. I'm nothing but baggage galore."

Rina smiled. "Zoe, come on. That man adores you. I saw it that day when he asked you to go home with him. He wants you. You don't see that? He probably just needs to process having a baby. You guys met in an unusual circumstance and have been moving so fast. You have to tell him about Mark. He physically hurt you. Maybe it isn't so strange to think he killed Mills like Dee threw at him the other day."

Zoe sucked in a breath. "You really think that? Mark, a killer?"

"I don't know, but he did hurt you and threatened you. Tell Zeke, please." Rina propped a hand on her hip. A very foreign gesture for her. "I'll tell Dee, who will go all out demon on you."

"Please don't do that," Zoe said with a depressing smile. "You know how she gets."

"Tell him then. He's a cop, if nothing else."

Zoe sighed, wiping a few more tears that escaped. "I'm just so raw right now. I need to go home. I know I've been doing that a lot lately, but I can't help it. Can you tell Ms. Black I'm leaving?"

Rina nodded. "Sure."

Zoe thanked her, grabbed her purse from her desk, and walked out.

BEN SAT at his desk going over every aspect of Murphy's life. Nothing strange was popping up yet. He broke a pencil he'd been twirling, flipping a page as he did. His desk phone rang as he started to reach for a new pencil.

"Detective Stoyer speaking," he said with little enthusiasm.

"Hi, Detective. This is Rina Chastain. I was looking for Detective Chance. Could I speak with him, please?" she said quietly into the phone.

Ben sucked in a breath at her smooth voice. "Yes, Ms. Chastain, I remember you. He's not at his desk right now."

He heard her sigh heavily. "Is everything okay? With you? With Zoe? You can tell me whatever you wanted to tell him if you're comfortable with that." He suddenly had the urge to see her beautiful face again. God, how pathetic.

"Well...I think I should tell someone. I know they haven't been seeing each other for very long yet and it's been an interesting relationship so far."

"He really cares about her. He has a funny way of showing it sometimes. But trust me when I say he's never felt more strongly about a woman than he does for Zoe. Whatever it is you think you should tell him...me...then I think you should. Trust your instincts," Ben said, his heart pounding a bit.

Every time her voice pricked his ears, his body shivered with anticipation. It was unlike any emotion he had ever experienced when it came to a woman.

"She's apprehensive right now about him. With good reason. Especially with a baby on the way and he's not happy about it. I—"

"Wait, what?" Ben interrupted her. "What do you mean a baby? She's pregnant?"

Rina inhaled a deep breath. "You didn't know that?"

"Hell, no, I didn't know about that. No wonder he's been distracted as hell today."

Why would Zeke keep something like that from him?

He picked up another pencil and started to twirl it like the last one. "I can't imagine he's not happy. Like I said before, he adores Zoe. He'd do anything for her—especially be there for her every step of the way with this pregnancy. Tell me right now what's bothering you?"

"Her ex-boyfriend...one of the reasons she went to the bar that night...he works here at our office. Mark Johnson. He cornered her in the break room. He said he wanted to get back together with her and she said no. He grabbed her arm and left a bruise. She's scared. I'm scared for her. He said she'd regret it—doing that to him."

Ben broke the pencil and sat up straighter in his chair. "Is she all right? How bad is it?"

"She was shaken up and left work. I walked in right after it happened. His fists were clenched. I'm honestly not sure how far he would've gone if I hadn't walked in. I told her to tell Zeke and she was...apprehensive about it. I called because I had to make sure he knew. I'm worried about her. I don't want to cause tension anywhere, especially our friendship, but I just want her to be safe."

"You did the right thing, I promise you that. He won't lay another finger on her. Zeke, or even I, will never allow it to happen again. Is he still there?" Ben asked with quiet anger lacing each word.

"Yes," Rina whispered, making him wonder if Mark was close-by. That thought didn't sit well with him.

"Is he near you?"

"Not right now."

"Good. Don't say anything to him or give him the impression you called anybody. We'll be there soon," Ben said firmly.

"What? Well, maybe—"

"Listen to me. He assaulted her. He left a bruise." Ben sighed. "It raises suspicion as well that he could be violent like that. He worked with Mills and Murphy."

"The same thought crossed my mind. I don't want to cause an issue."

"Trust me. You didn't cause anything. Mark did the moment he laid a finger on Zoe. You called us because you knew we would do something. Well, let us do our job."

"Thank you, Detective Stoyer," she said softly.

Ben took a small breath. This woman could break his heart with her soft words. "Call me Ben. You're welcome."

Ben hung up with Rina and leaned back in his chair as he processed everything. Zeke was going to flip out when he told him. Before he could decide how to break the news gently, Zeke walked back in, sitting at his desk.

"Man, the lab had nothing. They tried retrieving those

deleted files on Murphy's computer with no luck. So unless we find that flash drive, we won't know what was on there." Zeke sighed, rubbing a hand through his hair. "Did you find something good for us yet in all that crap lying on your desk?"

Ben glanced down at the paperwork, sighed, and shook his head. "I got an interesting phone call from Rina, Zoe's friend." Ben paused, trying to find the right words. "When were you going to tell me Zoe's pregnant?"

Zeke almost fell out of his chair. "Shit. She called you to tell you that. What the hell?"

"No, that's not the reason, but she blurted it out, saying Zoe told her you weren't taking it well. That you don't like the idea of a baby. You have been slightly off today."

"That's not true. I'm over the moon. I can't wait to tell my mom, who's going to freak and hopefully look past the fact we're not married yet. I've been distracted because I got home yesterday and found out she's pregnant. She said she was pissed about it. She doesn't want a baby with me. Now she's stuck with one. Yeah, I'm distracted," Zeke yelled, glancing around, noticing a few people looking at him. "What? What are you all looking at? Mind your business."

Ben frowned at Zeke. "Then keep your voice down. You want the captain to know you're sleeping with a potential witness in our case?"

Zeke took a few deep breaths. "I'm dating her, not just sleeping with her. I'm freaking inside and out, man. The way I feel about her in such a short amount of time should scare me. It doesn't. What scares me is losing her. I don't want to lose her. I feel like I am."

"You need to talk to her then. Talk to her about the baby. Reassure her, make her see this is a good thing. We need to keep her safe. We have issues here."

Zeke knitted his brows in confusion. "What issues? Why did Rina call? Does Dee know? Because, you know, she'll probably cut my balls off. I don't need that worry."

Ben laughed lightly. "I have no idea if she knows. Rina never said if she knew or not. I think it's safe to say that if Rina knows, Dee knows."

Zeke groaned as Ben blew out a breath. "Did you know her ex-boyfriend, Mark, works at the same office as her?"

"No. I didn't know that. I never asked," Zeke growled.

"He's the same ex-boyfriend who made her feel unworthy enough to go to a bar late at night dressed to kill in a slinky dress," Ben said, gauging Zeke's emotions. They weren't looking good.

"Do you have a point? Other than royally pissing me off that she works close to someone she once dated."

"I need you to keep calm and not go crazy on me," Ben started.

Zeke frowned.

"He spoke with her today in the break room. He wanted to try their relationship again. He—"

"Please, Ben. Please don't tell me she's leaving me for that jerk. I can't handle that," Zeke said quietly, the torture written on his face.

"No, calm down. She told him no. He didn't take that very well and he grabbed her, bruising her arm. Left a mark that Rina saw with her own eyes. She interrupted them. Mark had his fists clenched and she wasn't sure how far he really would've hurt her. He told Zoe she would regret it. It makes me think we might have a suspect in our murder cases."

When Zeke didn't speak but continued to stare at Ben as he clutched the edge of his desk, Ben said, "We have to take him in. Question him about the murders. Dig deeper into his background. He ditched her over a month ago—not kindly either—and now suddenly wants her back. A missing flash drive. Maybe he thinks she has it. Raise any funny bells to you?"

Ben sighed, suddenly worried about his partner. "We need to arrest him. He assaulted her. I need you to say something. You're freaking me out because I expected an extreme outburst here, not calmness."

Zeke continued to stare at him with immense fury pouring from his eyes. With quiet wrath, he said, "I'm just trying not to get up out of my chair and put a bullet through his brain, because that's exactly what I want to do right now. Why didn't she call me? Why did Rina call?"

"I don't know why. I'm worried about you. You can't go shooting the guy. Arresting him is entirely a different story," Ben said, standing up from his desk.

Zeke stood up as well. "I want to see Zoe first. I need to see...see what he did."

Ben sighed. "Rina said she went home. Perhaps we—"

"Don't argue with me, Ben. I need to make sure she's okay."

Ben nodded. "Okay. Let's go."

8

ZOE SAT on the bed staring at the deep-red mark on her arm. It still wouldn't go away. She had a sick, gut-wrenching feeling it wasn't planning on it either. Zeke would see it, giving her no choice but to tell him.

Why would Mark even hurt her? He had never given the impression that he was a violent man. They had worked together for two years before they even started dating. He could be abrupt, sometimes even rude when he worked with people, but never with her. He was a pure gentleman when he stepped out of the office. She dated him for three months before he uttered those disastrous words.

Now, nothing but confusion and fear. Why did he want to get back together? It made no sense.

Zoe turned her head toward the hallway. The front door had slammed closed. Then Zeke's voice floated down the hallway as he called her name.

What was he doing home already? She took a deep breath, pulled down her sleeve to cover the bruise, and walked out of the bedroom to the living room. Ben stood with Zeke when she walked in. Zeke didn't look happy to see her.

"Zoe, are you all right?"

"I'm fine. Why are you both here? Do you want me to leave finally? Ben here to throw me out?"

Zeke looked shocked, as did Ben. "What are you talking about? The last thing I ever want is for you to walk out that door. I fear it every single minute of the day. I want you in my life. You...and the baby. I couldn't be happier about that. But I know you're not, so it was hard last night to keep in my joy. You said you were pissed that you were pregnant." Zeke paused as he brushed a hand across his jaw. "Is the baby even mine?"

Zoe instantly took a step forward as the temptation to slap him flooded her. "How dare you say that to me? Insinuating I sleep around. Are we back to me being a hooker? You have a funny way of telling me how important I am to you when you keep insulting me in such a manner. If you didn't come to throw me out, well, maybe I should leave on my own."

"It could've been your ex-boyfriend's baby. You broke up with him the same night I met you. How should I know? How close were you with him? He just tried begging his way back into your life today," Zeke snapped, taking a step closer to her. "You keep wanting to leave. If that's what you want to do, I can't stop you. But if that baby is mine, you won't be able to keep me away. I will be a father in that baby's life."

"I slept with him once over two months ago. It's not his. Regardless of what you keep thinking about me, I don't flaunt myself around. One night of insanity apparently gives you that impression. I never date much, to be honest with you, because men don't seem to find me appealing. Not sure what the hell you see in me."

Zoe backed up as she wrapped her arms around her stomach. "I wasn't pissed about the baby. I was pissed the damn stick took so long to tell me. That's what I meant by that. It was just taking way too long, and the suspense was killing me. I was worried you would hate me for it."

Zoe started to heave deep breaths to keep the tears back. She would not cry in front of him. "You didn't say you were happy. You didn't do anything. You walked out of the room without a word about how you felt. What was I supposed to think? I would never keep the baby from you, unless you got physical, that is."

Zeke immediately walked up to her, grabbing her hands. "I would never hurt you. Never. Do you hear me? Never lay one finger on you. My way with words sucks. What can I say other than I'm an idiot? I want this baby. I want it with you, and I want you to stay."

He glanced down at her arms. "I know Mark asked to get back together with you, and I instantly worried you would want to go back to him. We haven't talked much about our past relationships, especially your last one. I know—"

"I would never go back to him. I wouldn't," she whispered.

Zeke let go of her hands and gently cupped her face. "I know he hurt you. I want to kill him for even laying one finger on you."

He gently grabbed her arms. She winced as his hand touched her left arm. He hesitated, then moved her sleeve up. Rage poured from his eyes as he stared at the deep-red bruise. She tried to cover it up, but he wouldn't let her.

"Why didn't you call me? Were you going to keep this from me? I'm here to protect you, Zoe. Please trust me."

"I'm scared. Crazy ex, baby unwanted. I figured it would

be too much and you wouldn't want me anymore," she whispered.

He let go of her arm, grabbing her face into his soft hands again, and kissed her lightly on the lips. "I will always want you, no matter how crazy life gets. I want this baby so much. You have no idea."

She smiled tentatively. "Really?"

He kissed her again. "I guess we need to learn how to communicate better. We could have avoided this whole baby argument. I never thought you slept around. You did recently break up with someone. It was a fair question."

"I swear it was only once." She smiled deviously at him as she whispered, "It compared nothing to you. Nothing compares to you."

Zeke pulled her into his arms, embracing her fiercely. "I could take you right now. You mean the world to me." He lowered his mouth, kissing her deeply. Zoe moaned in delight as his tongue tangoed with hers.

A throat suddenly cleared behind them. "I can see you two clearly made up, but we do have a murder to solve."

Zeke pulled away from her, winked, and put his arm around her side. "Sorry, Ben. You know how it is."

Ben shook his head with a smirk plastered on his face. "No, I don't. Never been in love before."

Zoe inhaled sharply.

"Well, maybe you should try it," Zeke said, glancing at her. "I should go. I wanted to make sure you were all right. I never meant to fight with you. I guess we're just good at it."

"Where are you going? It wasn't—"

"Don't you dare say it wasn't a big deal," Zeke interrupted her and gently grabbed her arm, taking care to avoid the bruise. "This is a big deal. He bruised you. I'm going to arrest him. Then I'm going to question him about his where-abouts when Mills and Murphy were murdered."

"You think he killed them," Zoe murmured, a slight tremor running through her body.

Zeke pulled her closer. "He works there. He hurt you. He's capable of violence."

Ben stepped closer to them. "Think about it, Zoe. Over a month ago when he broke up with you—how was his demeanor?"

Zoe cringed, hating to think about it. "He was distant. He wasn't nice about how he dumped me. If I'm honest, it wasn't that great of a relationship. We didn't connect that well. Today he said he had personal issues around that time. I don't know what kind of issues."

"How was he today? Besides the obvious, with grabbing your arm," Ben asked softly.

"He acted sweet, like he cared. He said he made a mistake and that's when he mentioned he had issues. He didn't like my rejection, although I wasn't nice about it. He said he wanted another chance...no...needed another chance. He grabbed my arm. He scared me with the look in his eyes. I told him to let me go and I was seeing someone anyway, that it didn't matter. That's when he squeezed hard-er," Zoe said as she started to shake.

"It's okay, honey. Did you tell him who you were seeing? Did you tell him it was me?" Zeke asked.

"No, I didn't say who. I told him to let me go because he was hurting me and he did. I told him I would call the police. That's when he got that really terrifying look on his face. He told me not to call the police or I would regret it. He looked like he was going to advance at me when Rina finally walked in. I didn't know how I was going to get out of that room," Zoe said, a few tears falling down as she finished. Her voice cracked as well.

Zeke pulled her into his embrace, rubbing her back lightly as she started to cry. "It's okay, Zoe. He won't hurt you again. I swear it."

"I'm afraid if you lock him up, he'll come back and hurt me. Maybe we should leave it alone," she cried into his chest.

"No, Zoe. I'm not leaving this alone. I'm arresting him for assaulting you. That's final. Don't you see? He was cold, heartless even, when he broke up with you. Now he's acting all sweet, gets angry when you deny him. He could be the one looking for that flash drive. Maybe he thought buttering up to you would work better than stalking you. I won't let him hurt you again. Do you understand me?" Zeke said softly, as he continued to rub her back.

His calming touch always made her feel better. He was doing a remarkable job. She didn't want him to leave.

"You know I can go get him myself. Why don't you stay here with Zoe?" Ben offered.

Zoe sniffed, trying to stop the tears. She pulled away from Zeke, wiping at her eyes. "I don't know why I'm crying like this. I'm normally not this emotional."

Ben laughed lightly. "I'm no expert, Zoe, but I'd have to say it's called being pregnant."

Zoe turned her mouth up in a mild grin. "I guess so. You're probably right. I keep feeling things I normally don't feel. Like the urge to throw up right now." She grabbed her mouth and rushed out of the room.

BEN'S FACE went into shock. "Is she going to be okay? Was she kidding?"

Zeke frowned. "I don't think so. You did remind her she's pregnant. I guess that's what happens when you're pregnant."

Ben started laughing loudly. "You are so in for it. I can't wait."

"What's so funny? In for what?"

"Hormones. Nine long months of hormones—raging pregnancy hormones."

Zeke scowled at Ben as he continued to mock him. "Midnight food runs because nothing sounds good to her, hogging of the bed because she needs the space, complaining of every pain imaginable, sensitivity to what you say. Make sure to be absolutely clear when you speak so she doesn't misinterpret anything you say, sort of like what happened last night. Hormones, my friend." He smirked real wide. "And no sex, too. They can't handle it when they're pregnant. Women feel fat or they're going to hurt the baby or—"

"Please stop." Zeke held up his hand, a horrified expression on his face. "Please do not go any further, because you have no idea what you're talking about. Absolutely no idea. Since when are you some big expert on having a kid? Oh yeah, you already said you weren't an expert. Plus, you don't have any."

Ben chuckled and crossed his arms as if he knew what he was talking about.

"You're right on one thing, though. From now on, I need to be as clear as possible with her. I did walk out of the room, afraid she was angry about it, and I should've just asked her. Could've cleared that whole mess up last night. I hope the crying stops, at least. I can't stand her tears, especially if I'm the cause. They tear my heart to pieces."

"They kinda tore me up, too. I can handle taking care of Mark." Ben grinned lightly. "And I have four sisters. Three have been pregnant before. I know what I'm talking about."

Zeke turned toward the hallway, indecision on his mind. He turned back toward Ben, the pain on his face. "I hate to leave her. I hate to let you go alone because I want to beat that man within an inch of his life."

Ben sighed. "That's probably why you should leave it to me. I might actually let you do it because he deserves it."

"I can handle it. I wouldn't do it, no matter how much I want to. I can't afford to lose Zoe by getting myself locked up." Zeke raked a hand through his hair, squeezing his eyes shut in frustration. "I don't want to leave her, though. She seems so fragile right now. I hate this."

A light hand touched his shoulder. He turned slightly to see Zoe. "Please don't worry about me. I'm okay. You should go with. I would hate it if something terrible happened to Ben because you weren't there to back him up."

Ben looked wounded. "Hey, I can handle myself. I don't need lover boy here to be the big man. I could take this Mark guy with one hand behind my back."

Zoe curled her lips in a gentle smile, while Zeke laughed heartily.

"I don't know, man. My beautiful lady here is one smart cookie. She knows strength...and weakness when she sees it."

"Very true. She's going to bring you to your knees one of these days jamming your weakness. Watch it," Ben retorted with a wicked grin.

Zeke lowered his smile to a glower. "I'm going to bring you to your knees right now."

"Boys, let's calm down. I didn't mean you couldn't handle it, Ben. I'm sure you could—can." Zoe glanced at Zeke. "You have a job to do, and I don't want you to worry about me. I'll be fine here. I'm not going anywhere."

"Promise?" Zeke asked as nervous energy flowed through him every time she talked about leaving.

"I'm not leaving. I promise." She glanced back at Ben. "You can always ask Dee for help if you can't handle it. She abhors Mark and would gladly knock him on his ass."

Ben chuckled. "No, thanks. She doesn't scare me either."

Zeke's eyes glimmered with laughter. "No, but Rina does."

Zoe looked confused. "Rina scares you? She wouldn't hurt a fly."

"Listen here. That woman scares the pants off me with her quiet tones. It's unnerving," Ben said with a slight tremor.

Zeke smirked. "I could think of another reason she'd scare the pants right off you."

Zoe's eyes bulged out. "You like Rina?" She lightly laughed. "Never mind. That's a dumb question. Everyone likes her. She's gorgeous and doesn't realize it."

Ben walked closer to her. "Look, Zoe, I know you're with Zeke—and let me tell you, he's one lucky guy. You're gorgeous, too. You made a comment why he would even be interested in you. It's plain to see why he is. Like I said, he's a lucky guy."

"That's all obvious stuff. I have a gorgeous woman. I am damn lucky. So you like Rina?" Zeke pressed on, a wicked grin on his face.

Zoe blushed lightly at Ben's words as she laughed at Zeke's, while Ben pursed his lips in a perplexed manner. "She's something else. Let's say that." Ben sighed. "She has this sweet, smooth voice on the phone. What am I saying? No, I don't like her."

Zoe started to laugh, then paused with confusion. "When did you talk to her on the phone?" She looked over at Zeke. "How did you know what happened today?"

Zeke grabbed her hands. "She was worried, honey. She told him what happened because she was concerned you wouldn't have told me. Were you going to tell me?" He glanced at the long sleeve covering her arm.

Zoe bit her lip in guilt. "I don't know. Probably...maybe. I was scared, okay. You probably would've noticed it anyway."

"Zoe, please don't be mad at her. She felt bad calling. She was only worried, like Zeke said. She had your best interest at heart. I forced it out of her," Ben said.

"Forced it out of her? She called you, Ben," Zoe said matter-of-factly.

"Very true. But please don't be mad at her," Ben insisted.

"Because you like her," Zoe said with a grin.

Zeke chuckled as Ben's jaw dropped. "Wow, you two are perfect for each other. It's sickening."

"So, that was a yes?" Zoe asked.

"Why are we having this conversation? We have a man to arrest. Come on, Zeke," Ben said, gesturing toward the door.

Zeke pulled Zoe into his side, grinning like an idiot. "My sweetheart asked you a question."

"I hate you both. I really do." Ben shook his head as he walked toward the door, then he turned back around. "What? Does it matter? Come on, Zoe. You're honestly going to tell me a gorgeous, sweet, silent-violent woman like that is available."

"Silent-violent?" Zoe asked, curious.

"Yes. I told you, her quiet demeanor could peel paint off the walls when she's upset. I would hate to tango with her in a real fight. She'd rip me apart, scaring my pants right off," Ben said with a shudder.

"You like her. Like I said the other day, we can double date," Zeke said happily. He turned to Zoe, kissing her on the mouth, relishing in her sweet, delectable taste for a brief moment, then pulled away reluctantly.

"We should go. We have a lot to do. I'll be gone for a while dealing with this. Maybe you should call Rina...and Dee." Zeke hesitated on that last part. "Have them come over and keep you company. Tell them to keep quiet about me. I don't want anyone at your company suspicious. I know it was someone there who killed those two. I don't have physical evidence to support that— just my instincts. I can't ask you to quit your job, so I'm asking you to pretend—at least at work—I'm not dating you. No one will think to look for you at my house, especially if they don't know we're together."

"I can do that. I would hate it if Mark hurt you. I need you—in more ways than one," Zoe said, rubbing a hand over her belly.

Zeke grinned as he bent down to kiss her belly. "I love you in there, my little monster." He stood back up. "Nobody's going to hurt me. Or you. Order pizza or something. Stay inside with your friends until I get home. Take it easy on Rina. I've got a funny feeling she'll have a lot on her plate with that nut over there."

Zoe grinned at Ben, who turned red and looked away. "I'm not asking her out. Let's go, Zeke." He headed for the door. This time he kept going, pulling it open and walking out.

Zeke gave Zoe another light kiss. "I hate leaving you. When we solve this case, I'm taking some time off so we can laze around."

"I'd like that. You should go," Zoe said, glancing at the door as she rubbed her belly.

He placed a comforting hand on top of hers. "I already love this little monster inside you. I did the minute you told me, even if I freaked out a bit." He paused a moment, inhaling a deep breath. "Just like how I love you. I know it hasn't been long for us. I can't explain it. I just know. I can't imagine my life without you. That tells me it's love, because I've never felt this way before. Never in my life. I'll be the best father to our little monster and the best man in your life as well. I swear that to you."

A lone tear rolled down Zoe's cheek. Zeke swiped away the tear. "I didn't mean to make you cry. Please don't cry. It tears me apart. I should have—"

Zoe kissed his lips to quiet his words. She always had to interrupt him. Would he ever get used to that? Of course, he didn't mind this kind of interruption.

Zeke grabbed her ass, pressing her into him, groaning into her mouth with the passion he felt. His feet stumbled a bit as she backed him up to the wall like that one disastrous night, assaulting his tongue in a fervor. He almost wished she had on his favorite dress so he could inch his hands up her beautiful body, feeling nothing but sweet, silky skin.

He broke the kiss briefly, whispering against her mouth, "I have to go, honey. Ben's waiting for me in the car. The things I want to do to you right now, you have no idea."

Zoe grabbed his head in response, pulling his mouth back to hers. She fought with his tongue, pulling back slightly, biting his lip in sweet delight. He groaned as she pressed into him, bringing her hands through his hair, down his arms, sliding them in between their heated bodies to grasp at his belt buckle.

Zeke grabbed her hands, breaking the kiss. "I can't, Zoe. I swear I want to. You're killing me here."

"I can't help myself. You do things to me." Zoe lightly nipped his lip again. "I'm scared, Zeke."

He placed his hands gently on her face. "Why?"

"Because you love me. Because I should say it back," Zoe whispered.

"You don't have to say it back. I won't rush you. Please, trust me from now on. Call me the minute something happens. I can't stand to think if something happened to you."

"I will."

"Swear?"

"Yes." Zoe grabbed another kiss, pressing lightly into him again. "You should go now."

Zeke pulled her deeper into him. "Yeah, I should. I want to say don't wait up for me, but—wait up for me."

Zoe grinned, backing away. "I can see that as a possibility."

"Call your friends. Have some fun. Say good things about me to Dee. I really need her to start liking me." Zeke grinned as he headed for the door before he changed his mind and wrapped Zoe up in his arms, taking her to his bedroom.

"I've already been trying," she said with exasperation.

"Try harder," he said with a grin as he opened the door. "I love you."

He waited for a brief second, waiting for anything, receiving a small smile in return, then closed the door gently behind him.

"UGH. THIS IS DISGUSTING," Zoe cried as she threw her piece of pizza back on the plate.

Dee raised a brow in disbelief. "You love sausage and pepperoni pizza. What's going on? Are you...no, please tell me it didn't come back positive. I will kill that man with my bare hands."

Zoe sighed. "Please, Dee. Please like him. Try to give him a chance. We've both made mistakes in this relationship, as weird and crazy as it's been. I'm pregnant. I'm excited. He's excited."

"So you talked with him? Because earlier you said you didn't think he wanted the baby," Rina said tentatively.

Zoe smiled at Rina. "Yeah, we talked right before I called you guys to keep me company. It was a misunderstanding. It's something we both want, not that we asked for it, but we want it."

Zoe looked down at her arm, lightly rubbing it, wincing as it still hurt to touch. "I know why you called him, Rina. I'm sorry I made you think you had to do that. I should've called him myself right away. I'm not mad at you." Zoe looked up. Rina grinned with relief.

"I was afraid you would be mad, but I had to do it. If Mark did something even worse—I wouldn't have been able to live with myself." Rina looked over at Dee, who chewed her pizza with silent, angry vibes rolling off her. "Give him a chance. He does care for her. Not all men can express their emotions right away. These two are meant for each other. It was destined."

Dee looked annoyed. "Destined? Rina, get the stars out of your eyes. He could still hurt her. Leave her with a baby without a glance good-bye. He—"

"Loves me," Zoe finished for her, glancing back and

forth between the two, watching as the surprise splattered all over their faces.

"Just because he shows sweetness, slick words that run off his tongue, does not mean he loves you, Zoe," Dee said wryly, covering her shock up quickly.

"He loves me because he told me right before he left. I feel it every time he places a soft hand on me, or the way his eyes glance at me, and even the way his slick words slide over my body. I believe him. I want you to give him a chance because I can't handle any more nerves running through me. You two not getting along brings those nerves out full force. Please, Dee."

"I don't want to like him or give him a chance." Dee scrunched her lips up in a measured manner. "I'm sorry. I don't want to see you hurt again like you were a month ago, but I'll try."

Zoe blew out a calming breath, the sudden anxiety slowly releasing from her body. "Thank you, Dee."

"So, you love him, too?" Dee asked with a funny face.

Zoe shifted in her seat, rubbing her belly faster. "I never said it back. My emotions are haywire right now. I do trust him with my life, but my heart is still a little leery. I'm so used to rejection from the men I date that I'm afraid. I'm going to try, though. I'm not giving up on us."

"Take your time, Zoe. You both have the rest of your life to figure it out," Rina said softly, the happiness shining in her eyes mingled with relief.

"Yeah, I know. He understood. He said he wouldn't rush me." Zoe glanced over at Rina with a sly grin. "So, you talked to Ben today?"

Rina glanced away. "Yes, I did. Zeke wasn't available, so I had to tell Ben."

"Who's Ben?" Dee asked.

Zoe smiled brightly. "Zeke's partner. Remember the other guy in Mills's office that day they delivered the news he was murdered. He was also with Zeke knocking on doors in the neighborhood when my house was broken into. He's cute, don't you think, Rina?"

Dee bawled out laughing as Rina blew out a nervous breath. "Do you like this man, Rina?" Dee teased. "Where's my hunky detective? This suddenly doesn't feel fair."

"I don't like Detective Stoyer like that. He seems like a very nice man, though," Rina said shyly, glancing at her nails.

"I'll ask Zeke who would be perfect for you, Dee, don't worry," Zoe said.

"You better. I feel left out," Dee pouted with a twinkle in her eye. She glanced at Rina, who was still poking at her nails. "Rina, I've never noticed you to blush over a man before. You always quietly brush them off with ease. You like this guy. Don't lie to us."

"I don't brush anyone off because men don't like me like that," Rina said as the other two scoffed at her with disbelief. "What? They don't. Men make me nervous."

"Give me a break. I've never once seen you nervous around a man. Unless you never really liked them as you do this Ben guy," Dee said with a crafty smile.

"He seems nice, but I can't say I like him." Rina bit her lip lightly, glancing at Zoe. "Why? Did he say something about me?"

"Oh, he was just as nervous talking about you as you are talking about him. Getting red in the face, denying liking you, raving about how smooth your voice is over the phone. He likes you," Zoe said matter-of-factly.

"Man, you both are falling like rocks. I'm sitting over here taming my hair so I can hopefully see a man through the mess of it all," Dee said with misery slightly pouring out of her eyes.

"I don't have a man," Rina said.

"But you could with one simple, delectable moan from your mouth. I dare you to try it and see if he ravishes you silly," Dee said with a sexual gleam in her eye.

"Dee, stop saying things like that," Rina said, embarrassed. "I don't moan."

"No, not even while you're having sex? You do make these silly sounds sometimes when you're eating something delicious. He might even take you over the table if you went out to dinner with him," she replied deviously.

Zoe started laughing. "Oh geez, you two are too much. I couldn't ask for better friends. Dee, leave the poor girl alone. I was teasing." Zoe glanced at Rina. "I think he likes you, though. Maybe you should give him a chance if he asks you out. You rarely date when you could probably have any man you want."

"I don't like dating for a reason," Rina said quietly.

"Yeah? What's the reason? Dish already," Dee demanded.

"Men make me nervous. I told you that already. I need another refill of my tea. Excuse me," Rina said, standing up.

Dee turned to Zoe. "I didn't mean to upset her. She can be so sensitive sometimes. And she's not even pregnant like you."

Zoe sighed. "Give her time. Ben seems like a great guy. Maybe she just needs the right man to open her eyes." Zoe picked up a piece of pizza. "Let's talk about something else. No need to upset her anymore." She took a small bite as she glanced at Dee, who nodded in agreement.

Rina walked back into the room, sitting quietly down on the sofa. Dee glanced at her, then turned her attention to

Zoe. "So, what's going to happen to Mark? I hope they slam the book on the jerk for hurting you today. Zeke's going to beat his ass I hope."

Zoe laughed lightly. "He wants to. I almost forgot to tell you guys that he doesn't want anyone at the office to know I'm dating him. If it isn't Mark who killed Mills and Murphy, he thinks it's someone else there. He wants it a secret where I am so no one can find me. They're going to arrest him for the assault and question him about the murders."

"I told you he could have done it," Dee said with certainty.

"I thought you were kidding, Dee," Rina pointed out.

"Well, I was kidding—kind of. Look at what he did to Zoe. Repressed violence like that is just asking to be released. He's totally capable of it. He's always been a little douchey—we all know this. I never understood why you dated him in the first place, Zoe," Dee said as she scrunched her face like she was revolted by the thought.

"I would've never met Zeke if I hadn't. That's what I'm telling myself. I don't have any other excuse except insanity," Zoe said sadly.

"I'm glad you met him. Especially now that he's here to protect you from Mark, so he can't hurt you again. He scared me today. I saw the violence, the rage in his eyes," Rina said quietly.

Zoe and Dee glanced at Rina in a new light for the first time. Then they shared a look, silently communicating that maybe they had missed something in Rina's demeanor the whole time they'd known her.

"Well, there are two hunky detectives on the case to thwart any further violence. Let's all cheer to that," Dee said jokingly and picked up her drink, holding it out for the other two to clink glasses with her.

Rina gave a halfhearted smile, raising her glass to meet Dee's. They both glanced at Zoe, who started to pick up her glass, then changed her mind, throwing her pizza down on the table, nearly missing it by inches.

"I think I need to throw up again. I hate pizza," Zoe exclaimed as she stood up quickly from the couch, rushing to the bathroom.

"Whoa. Not sure I ever want to be pregnant if that happens frequently. She loves pizza," Dee said.

"I guess the baby doesn't," Rina said with a small grin.

Dee glanced over at Rina. "Well, cheers to you then. We're going to be aunties. That's good enough to cheer away. Let's baby shop one of these days."

"That's a nice idea. She would enjoy that," Rina said, clinking her glass one more time with Dee.

9

"SO TELL ME, Mr. Johnson, do you like hurting women—people in general?" Zeke asked as he scowled at Mark from across the desk in the interrogation room.

"I have no idea what you're talking about or why you even arrested me. You made me look like a criminal in front of all my colleagues. This is ridiculous," Mark growled, slamming his handcuffed hands on the table. Zeke didn't flinch by the outburst, although his rage simmered below the surface to pound the guy into the floor.

"I would watch your violence with us, Mr. Johnson. We know how to fight back," Ben said straight-faced as he stood slightly behind Zeke near the door with his arms crossed.

"I want my lawyer. I'm not saying anything else until my lawyer gets here because I didn't do anything wrong," Mark said smugly, leaning back in his chair.

"Sure, we'll get your lawyer. Have a quick look at this picture first. You don't need to say anything because we all know you did do something wrong. You put your filthy hands on a woman, bruising her arm. In my book, that's called an assault. In the law's book, that's also called an assault."

Zeke smiled menacingly as he opened the folder, took a photo out, and laid it on the table in front of Mark, glad he thought to call Susan and have her swing by his house to take crime scene pictures of Zoe's bruise. Thankfully, she had responded right away.

Looking at the photo himself, he could feel his fury bubbling rapidly to the surface, but he squashed it down, not wanting to ruin the case in any way. Mark was going to pay for what he did. The correct way.

Mark started to get red in the face as he leaned forward, resting his clenched hands on top of the table, staring threateningly at the picture.

"Still nothing to say, Mr. Johnson? No excuse why there's a bruise there. You threatened her. You told her not to call the police or she'd regret it. What did you mean by that? What would she regret? More physical harm?" Zeke edged further, trying to break the dam waiting to burst within Mark. He could see the intensity pouring from his eyes, wanting to reach inside the picture and inflict more pain on Zoe. Over his dead body would Mark ever lay another hand on her.

"I didn't hurt her. She's a damn liar. Zoe's nothing but a liar. She did that to herself," Mark yelled, slamming his hands on the picture, shoving it away.

Zeke grabbed the photo before it went flying to the floor, slamming it down in front of Mark. "Look! Take a good look. I see only a picture of an arm. I don't see a face. Who in the hell mentioned Zoe? You're the liar."

Zeke shoved it closer. "She upset you because she wouldn't go back to your filthy self. She knocked down your insecurities, making you look pathetic. You don't like it when a woman does that to you, do you? What other rage do you have simmering inside? Did Mr. Mills and Mr. Murphy upset you somehow, too? Did you unleash some anger on them and kill them? Are you planning on showing her the regret by killing her? Tell me, damn it."

"That bitch deserved it. She was pissing me off, leaving me for someone else. When I find out who it is—"

"You'll what? Tell me. You'll hurt him, too? I'd like to see you try," Zeke said with cold malice in his voice. "Are you a killer, Mr. Johnson? I'm starting to think you are."

"I didn't kill anyone. I want my lawyer now. I'm done talking." Mark pressed his lips closed.

"Sure, Mr. Johnson. Let me get that lawyer for you. You're going to need it," Zeke said, grabbing the photo and sliding it into the folder.

"I'll be out of here in no time flat, detective. Make no mistake about that. My father is the best lawyer in town," Mark said with arrogance.

Zeke smiled calmly. "Is that right? Well, my father happens to be the best judge in town. We'll see how fast you actually get out of here."

Zeke turned around after he enjoyed the look of surprise on Mark's face, then stepped out into the hallway with Ben.

Ben closed the door, whooping with laughter. "Whew. I swore you were going to deck the man. You had me going there."

"I almost did. I can't stand it that I couldn't. He hurt her, Ben," Zeke said, breathing hard, his chest heaving in pain.

Ben clapped a hand on his shoulder. "She's safe now. He can't hurt her again. Plus, I guess you're bringing dear old dad in. You never use your dad for anything."

Zeke looked Ben in the eye. "I've never loved a woman like I do. I'll do whatever it takes. When my dad hears he's going to be a grandpa and his only son is taming down, I don't think he's going to care."

"I'd love to see that conversation." Ben chuckled.

"Well, what the hell you waiting for? Let's go," Zeke said with a grin as he headed down the hallway. "Better make our move now before Mark's dear old dad gets here."

ZEKE QUIETLY CLOSED the front door. All the lights were out in the living room. A loud sigh escaped as disappointment swept through him that she went to bed without him. He shouldn't be surprised. It was almost eleven o'clock.

Ben had issued a few more unwanted pregnancy advices, according to his knowledge, that were debunked in Zeke's mind. He mentioned that pregnant women get tired —a lot. Adding in with a sly grin, which was why they don't like sex. Zeke had grinned despite himself, as he knew Ben was only trying to get his goat. It slightly worked because he couldn't imagine not taking Zoe whenever he wanted. The urge seemed to strike with the least amount of effort on her part. A simple glance his way and he wanted her without thought. She simply did things he couldn't describe. Probably the reason he fell so hard, so fast.

He silently made his way down the hallway. A dim light spilled out from underneath his bedroom door. His lips curled in delight. She waited up for him. He opened the door. She sat propped up in bed, a laptop resting nicely on a pillow on her lap.

One brief glance and he was hard as a rock, wanting to take her to the height of pleasure and show her the love he truly had. He felt no dismay—yet—that she couldn't say I love you. They were moving fast. He wouldn't rush her, like he told her earlier today. He had faith she would eventually say it.

"You look wiped out. Come here," Zoe said tenderly as she closed the laptop, setting it on the nightstand, and then patted the spot next to her.

"I am wiped out. It was a long day. I worried about you constantly," Zeke said as he unholstered his weapon, laid it on the nightstand next to his badge as well as his phone.

"I'm okay. You saw for yourself. Plus, you arrested Mark, right?" Zoe asked with a slight quiver in her voice.

Zeke took his shirt off and hurriedly tossed his pants off as well. He climbed into bed and pulled her into his arms. A tremble passed through her body. Sadly, he knew it wasn't from his touch, but from the thought of Mark hurting her again.

"Yes, I arrested him. I basically got a confession from him about hurting you. I might've provoked it out of him, though," he said with a grin. "He'll be spending the night in jail. He'll most likely get out tomorrow."

He framed her face and lightly kissed her. "I worry about you because I can't help myself. We have two unsolved murders, a crazy ex-boyfriend, and an unknown person trying to get something from you that you don't even have. I'll always worry, even when life goes back to normal."

He kissed her again. He would always make sure she was safe. And he would always worry. No doubt about that.

"Don't worry. I'm fine—really. Maybe a little nervous to see Mark again. He'll probably get out tomorrow, huh?"

"Yeah, he would've gotten out tonight because his dad is Lawrence Johnson, best criminal defense attorney in the city. He pushed hard to get him out. We pushed hard right back, especially about Mills and Murphy."

"So, I'm guessing he didn't confess to that."

"No, he didn't confess to that. Tell me, how well do you know him?"

Zoe frowned. "Why? Does it matter? I already feel so stupid for dating the man."

Zeke cradled her face, caressing lightly. "Don't feel stupid. I'm curious for the case. Because honestly, I want to forget he exists, or that he ever held you in his arms like I'm doing now."

"He never held me in his arms like you are. It wasn't that kind of relationship. He was never touchy-feely with me. He told me in the break room that I was hot and cold for him. I guess he blames me for that, and I'm not sorry either. I took him breaking up with me hard because of the way he did it, the words he said to me. They hurt." Zoe frowned. "I'm not sure what you want to know. I've never even met his parents."

"I want to know anything that struck you as odd. I want to know what you did together. Did he seem distracted? He told you he had a personal issue and that's why he broke it off."

"We mostly went out to dinner, a few shows, hung out at my place a few times. Never his place. He never offered to take me there. I thought that was slightly odd. We talked about work, nothing strange about that. Nothing where I thought he was digging for information, if that's what you're wondering. We only slept together one time. And I'm not sure why I even did," she said, looking away from him.

He nudged her chin back his way. "You're mine now. For as long as you'll have me. I hate the way he made you feel. But what he did brought you to me. So, I don't hate that. I'll keep digging to find out what personal issues he had," he replied, kissing her on the lips. "I love you."

She smiled slightly, but made no response.

"I make you uncomfortable when I say that, don't I?"

She shifted in his arms. "Maybe."

He shifted closer. "Better quit squirming with me. You know how my body reacts to sudden movement." She grinned at him deviously as he continued, "And you better get used to hearing me say I love you. Because I do and I'm not afraid to tell you. We need to be clear with each other since we have this crazy experience misunderstanding each other all the time. If I have to repeat it all day, every day, then that's what I have to do. You'll get used to it, I promise. I love you."

He started to shift on the bed, bending toward her stomach, and lifted her nightgown to reveal her delicate, soft skin. "I love this little monster, too." He kissed her and glanced at her as she smiled brightly.

"Why must you call our child a little monster?" she asked with a chuckle.

"Don't know. You can be very scary when you're angry. Turns me on. Although, who am I kidding? Almost everything you do turns me on."

He winked at her, then peppered a few more kisses on her belly, making a small trail until he reached her mouth. He devoured her mouth, moving expertly over her body when he whispered against her lips, "You're not gonna deny me sex or anything because you're afraid we'll hurt the baby, will you?"

"No. Why? Could it hurt the baby?" A deep worry suddenly filtered out in waves.

"No. Heavens, no. The baby will be fine," Zeke replied with a rushed breath.

She grinned, her body relaxing. "Then why did you ask?"

He shifted his body so he was lying next to her instead of

on top of her. "Ben has a big mouth. He put a few whispers into my head how pregnancy can be. He's trying to mess with my head."

"Obviously, he's doing a good job. I thought he said he wasn't an expert."

"He's not, but he has four sisters and they've been pregnant before. Hell, I have a sister and she has three kids. I know things, too. Sex will not hurt the baby." He grabbed her hand. "Don't deny me, please."

"I won't. Unless, of course, the doctor says so," she said with a giggle.

"Did you make an appointment? I want to be there for everything, every step of the way."

She shook her head. "No. I didn't even think about it. It's all a little scary. I didn't even tell my parents yet. I might wait a bit on that. I'd hate for my dad to pull the shotgun out because his little girl was knocked up before marriage."

Zeke grimaced. "He's gonna hate me, is what you're saying?"

"Well, he's not going to like it, but he won't hate you. I don't think so anyway. I've never brought a man home to meet the folks before, let alone one that made me pregnant."

"Oh man, I'm dead meat. I don't want your parents to hate me."

She cradled his face in her free hand. "Don't worry about it. They're good people. Once the initial shock wears off, I'm sure everything will be fine. I'm going to wait until this whole murder mess is dealt with. I don't want them to worry about any of that. I'd have to explain everything and I've never been able to lie to my parents."

"My dad took it well."

"When in the world did you have time to tell your dad?"

"Oh, well, about that. Mark threw his dad's name out there, all smug, thinking he'd be out in a snap. He probably would've been, but I went to my dad and got all smug back. I don't normally use my dad or his position, and quite frankly, I try to avoid dealing with my dad at all costs when it comes to work. I didn't want Mark out right away, so I did. My dad's a judge. He knows I never come to him for stuff and he respects that. Me doing that out of the blue, well, it raised some red flags. I had to confess. He was delighted and insisted on meeting you...soon. Like...tomorrow night for dinner."

Zoe immediately shrank back from him. He wasn't about to let her pull away. Not like that. He pulled her back into his embrace, wrapping his legs around hers. "Why do I get the feeling you don't like that idea?"

"Meeting the parents is a lot, Zeke. What if they hate me? What if they ask how we met?" She tried to move away again, but his arms tightly pressing on her back and his legs encircling her made it impossible. "They will ask that. What do we say? That I was dressed like—"

"A beautiful woman and I couldn't, not for one minute, take my eyes off you. That you pulled me in with one gorgeous glance and I was sunk. I still haven't resurfaced. They will love you, especially my mom. I swear. Will you come with me tomorrow? It wasn't really a question my dad asked. It was more like an order. Which means he told my mom to expect us, and I'm sure she's already planning a ridiculous meal. Please, Zoe."

"Ask me when you're not holding me like this," she whimpered.

"Hell, no. Then it'll be a straight no. I told you before, I use what works. Do I need to start nibbling on your delicious body as I ask?" He lowered his lips toward her neck to start the torture, but she moved her head away.

"No. That's not fair."

"Of course not. That's the point," he said, grinning.

"What will we say?"

"The truth. I met you one night when I was having a drink. The rest stays between us. It is the truth. I did buy a drink that night. You had one as well. No specifics have to be said. Trust me. I don't want my dad to know. He'd be ashamed of me and the way I acted while I was supposed to be working. I'm ashamed with myself. But in the end, it brought me to you. That's all I care about."

He sighed, brushing a hand over her hair. "I'm sorry. For everything. We don't have to go. I'll make up an excuse. It'll be fine."

"I'm sorry."

Zeke sighed heavily again. "You have nothing to be sorry for. Why are you sorry?"

"For enticing you that night and making you lose focus. For making you forget you're a cop. I didn't know I was so potent like that. It'll never happen again," Zoe replied, a slow grin crawling up into a wide smile.

"Oh, don't say things like that. I like losing focus when it comes to you," he said, smiling as he rolled her and hovered above her.

"I'll go tomorrow. For you," she whispered, slowly rubbing her hands down his back.

"Everything will be fine. I promise," he said, shivering in anticipation. "Now let me love you. I've been waiting all day for this."

"I don't know what you've been waiting for. I've been waiting since you walked into the room."

He cut her smile off as he dipped his mouth down over hers and began to show her the love he felt.

"I'VE ALSO HEARD that the first night home from the hospital is the worst. It starts the routine of no sleep, no sleep, and oh yeah, no sleep. Not to mention no sex for like six weeks, because, you know, she's healing down—"

"Knock it off, Ben. I've had it up to here with your talk about pregnancy and your so-called knowledge. You don't know what the hell you're talking about," Zeke said, throwing another pencil at him for the third time that morning.

"But I do. I have four sisters."

"Yeah, big talker. I have one and she's been pregnant three times. I'm no shy goose when it comes to this stuff. I've babysat before and listened to her and Mom talk pregnancy crap."

"Not the same, man. I'm telling you. You're in for it. Four sisters trumps one. I was actually in the delivery room for one of them and nearly passed out from the pain she endured. The screaming and cursing she carried on. I mean, the one thing she kept saying was...No. Sex. Ever. Again," Ben said with a serious expression.

Zeke leaned back in his chair and frowned. "She did not say that."

"Okay. Maybe she didn't say that, but she was moaning and groaning from the pain. She was definitely thinking it at the time," Ben replied, chuckling, as Zeke rolled his eyes.

"Can we focus back on the case, please? I have enough to worry about already. I convinced Zoe to meet my parents last night, and this morning she was hedging about going. I had to pull her into my arms and convince her again," Zeke said, shuddering at the glorious memory.

"Why would you have to pull her into your arms for that?"

"To convince her."

"I get that, but do you have to be touching her to convince her?"

"Hell, yes. She gets weak by my touch. Can't resist me. I use any weapon necessary to get my way. I'm evil like that," Zeke said with a grin. "Plus, she feels delicious in my arms. Something you have no idea what it feels like because you aren't getting any."

Ben frowned this time. "That's just mean. And cruel."

"I could always try to set a double date with Rina and—"

"I'm done talking about your sex life. It was nice while it lasted," Ben said, picking up a piece of paper.

"I don't get why you get all gun-shy when it comes to talking about her. You should ask her out and—"

"I'm done, Zeke. Not going there. She's a woman I will not tangle with."

"Why not?"

"She's too beautiful, for one."

Zeke laughed in disbelief. "You don't think you're good enough for her. Wow. You're an idiot."

"So are you. Let's not go down the list of reasons why. Shut up already about Rina."

Zeke held a retort on his tongue when he saw Young walk into their domain. "Heads up, Young's coming this way."

Ben turned slightly as Young stepped up to their desk. "May I speak with you, detectives?"

"Sure, Mr. Young, grab a seat," Zeke said, pointing to a chair not far from where he stood.

"I'll stand, thank you, detective. I'd like to know why you made a spectacle last night and arrested one of my employees."

Zeke grabbed the folder that sat on the corner of his desk, whipped it open, and threw a picture in his face. "I'd like to know why you employ someone who assaults another employee. Unless, of course, you have no problem with him physically abusing a woman in your break room."

Young took the picture with a trembling hand and stared in surprise at the sight of Zoe's arm. "I had no idea. This isn't what Mark told me this morning."

"Yeah, well, he's a damn liar and there's your evidence to prove it. Makes it suspicious enough to raise our curiosity about the deaths of Mills and Murphy," Zeke said.

"You honestly think he could've killed them," Young said, incredulous.

"Or you," Ben threw in.

"What? Why would you say that? I've been nothing but cooperative since everything happened," Young exclaimed.

"Not really, Mr. Young. You've given us access to the company, yes, but you're hiding something. You received a phone call that same day we found Mills's body. You've yet to divulge who called you and why you went running out. Liars usually equate to guilt. Proven fact," Zeke said, grabbing the photo from him and shoving it back inside the folder before his rage boiled over from seeing it.

Young ran a rough hand through his hair and cursed viciously under his breath. "It has absolutely nothing to do with the murders. I did not kill them. They were my friends and my colleagues. My partners, for God's sake. I swear I didn't do it. I'm sleeping with Carly Murphy."

He paused, glancing at their shocked expressions. "Carly called me that morning after you left the house telling her about Mills's death and that her husband was missing. She was frantic and worried about Murphy. I wanted to calm her down. I deeply care about her and it scared me when she called. I didn't mean to lie about it, but neither of us killed them."

"Pretty damn good motive to kill them," Ben retorted.

"Murphy maybe, I'll admit, but Mills? Why would I kill Mills? I did not kill my friends. I'm not lying about anything else. You can tear my company apart, my life apart, and you will not find anything to tie me to their murders. I didn't kill them," Young said firmly.

"You just admitted that you could have reason to kill Murphy," Zeke pointed out.

Young ran a hand over his face in frustration. "Look, he wasn't the world's greatest husband, but he was better than most. I'm sleeping with his wife. I'm merely saying how I could look like a good suspect. I didn't do it, though."

"We found Mills in the morning, but he was killed the night before. Where were you that night?" Zeke asked. He had originally told them he was home alone.

"I guess you can get me for lying. I was with Carly. She was at my house. She was contemplating divorce. There wasn't any love lost between them. And if we're really honest here, I think he kinda knew she was seeing someone. Maybe not that it was me, but he suspected. He made a brief comment about it. And you know what? He didn't seem too concerned. He had other pressing issues on his mind. Like the fight between him and Mills. I don't know the real issue between them either. I truly don't. And I wish like hell I did."

"Do you keep information about your company on flash drives?" Ben asked.

Young looked confused. "Of course not. We keep everything on our company computers. We also use another company to back up all of our data. We would never use a simple flash drive to back up our information. I honestly can't say if these murders are related to the company. I've had Deena O'Malley, my secretary, comb through every little piece of information and she found nothing odd. She would, too. That's why she makes such an excellent secretary."

"Not gonna lie, you're still on the list of suspects. Being with Carly that night doesn't look good either, or the fact you lied about your alibi," Zeke said.

"I didn't do anything and neither did Carly. I'll continue to help in any way I can. If I'm not available, then ask my secretary for whatever you need. I need to get back to work. I have an issue I need to deal with now," Young said, glancing at the folder that held the photo of the bruised arm.

They nodded at him and watched as he walked away. As soon as he was out of earshot, Ben said, "Well, that's a development I didn't see coming."

"I guess we know why Carly wasn't so forthcoming with us when we informed her of her husband's death. And why they were having marital issues. It's a good motive to kill Murphy, but like Young said, not really for Mills," Zeke replied.

"Carly did say she was worried Murphy killed Mills. Maybe Murphy did kill Mills and then Young and Carly killed Murphy."

"No. That's way too convoluted. Young admits to being with Carly the night Mills was killed, which means Carly lied that she was home alone waiting for Murphy to get home. I honestly think he's telling the truth. Those two were getting it on when Mills was killed. Do we have an estimated time of death for Murphy? Coroner's report come back yet?" Zeke asked.

Ben shook his head as he grabbed for his phone. "I'll call Susan and see if she processed everything yet. You call Dr. Everly and see if we got a time of death. And then let's head back to Carly's house and see her squirm when we ask her why she lied."

Zeke laughed. "Please. I guarantee you that Young called her the moment he walked away from our desks. She'll have had time to get her bearings down."

"True, but we can threaten an obstruction charge for lying to us and see if she slips up anyway. We should arrest both their asses just for lying. Running around in circles when we could've cleared that up in the beginning," Ben muttered as he dialed Susan's number.

Zeke nodded in agreement, picking up his phone as well.

Zoe pressed her hands over her knees where her dress kept riding higher. She wriggled around in her seat, pressing her hands down one more time to straighten her dress out again.

"Stop moving around like that. I'm liable to pull over and ravish you silly. You look perfect," Zeke said, putting a hand over hers that sat barely above her knee.

"I should have never worn a dress. It keeps riding up and it's—"

"Getting me hot just looking at it," Zeke said with a devious grin as his hand started inching up her thigh, moving the dress along with him.

"Stop," Zoe exclaimed, moving his hand back to his own

lap. "Focus on driving, please. Next time you insist on packing my clothes, pack more pants, not dresses."

"First, I didn't want you going in your home the day of the burglary because it was not a pretty sight. Second, I love you in dresses. That'll never change, honey. Of course, if it's up to me, I'd take you naked as well."

"Get your mind out of the gutter, please. This is important," Zoe said, frowning, as she gazed out the window, watching as the houses passed by in a blur.

Zeke grabbed her hand, planting a light kiss on it, and then kept holding it as he gently placed it on his lap. "I know this is important. My parents will love you. Stop worrying so much. What else is on your mind? What's bothering you? Remember that communication and understanding we need to maintain. Talk to me, honey."

Zoe sighed. "Mr. Young fired Mark today. He didn't look happy when he passed my desk. Mr. Young walked him out of the building so he didn't stop, but I could tell he wanted to. I'm scared he's going to retaliate against me. It's my fault he was fired."

"Damn it, Zoe, it's not your fault. I can't believe you didn't tell me this right away when you got home. That's great he was fired. I didn't like knowing that bastard was anywhere near you. He made the decision to lay a hand on you, not you. If he comes anywhere near you again, he'll wish he never had. I'll crush him like a bug. Do you hear me, Zoe? I love you. I won't let anyone intimidate you or scare you. Or hurt you."

Zoe glanced at him, his piercing blue eyes shining at her with the love he so desperately expressed to her constantly. "You need to keep your eyes on the road before we get in an accident."

Zeke turned back to the road and squeezed her hand. "Did you not hear any word I just said?"

"I heard every word. You make me feel safe, but Mark scares me now, and you're not always around."

"I can change that."

"You have a job, Zeke. And some murders to solve. Solve them, please. You can't be around me 24/7. It's not feasible. Nor wise."

"Why isn't it wise? I love you."

"Must you say that every other minute," Zoe said, trying suddenly to extract her hand from his.

Zeke held tightly to her and grinned. "Yes. I'm a deep, passionate man. I can't help how you make me feel. Plus, you're the mother of my child now. I can't help but love you even more. And I love our little monster."

Zoe groaned. "Again with the little monster."

"Uh-oh, my little monster next to me is coming out. Are we about to fight? Do I have to pull the car over and ravish you silly?"

"Keep your focus on driving."

He glanced at her out of the corner of his eye, smiling. She finally caved in and offered a small smile in return.

"I'll change the subject. Don't worry about Mark. I'll take care of him."

"That's not changing the subject." Zoe laughed as he scrunched his brows in mock annoyance.

"Okay, how about this? Did you know Mr. Young was having an affair with Mr. Murphy's wife, Carly?" Zoe's shocked expression told him the answer. "I guess not. Took Ben and I by surprise, too."

"When...how did you find that out? Are you sure?" Zoe asked.

"Yes, honey, I'm sure. Came straight from Young's mouth

himself." Zeke gave her an exasperated look. "You know, it comes easily to tell you things. It's not something I should be telling you. Keep it to yourself, okay? I don't know why I always forget I'm a cop when you're near me."

"Because I turn you on and make you wanna ravish me silly," Zoe said with a come-hither smile.

"Honey, you're seriously begging me to pull this car over at every turn. And you're damn right. I do believe that's why I lose my mind and forget everything. You do something to me, Zoe. It's scary as hell and I love every minute of it."

"I'm almost thinking you need to pull the car over now," Zoe said, moving her hand still within his even closer to the spot she craved.

Zeke glanced down and then quickly at her. "Oh, honey, I love you."

Zoe merely smiled and then frowned. "Zeke, I don't think we should do any hanky-panky in someone's driveway. I was kidding."

Zeke stopped the car, put it in park, and shut it off. He kept hold of her hand, still in the same delicious spot, reaching over with his other hand and unbuckling her seatbelt. He pulled her closer, almost into his lap, and kissed her soundly, deeply, and passionately.

"I would love nothing better than to do some hanky-panky right here, right now. But this is my parents' house. They could look out the front window at any time. Not sure I want to see my mom's surprised expression at her son getting it on in her driveway." Zeke kissed her. "Ready to meet my folks? Not sure I am anymore with this raging hard-on. Thanks a lot."

"I think I am now. It's better if we're both uncomfortable. I won't feel as out of place."

"Don't feel uncomfortable. Don't feel embarrassed. Just

be your beautiful self. And maybe move your hand already. It's not helping right now."

Zoe smiled wide. "Then let my hand go. You're the one holding me there."

"Damn. We need to get out of this car." Zeke brought her hand to his mouth and kissed it hard.

The minute she lost his touch, her nerves came back full force. She could get through this dinner. It was no big deal. Although, it felt like a huge deal as she got out of the vehicle and her mind spiraled thinking about their entire crazy relationship.

ZEKE TRIED to adjust himself without looking at Zoe, knowing he'd never settle down if he did. Still slightly uncomfortable, he met Zoe by the front of the car where she stood fidgeting with her dress again. "You look beautiful. Stop messing with the dress."

Zoe sighed, as he grabbed her hand again and led her to the door where he knocked once and then let himself in. "We're here. Oh man, Mom, that smells delicious, whatever it is," Zeke said, sniffing the air, his mouth watering instantly.

Before he could say another word, his mom popped into the hallway with a gleeful smile on her face.

"You're here. Richard! They're here!" his mother hollered as she walked up to Zeke, pulling him into a big hug. Without waiting for an invitation, she pulled Zoe into a hug next.

"You did good, Zeke. She's gorgeous," his mother beamed with pride. "You're gorgeous. I'm Debbie. You can call me Mom, if you like. Oh, and how is this little one in here?" She instantly rubbed Zoe's belly.

Zeke grabbed his mother's hand and backed her up. "Mom, you're probably scaring her. Shouldn't you ask permission to touch her stomach at least? It's not like this is your first grandchild."

"Heavens, no. We're family here. Family's allowed to touch without asking. And it's not my first grandchild, you're right. But it's *your* first, so it's different," she said with excitement. She glanced at Zoe. "Did I make you uncomfortable, dear? I didn't mean to. I'm so happy and proud. I can't wait to hear all about you."

Zoe smiled. "It's okay, Mrs.—"

"Nonsense. Don't call me Mrs. nothing. It's Mom or Debbie," she said, cutting her off with a disapproving look that said no argument would be tolerated.

"I'm still getting used to the idea of being pregnant, but thank you for welcoming me into your family. I guess you can touch my belly. It's still pretty flat, though," Zoe said with a laugh.

Zeke could hear the nervousness in that simple laugh. He squeezed her hand in reassurance and felt a small squeeze back.

"Doesn't matter. There's a little being growing inside already and they hear everything, feel everything. They have to know grandma's here and loves them. Yes, I do, little one," she said as she rubbed Zoe's belly again.

"Mom..."

"Oh, stop. She said it was fine. Come, come. Dinner's almost ready. We're having honey-mustard chicken with baked potatoes, broccoli, and a delicious red velvet cake for dessert that I whipped up today," Debbie said, pulling Zoe along, leaving Zeke to follow.

He started to follow them with quick footsteps to derail

his mom's smothering, when he saw his dad gesture from the study to have a word. Zeke hedged for a brief moment, then decided Zoe would be fine for a few minutes with his mom alone.

He walked into the study. "Mom's excited I see."

"What the hell did you expect? You're giving her a grandchild like she's been dying to have. We can't talk long because she's going to be asking that poor girl when the wedding is. When is the wedding?" his dad asked with a stern face.

Zeke grimaced. "It's complicated, Dad."

"Uncomplicate it for me then. You were taught better than this. What's going to happen?"

"Whatever she wants to happen, Dad. I love that woman with all my heart, but it's complicated. And no, I'm not going to get into it with you why. When she's ready to walk down the aisle, or even ready for me to ask, then it'll happen. I don't plan on letting her get away. Please hold Mom off with any wedding plans. Zoe's a bit on edge about our relationship as it is."

His dad laughed with absurdity. "Good luck with that, son. You know your mother. She's been dying for you to get it together, to get married and have kids. If you can't convince your own woman, your mother will do it for you."

Zeke groaned and started to walk out of the study when his dad said, "Not the only reason I called you in here."

Zeke turned back around. "I was afraid of that. What did I do wrong?"

"Nothing. Except knock a woman up before marriage."

"Geez, Dad. Can we move on from that, please?"

His dad gave him another piercing stare. "Give me an update on these murder cases and Mark Johnson. I don't like that my future daughter-in-law is involved and neither would your mother if she knew. I didn't tell her about that. Expect a talking from your mother why you came to me about the pregnancy and not both of us together. I didn't want to worry her."

"Thanks a lot, Dad."

"You want your mother to worry, do you?"

"No, of course not. But what the hell am I supposed to say to her?"

"Figure something out. Not my problem. Update me."

Zeke sighed. "Dr. Everly confirmed time of death for Murphy to approximately a week ago, around the same time as Mills. He can't pinpoint an exact time because of the body's condition from the water. We're thinking they were killed the same night. But we'll never know if Murphy really went home that night because his wife's having an affair with Young, another partner in the company, and she wasn't home. She was at Young's house. So, their alibis suck because they could've killed them, but Ben and I aren't feeling that angle."

"That's an interesting angle, though," his dad said as he sat propped on the edge of his desk.

Zeke nodded. "Ballistics came back matching the same .40 caliber handgun used in Mills's murder. Susan also found a key on Murphy's body hidden within his suit jacket. We think it's for a lockbox. We're hoping the flash drive is inside. Although not sure, because how could Mills or Murphy, if Murphy got the flash drive from Mills somehow, have thrown it into a lockbox that night when the banks were obviously closed. But we need to make sure it's not."

He rocked on his heels as the weight of everything started to bring him down. "Now we have the headache of searching for the lockbox because the key has no identifying markers on it. Only a number. We have nothing to tie Mark to the crimes, but I feel like he's involved somehow. He hurt Zoe."

Zeke blew out a breath and lowered his voice. "Zoe informed me that Mark was fired today by Young. So that makes me feel better. Except Zoe's worried he'll try retaliating for losing his job. She's absolutely right, and I'm freaking out inside, Dad. I love this woman and I love that child growing inside her." He ran a haggard hand over his face, letting it sit there for a brief moment.

Zeke glanced to his left when he felt a hand on his shoulder.

"Zeke, things will be fine. You'll figure it out because you're a damn fine detective. It's nice to see my only son finally in love and ready to settle down. I never thought I'd see the day." His dad grinned and lovingly squeezed his shoulder. "Don't hesitate to come to me for anything— warrants, advice, support. You name it, I got it. I want to be regularly updated about this case until it's solved. Understood?"

"Sure, Dad. I hate—"

"Yeah, yeah. I know. You hate coming to your dad for work stuff. I don't know why the hell not."

"I don't know. Maybe because you're so damn critical about every little thing. You tear me apart like I'm a teenager in high school."

"No other judge is critical when you present them a warrant?" his dad asked with an amused expression.

Zeke groaned and rolled his eyes. "Yeah, sure. Judge Thompson was critical last week, but he doesn't have that same tone of voice and look in his eyes when he knocks me down a peg or two."

"I told you once about your grammatical error. One grammatical error, and you've yet to step back into my office until yesterday. All your warrants should be tight and precise."

"Like I said, Dad. It's the way you say it." Zeke glanced down at his feet and shrugged helplessly. "I hate disappointing you. I've already disappointed you when it comes to Zoe. I disappointed myself."

Richard pulled Zeke into his arms and hugged him tight. "I can't have my son thinking I'm disappointed in him." He let go and clapped him on the back. "I wish you were married first, of course, but you've never disappointed me. Even about your warrants. I can give you a hard time if I want. You're my son."

Zeke smiled. "You always give me a hard time."

"And that'll never change. Now let's go save your girlfriend. I'm sure your mother has already been feeling her belly twenty times by now. You do recall how she was with Cassandra when she was pregnant each time. Your sister nearly went off the deep end with your mother's fussing."

"You're probably right. She's just excited." Zeke followed his dad out of the study and into the kitchen where Zoe was busy helping his mom prepare the food.

"Oh, there you are, silly men. It's almost time to eat," Debbie said as she bustled around the oven and pulled the chicken out.

"Nothing but a little shop talk, dear. Our bellies are grumbling, though. Smells delicious, like always." Richard grinned at his wife lovingly and then walked up to Zoe. "It's a pleasure to meet you, Zoe. I'm Richard. Call me Rick, Richard, Dad, Hey You. Whatever you feel comfortable with."

Zoe shyly laughed. "It's very nice meeting you...Hey You."

Richard burst out laughing and pulled Zoe in for a hug.

"This one's a keeper, Zeke. I like her. I hope Deborah hasn't been too in-your-face already."

Debbie cleared her throat and shot a glance at her husband. "What does that mean?"

"Darling, you know what that means. Need I remind you how you were with Cassandra each pregnancy. We just met this beautiful woman. Give her time to adjust to us." Richard winked at Zoe and walked up to his wife, pulling her into a hug, kissing her soundly on the mouth.

Zeke walked over to Zoe and pulled her into his side. "I didn't mean to leave you alone with my mom. Dad wanted a quick word. You're not mad, are you?" he whispered.

"Your mom's wonderful. Belly touching and all," she whispered back with a laugh.

Zeke chuckled, grabbing a quick kiss.

"Let's eat. I can't wait to hear more about you, Zoe, and how you two met," Debbie said, beaming with excitement.

Zoe tensed beside him. He grabbed her hand and squeezed in reassurance. "It's nothing spectacular, Mom. I'll help you bring the food to the dining room and give you the short version."

"Oh, I have all night. I want to hear the long version," she replied, walking out of the kitchen with the chicken.

10

"I love this. You should get this," Dee said, holding up a small pink dress with a beautiful flower adorned in the middle.

"What happens if I'm not having a girl? Shouldn't I wait to buy baby clothes?" Zoe asked, grabbing the dress from Dee. "It is adorable."

They stood in the middle of the baby store, perusing the clothes. They hadn't seen much of the front because Dee had bee-lined it to the clothes immediately. They had every intention of going through the entire store. If they could distract Dee long enough to look at something else, of course.

"Geez, the way you two go at it, you'll be popping out babies like a factory. Save it for the next one if you don't have a girl," Dee said, rolling her eyes.

"How do you know what we do?" Zoe asked, blushing.

"You have this, like, glow or something," Dee said, waving a hand around her face.

"I think that's called the pregnancy glow," Rina said softly, holding up an outfit. "I like this one. It's neutral, too."

Zoe took the green jumper from Rina and smiled. "This is cute. Oh, what the hell. Let's get 'em both. Let's move on from the clothes because, honestly, it's all really cute and I'll buy the whole store up. Let's go look at cribs."

"We're buying a crib today?" Dee asked, snatching another dress, purple this time, from the racks.

"Put it back, Dee," Zoe said, catching her in the act as she made her way toward the cribs. "We're only looking today. I think Zeke would like to go shopping with me. He said as much."

"I'm not putting it back. I'll buy it and it'll be from Auntie Dee. This baby girl is gonna be the best dressed girl on the block," Dee said, clutching the dress to her chest in case Zoe attempted to snatch it from her.

Zoe stopped. "Who says I'm having a girl? What happens if it's a boy?"

"Then it's for the next baby. I told you, you'll be popping babies out like nobody's business. Tell me, did you get some this morning?" Dee asked, propping a hand on her hip.

"Is there relevance in that question?" Zoe asked, snatching the dress from her. "What is this obsession with you and dresses? I'm not sure I'm a fan of them anymore. Trying to dress my baby girl in dresses. Don't you dare put any slinky dresses on my baby girl, Auntie Dee."

"I'll take that as a yes, you did get some this morning. Pop, pop, pop. I'm buying it," Dee said, snatching the dress back. "And I won't start giving her the slinky dresses until she's at least eighteen. I have some decent morals. You know Zeke loves you in slinky dresses." Dee laughed as she took the lead.

"She makes me nervous sometimes," Zoe whispered to Rina.

"Yeah, but she's a good friend. She'll be a good aunt," Rina whispered back. "They are cute dresses."

"Yeah, I know. Makes me wish it's a girl. But a healthy baby is what matters in the end." Zoe slowed her steps when she saw the cribs emerge. The selection made her eyes bulge. How would she pick one?

"Ugh, look at this price," Dee exclaimed, holding up the price tag. "Who in the hell pays a thousand bucks for a crib?"

"It looks nice," Zoe said, walking over to her. "A beautiful mocha color, carved pretty, and...oh look, it turns into a toddler bed when they get bigger."

Dee leaned closer to look at the description underneath the price tag. "A thousand dollars," she reiterated in a disgusted tone.

"Is that normal?" Rina asked, as she walked around looking at the other cribs. "This one's mocha and it also turns into a toddler bed. It's only eight hundred."

"Seriously. That's way too much money. That's ridiculous," Dee said, scrunching her nose up as if appalled by the price tags.

"How much do you think I should spend, Dee?" Zoe asked, walking around as she checked them all out. "I like the mocha color, or maybe something light, light tan."

"A couple hundred, two, three, maybe. But eight or a thousand...geesh. I'm never getting pregnant if it's gonna cost this much and the baby isn't even here yet," Dee replied.

Rina laughed lightly. "Nothing's cheap these days, Dee. Especially having a baby. You have to get a nice, decent, durable crib. So many things could go wrong if you don't."

"I don't even want to know what could go wrong. Now

I'm worried. What could go wrong?" Zoe said as the panic sliced through her veins and out through her words.

Rina walked up to Zoe, who stood near a light-tan crib with a matching changing table, and gave her a small, reassuring hug. "I didn't mean to worry you. You hear things in the news, and I guess that's what I was thinking about. I didn't mean to upset you."

Zoe nodded in understanding. The news did portray some very disturbing things. She always turned the television off when she couldn't take it anymore.

"Maybe I should buy a pregnancy book. There are way too many options here and I have no idea what I am doing." Zoe lifted another price tag to a crib that said it was twelve hundred dollars. She dropped it as if it burned her hand and took a step back.

"That's a great idea," Rina said.

"Forget the cribs then. Let's go back to the clothes. I wanna get that yellow dress I saw when we walked away. Then let's hit up the bookstore and grab a bite to eat for lunch. People watch, laugh a little, puke a little...you know, because you haven't done that yet," Dee said with a grin.

"Don't remind me. I just might," Zoe said with a laugh. "We don't need the yellow dress."

"Oh, I'm getting the yellow dress," Dee said as she power walked to that area and whipped it off the rack. "Oooo, and this beauty. Look at this shirt. It's perfect for my niece with this saying, I'm sweet, sassy, and downright classy...just like my auntie!"

"I'm getting this strong feeling you want Zoe to have a girl," Rina said, glancing at Zoe, who laughed with her.

"You're sassy and a little classy, but sweet? I'd say more like spicy," Zoe said.

"Spicy. I like that. I should make my own shirt for her,"

Dee said, shaking her head as if the wheels of ideas were rolling around. "I'll be happy if it's a bouncing baby boy. I can go with spicy, dicey, making my truck look nicey...just like my auntie."

"You don't own a truck," Rina said with a chuckle.

"Okay, so that saying needs some work. Spicy. I still like that. Definitely keeping that," Dee said as she snatched the shirt off the rack.

"Let's go before you buy the entire clothes department," Zoe said, pushing Dee out of the baby clothes area.

Zoe quickly ushered Dee to the checkout line, laughing, as she snatched several clothes on the walk there. She found it hilarious Dee was into buying clothes more than she was. She loved walking through the clothes, admiring the dainty girl outfits, the pinks, the purples, and flowers galore. The handsome, sweet baby-blue outfits tickled her heart with joy as well, but part of her was holding back.

Zeke.

The way his eyes sparkled with excitement about wanting to be there with her through everything. Including shopping. She knew he'd enjoy it, already imagining the way his eyes would light up and make a sweet, silky comment in her ear about a baby item.

She wanted him here shopping with her. Not to mention she wanted to know what the sex of the baby was before she bought too many of the wrong clothes.

She listened as Dee and Rina talked to the cashier about the clothes, laughing inside at Dee's comment earlier. The way she and Zeke did go at it, they just might have a parcel of kids. That thought alone made her deliriously happy.

So why was she afraid to say I love you? She imagined a future filled with a bundle of kids with Zeke as the father, yet froze when the words wanted to leave her mouth.

"Earth to Zoe. Yoo-hoo," Dee said, waving a hand. "You with us? I'm done. Let's blow this joint and hit the bookstore."

Zoe glanced at the cashier and behind her, noticing she was standing in their way like an idiot as Rina and Dee stood waiting by the exit, bags in hand.

"I guess I zoned out a bit. I mean, geez, I'm having a baby," Zoe said with a small laugh, following them out of the store.

"Is that a symptom? Zoning out? Each time you do something new it reinforces my decision to have no kids," Dee said matter-of-factly.

"Are you really going to discredit it based on Zoe? Everyone handles pregnancy different," Rina replied.

"I have a lot on my mind. Sorry if I'm not as excited as I should be shopping and whatnot," Zoe said with a sigh.

"Girl, you're fine," Dee said, grabbing Zoe around the shoulder as they walked along. "Good thing we're buying a pregnancy book. You can make sure if zoning out is a symptom. Could be, you never know."

Zoe laughed, shaking her head in amusement as they walked along. The bookstore was at the other end of the mall and it took them twenty minutes to make the long trek. A little longer than normal, considering Dee had to stop and gawk frequently in the store windows at other baby clothes. Zoe and Rina had to push her along the way to prevent her from stepping inside each store.

"For someone who doesn't want kids, your fascination with baby clothes is mind-boggling," Rina said.

"Take the word baby out. Clothes. I love clothes. Doesn't matter who I'm dressing, as long as I can dress them up. I already said this baby was gonna be the best dressed on the block. I wasn't lying," Dee said as she glanced around the bookstore. "Does this joint have a sign that says pregnancy or what? What area are we looking for?"

"Pregnancy, did I hear? Who's the lucky lady?" an older woman with the nametag 'Carolyn' pasted on her shirt asked.

"I'm looking for some pregnancy books. Anything to give insight on...everything," Zoe said with a laugh.

"Oh, congratulations, my dear. Your first?" Carolyn asked.

"Yeah." Suddenly, tiny slices of fear propelled down her spine. She glanced behind her as the funny feeling increased. Except she saw nothing strange and turned back to Carolyn. "Do you know where we can find some of those?"

"Of course. Follow me," Carolyn said, leading the way to the right.

"Busybody, asking questions like that," Dee muttered under her breath.

"She asked two questions, Dee. At least she didn't touch her belly without permission. Some people are very brazen like that," Rina whispered back.

"Zeke's mom was like that. She couldn't stop touching my belly. I didn't want to be rude and shove her off. She's a nice lady," Zoe said, getting in on the whispering.

"Well, his mom, I guess you can't. But a complete stranger is getting their hand broken if they even attempt to touch your belly when I'm around," Dee said, raising a brow, waiting for someone to argue with her.

"Here you go, ladies. Congratulations again. My daughter just had her first child and I can't say how much of a blessing it is," Carolyn said, smiling brightly at her.

Dee stepped slightly in front of Zoe, hindering any potential belly touching. "Thanks a bunch, Carolyn."

Carolyn nodded with a strange look on her face, then walked away.

"Geez, Dee. Scare the woman why don't ya. She didn't even have her hand out to touch my belly," Zoe said, scanning the shelves.

"Doesn't hurt to be preventive. No need to give her an opportunity to try," Dee said with a smirk.

"That's why we love you, Dee," Rina said, scanning the shelves as well.

They meandered through the aisle, pulling books out frequently as they tried to decide which one would be best. Every so often, a strange spine-tingling feeling possessed Zoe into glancing furtively around her. She never saw anything suspicious, but the more she felt the unsettling feeling, the more nervous she became.

"Eww. This is disgusting," Dee exclaimed, slamming the book closed and placing it back on the shelf.

"What was it?" Zoe asked, shaking off another frightening shiver.

"Do you want to know? Because I didn't even want to know and now I do," Dee said, shaking her head with disgust.

"Yes, I want to know," Zoe said with a laugh.

"The birthing process. Quite disgusting. Giving great detail on what comes out and...yeah, need I say more? Disgusting. Don't buy that book," Dee said, moving away from it.

"That's the whole point we're in this aisle, Dee. She needs to know these things. It's part of the cycle of life and the beauty of creation," Rina said.

"Stop always being the voice of reason. It makes me sick," Dee said.

"Someone has to when you're around," Rina retorted

softly.

"And that's why we love you, Rina," Dee said, grabbing her around the shoulders for a hug.

Zoe laughed, shaking her head at their craziness when the corner of her eye caught a glimpse of something. A book fell from her hands. She walked unsteadily, yet swiftly to the end of the aisle to get a better look. Her feet froze in place as a gasp escaped.

"What is it, Zoe?" Rina asked, coming up behind her, Dee on her tail.

"I've felt someone watching me since we got in the bookstore. Now I know who it is. Mark. Do you see him?" Zoe said, pointing across the store where Mark stood outside the doors, leaning casually against the railing. They made eye contact, no fear present on his face. "He said I'd regret it. I don't like how he's looking at me."

"Let me help rearrange his look," Dee said, walking away without waiting for a response.

Before Dee made it out of the store, Mark gave Zoe one more terrifying look, and walked away. Dee disappeared from their view as she walked out of the store. A minute later, she walked back inside where Rina stood rubbing Zoe's back while she quietly talked on her phone.

"She called Zeke. Go grab the disgusting book and the one she dropped and buy them for her. We need to leave," Rina said quietly to Dee.

Dee nodded without one argument. Zoe tried to focus on anything other than the terror rushing through her, but nothing in her vision looked clear. The only thing clear had been Zeke on the phone. His voice, instead of calming her down, had raised her anxiety. The concern, even a small amount of terror had filtered in his words.

Would Mark hurt her? Kill her? Did he kill Mr. Mills and Mr. Murphy?

She waited with Rina by the exit doors as Dee rushed through the checkout line and met them a few minutes later.

"So? What's up?" Dee said.

"Zeke wanted to come here, but I talked him out of it. I think it's best if I go home," Zoe said, attempting to regain some of the composure she'd lost when she spotted Mark. She still had her friends by her side. "Do you think he'll try something?"

"Well, if he's trying to scare you, he's doing a damn good job, the douche. Let's go and throw a movie in. Not order a pizza, that's for sure. Can you handle Chinese food?" Dee asked.

"I don't know. I guess we'll find out," Zoe said with a lame chuckle.

"I think he's just trying to scare you. He'd be dumb to try anything. I think we'll be safe with Spicy Dee leading the way protecting us," Rina said.

"Lead I will. Spicy Dee. Sounds like an exotic drink. I like it," Dee said as she took the lead, making quick glances around them as they walked.

"Why do you encourage her?" Zoe whispered to Rina with a smile.

"Because she likes it and it made you smile," Rina replied.

Zoe smiled again, glad to have her best friends with her. What would she do without them?

They wasted no time walking out of the mall. Dee was on a mission, her steps quick, yet determined. Once they made it outside, she slowed her stride and glanced around the parking lot. "Coast looks clear."

"And why wouldn't it? You bulldozed us right out of the mall," Zoe said with a laugh.

"Just doing my job," Dee said, waving a hand for them to follow her to the car. "I'm starving. Let's order on the way home. You wanna do that, Rina?"

Rina nodded. "Do you guys want the usual?"

"Yes, please. I hope I still like it," Zoe said.

Dee blew out a strangled breath. "I do, too. We can hear when you're yacking up." Dee turned around to give her a joking grin when it turned into a horrifying frown. "Look out, Zoe!"

She tried to push Rina and Zoe out of the way together, except Rina was closer to Zoe, getting a better grip to shove her. Zoe managed to look behind her just in time to see the car rush at them and jump back with the small help from Rina. She rammed into a parked car and tumbled to the ground.

Gravel and dirt coated the palms of her hands as she lay there. A ringing sensation reverberated around her head as a slice of pain shot up her left arm. The thought of moving seemed like too much of an effort. Immobilized. Terrified.

Someone tried to run her down.

Mark, most likely.

Was he capable of killing? Apparently, he was.

She tried to sit up, but her body still refused to move as the ringing in her ears intensified.

"That son of a bitch!" Dee shouted. Zoe shifted her head to see Dee pull out her phone. "I got you now, bastard."

"Zoe, are you okay?" Rina asked, moving closer to her.

"I think I hurt my arm. It hurts. My whole body hurts," Zoe said, as she slowly lifted herself up.

Dirt hit her forehead as she swiped a hand across it. Dropping her hand, unable to keep up her strength, a small amount of blood transferred to her pants from a small cut after she swiped her palm across her leg. Or had that come from her forehead? Her head still rang with pain. Deciphering what sort of injuries she had seemed impossible.

"Did the car hit you?" Dee asked, covering the phone as if the operator were rattling off questions to her.

"No. I hit this other car hard and the ground. I think I just landed wrong." Her head started to pound like mad as she wiped her hand against her pants again. Not much blood smeared this time. Damn. Perhaps her head was bleeding.

"Make them send an ambulance, Dee," Rina said, turning to look at Dee, who nodded in agreement.

"I don't need an ambulance. The car didn't hit me. I'll be fine," Zoe said, trying to reassure her as she pressed a hand to her head again to make the ringing go away.

"Zoe, you're pregnant. You have to make sure the baby's okay," Rina whispered.

"My baby," Zoe gasped. "Our little monster."

That was the last thing she said before she saw nothing but blackness.

A COMFORTING SENSATION zapped through her hand as she opened her eyes. She blinked a few times before the room came into focus. Dull colors, a TV, and a funny looking table hit her sights first.

"Zoe, honey. Don't ever worry me like that again. Do you hear me?" Zeke said, squeezing her hand as her eyes finally trailed to him.

"Where am I?"

"The hospital. You have a concussion. You scared me

when you didn't wake up right away, going in and out of consciousness. The doctor said not to worry, but I couldn't help it. You had to get a few stitches in the head. Rina didn't notice the blood until you passed out. Don't ever scare us like that. Ever." Zeke pulled her hand to his mouth, lightly kissing, his hand shaking a little.

Zoe looked around the room again. The funny looking table made sense now. It was the kind that rolled over the bed so you didn't even need to leave it when you ate.

"How long was I out? I didn't mean to scare you. I knew I fell hard and it...it hurt, but... I don't remember much," she said, looking back at Zeke.

"You don't need to remember that. It should've never happened." He kissed her hand again. "You weren't out long, but long enough for me. I'm glad the car didn't hit you. I don't want to imagine how bad it could've been." He released a ragged breath.

"I don't want to think about it either. The baby—" Her eyes got wide. "Oh, my. Our little—"

"Monster is fine," he said, interrupting her as he squeezed her hand tightly. "He's fine. I swear. The doctor, after stitching your head, made sure. You and our little monster are okay."

"He? What makes you think it's a boy?" Zoe asked, trying to give a smile. The relief inside knew no bounds. It would've torn her up knowing she lost the baby to Mark and his horrible rage.

"Just a guess. I hear Dee wants it to be a girl. Already buying her dresses," Zeke said with a grin, leaning closer to her.

"She said she won't dress her up in any slinky dresses until she's at least eighteen."

"Zoe, honey, she's never dressing her up in any slinky

dresses. Over my dead body. I know what you look like in one, and heaven help me, no man is going to see my little girl like that. I'll kill them if they even look."

"Boy, you're going to have a fight on your hands with Dee then," she said with a sassy grin.

"Tell Dee to bring it on," he said, leaning even closer to kiss her on the lips. Before he moved away, he whispered, "Please, don't ever scare me again. You have no idea the torture I was in."

"Okay, I won't," she whispered, grabbing another kiss before his tender lips left hers. "Where are Dee and Rina?"

"You know how Dee is. Loud, crazy, in your face. Apparently, when she hasn't eaten, it's ten times worse. Rina took her to the cafeteria before she chopped off the heads of the doctor, nurses, and anyone else she came into contact with," Zeke said with a laugh. "She'd make a good cop."

"Please don't say that to her. Can you imagine putting a gun in her hand? She sees a suspect and stops them, yelling, *make a move, douche, I dare ya*," Zoe said in her best Dee impersonation.

Zeke laughed. "You make a very good point. I won't say anything to her."

"Where's Ben? You guys were working and now...you're here," she asked, wondering how to ask about Mark, yet not wanting to hear the answer.

"Dee got a good look at the tags. We also have the car on the mall's parking lot security cameras. It was definitely Mark. Ben, with some help, is hunting down Mark as we speak. I wanted to help, but I couldn't leave you." He looked down at her hand, rubbing soft circles on her palm. "I don't trust myself not to kill him. He tried to run you down and kill you. I can't even describe how that makes me feel. I can't lose you. I love you too much."

"I'm glad you're the first person I saw when I woke up," she said softly.

Zeke lifted his eyes and smiled tenderly. "I'll never leave you. Ever."

She held her eyes to his beautiful gaze, almost drowning in the love she saw. "Don't go killing him. He's not worth it."

"Of course not. My son's not that stupid. Or are you?" Richard said, walking up to the bed with a stern glare pointed at Zeke.

ZEKE HAD BEEN SO ENGROSSED LOOKING deep into her eyes that he didn't hear the door open. He wanted to kick himself in the ass for not paying attention. He needed to. Things were not looking good for Zoe.

"I'm not stupid, Dad. I'm royally pissed off, though. Which is why I'm desperately holding Zoe's hand and not out searching with Ben, because the temptation might overwhelm me," Zeke replied, glancing at his dad and then back to Zoe.

"Good decision. How are you, Zoe? You gave us a scare," Richard said, giving her a fatherly look.

"I'll be fine. I'm glad the baby's okay," Zoe said, rubbing her belly with her free hand.

"I'm glad about that, too. I can honestly say I didn't see this coming," Richard said.

"Me either, otherwise, I would've never let her go shopping." Zeke gripped her hand a little too tightly, the thought of her seriously harmed too much to contemplate.

"Let me?" Zoe asked with a sliced tone.

"Don't get like that with me, honey. When it comes to your safety and the safety of our baby, sometimes there's no discussion involved. It's just a plain old 'you're doing what I say.' I won't let you get hurt. Need I remind you there are two men dead already? Mills and Murphy. Mark tried to run you down with a car, and I have two unsolved murders. Do the math," Zeke snapped.

"All right, you two, settle down. No need to argue with each other," Richard interjected.

"Don't worry, Dad. We're good at arguing," Zeke said as he glanced away from them.

"Anger equates to scared. Taking it out on Zoe does not help," Richard said firmly, then he turned to Zoe. "He's right. You can't go around doing normal things right now. Not anymore. Until they get a better handle on these murder cases and find that flash drive, your safety is a priority. Especially considering what happened today."

"Is that why we fight like we do? We're both scared," Zoe said.

He whipped his head to her, hating the terrified look in her eyes. "My dad's a smart guy. I guess I do get mad when I get scared thinking about losing you. The thought of you walking out the door, leaving me, scares the hell out of me. You've mentioned it a time or two, and yeah, we fight when you do. The thought of you getting hurt scares me. I don't mean to sound controlling or demanding, but I don't want to see you in this bed with more serious injuries. Injuries that you possibly won't recover from. Yeah, I'm scared as hell."

"I'm scared, too," she whispered as a tear rolled down her cheek.

Zeke stood up, joined her on the bed, and pulled her into his arms. "I'll figure this out. I won't stop until I do. Once it's finished, we can focus on building what we have together. Baby or not, I want you in my life."

Zoe pressed her face into his chest, her tears soaking clear through his shirt and straight to his heart. Her sobs echoed throughout the room. All he could do was hold her, comfort her as best he could. He glanced over at his dad, who gave him a reassuring smile but said nothing. Zeke knew he didn't need to say anything. The look said it all.

"I don't know what came over me. I'm so sorry about that," Zoe said as she sat up and wiped the remaining tears from her face.

"Well, if Ben were here he'd probably say it was pregnancy hormones. It doesn't matter. You can cry on me anytime. I'll always hold you," Zeke said, kissing the top of her head.

Zoe laughed lightly. "He would, would he? He does like giving pregnancy advice."

"What does he know about pregnancy? He's never had a baby," Richard said.

"Four sisters. Three have been pregnant. He thinks he's an expert at it all, Dad," Zeke replied dryly.

"So he's jerking you around and you're letting him," Richard said with a laugh.

"No, I'm not letting him," Zeke said firmly with a slight pout lingering in the depths.

"I beg to differ. It circles your mind what he says, but you dish back about Rina, so I guess it's fair." Zoe nudged him in the stomach.

"Okay, maybe he gets to me a little. He just doesn't shut up about his so-called advice," Zeke said.

Richard laughed heartily. "You two and your antics. Thank goodness you didn't know each other growing up. My gray hair would've come much sooner than it did."

"Yeah, but the fun we would've had," Zeke said with a smile.

"Not to bring the conversation down again, but we need to talk about safety," Richard said, breathing a heavy sigh.

"Can you take time off work, Zoe? I'm not sure I feel comfortable with you going back right now," Zeke said.

"What happened to no discussion? That sounds like I have a say in the matter," Zoe replied.

"My anger got the best of me, remember? No reason we can't talk about this nicely. If I don't like the answer, then we might have an issue," Zeke said with a pointed smile.

"So basically you're asking me, but if the answer isn't the correct one, then you're going to put your foot down and argue with me anyway." Zoe arched a brow.

"Basically," Zeke said.

"So that's settled then," Richard said confidently.

"How so? Mark doesn't work there anymore. Where's the risk in going to work?" She looked at Richard with a devious gleam in her eyes. "I see where Zeke gets his attitude from."

"What attitude?" Richard asked with a teasing smile.

"Look, Zoe. You're right. Mark doesn't work there, but it doesn't mean it was only him involved. He honestly doesn't strike me as the type to pull those murders off. You weren't at the crime scenes, and they had a different feel to them. He was sloppy today, trying to hit you with a car. Mills and Murphy...well...I don't want to say too much, but they were a bit more clean and professional," Zeke said softly. "It involves that company somehow, and I don't want you there. I don't want to fight about it. But I will put my foot down if I have to."

Zoe sighed. "I guess a few days of rest wouldn't hurt. Mr. Young should understand."

"Thank you, honey. You have no idea how that makes me feel. I love you," Zeke said, grabbing a kiss.

"So that's settled then," Richard repeated.

Zoe chuckled. "I guess so."

Before Zeke could respond with a witty retort, the door to her room opened. Instead of seeing Dee and Rina as he'd expected, Ben walked in. "Hey, man. I hope you have good news. My temper hasn't tamed down to talk to that jackass yet, but good news would be...good."

Ben's expression didn't turn into a smile like he wanted. He tried a small lip curl for Zoe's sake, but Zeke saw through it.

"Not exactly. How are you doing, Zoe?" Ben asked.

"Fine, Ben. My head hurts and I feel sleep edging in, but I imagine I'm not supposed to do that with a concussion," Zoe said.

"No, definitely not, honey. The first twenty-four hours are crucial with a concussion. Doctor said it was mild, but I'd say severe considering how long it took you to wake up. A very lackadaisical doctor if you ask me," Zeke said.

"I'm awake and I'm fine. Give the doctor a break," Zoe replied, leaning her head on his chest.

Zeke hugged her tighter, glancing back at Ben. "So what's the news, man?"

Zeke caught Ben's subtle nod that he wanted to talk out in the hallway, but apparently, so did Zoe.

"Tell us, Ben. I can handle it," she said softly.

"Spill it already, detective," Richard said, sternly.

"We found Mark. His car was spotted on the side of the road heading out of town on Highway 24," Ben said.

"Why do I get a bad feeling with what's left to say?" Zeke said, holding Zoe tighter for emotional support. She would need it. And damn it, so would he.

"Clean wound, gunshot to the head. Makes me think a silencer was used. If I had to take a guess, ballistics will come back to the same weapon that killed Mills and

Murphy," Ben replied.

"Well, shit," Richard muttered.

Zeke glanced at his dad, feeling the same sentiment. Zoe shook in his arms, as he suspected would happen. She shouldn't have to fear anything. But the way things were going, she had a lot to be afraid about.

"You're definitely not going to work. So I'm taking a guess here, but I think Mark was working with someone. That someone killed Mills and Murphy. Mark's job, maybe, was to get the flash drive from Zoe. I'm guessing he broke into her house, which is why it felt personal. When he couldn't find it, he tried a different tactic—to get back in a relationship with her. That obviously didn't work. Now he's really feeling the pressure to get that flash drive. His anger gets the better of him and he tries to hurt Zoe. That someone doesn't like it and takes care of that problem."

Ben sighed heavily. "Sometimes I hate how well we think alike. They want that flash drive. We need to find it first."

"Get on with it then, detectives. Zoe will be safe with me," Richard said, sharing a look with Zeke. "I promise. She'll be safe with me."

Zeke squeezed Zoe tightly, kissed the top of her head, and whispered in her ear, "I love you, Zoe. I will find this bastard."

"Maybe you should take Dee with. She might be able to sniff this douche out for you."

Zeke laughed lightly, loving this woman even more. "You could be right. I'll be back soon."

"Where are you going? Zoe, you're awake. Don't ever scare us like that again," Dee demanded as she walked into the room with Rina.

"Who are you?" Richard asked, stepping closer to Zoe.

"That's my friend Dee. She can get a little loud. That's Rina standing next to her," Zoe said tiredly.

"A little is an understatement," Richard said, raising an eyebrow.

"And who are you?" Dee whipped at him.

"That's my dad. Be nice. He can get sensitive. You don't want to piss him off, Dee." Zeke stood up, his legs moving slowly. The thought of leaving Zoe's side was like a knife to the chest.

"Oh, I guess that explains it," Dee said, raising an eyebrow back at Richard, to which he gave her a sleek grin.

Zeke couldn't help himself. He stepped closer to the bed, leaned down, and kissed Zoe one more time. "I think you'll be fine with my dad and Dee in attendance. And Rina, too." He glanced at Rina and gave her a wink. Rina shyly smiled back.

"Where are you going? Did you find douche-man yet?" Dee asked.

"Did we ever," Ben muttered.

"What does that mean?" Rina asked quietly, her soft eyes glancing at him.

Zeke wanted to laugh as Ben stared at her for a moment before he responded, "He's dead, Rina. Probably by the same person who killed Mills and Murphy. Zoe needs to be alert, but you two should be as well. You work at the same place and it involves that place somehow. We aren't sure exactly how. Call it gut instinct."

Rina gasped.

Dee staggered back but recovered quicker than Rina. "Well, shit. I wanted to beat that douche myself."

11

"You okay?" Ben asked as Zeke drove to the next bank on their list.

"I'm good."

"You sure?"

"Yep."

"You don't sound good."

"Does this conversation have a point?"

"I'm worried about you, man. You've been quiet and sulky since you walked into work this morning. Every time I ask, you say you're good. You don't sound good."

"Well, let's see. It's been two days since Zoe almost died by getting hit by a car. Mark's dead. We've had zero luck on finding where this damn key belongs. Zoe's resting at home with my dad. I'm glad he could take the day off, but it should be me there. I won't leave her alone until this case is solved, and I have no idea what I'm going to do about tomorrow because my dad has to go into work. We're nowhere near solving this damn case and I'm losing my mind with worry. But instead of saying all of that because I'm pretty sure you know it, it's easier to say...I'm good."

"She didn't get hit by a car," Ben pointed out. "Barely. Her injuries are from jumping out of the way."

"Shut up, Ben."

"I'm just correcting part of your statement."

"Where's a pencil when I need to throw it in your face?"

"I might have one. Hold on," Ben said, opening the glove box. He moved a few papers, smiling in delight as he found a pencil. "Here you go. Will that make you feel better?"

Zeke glanced at Ben with a maddened expression. His lips scrunched in irritation as he eyed the pencil. He snatched the pencil, twirled it once, and flicked it at Ben, hitting him in the chest. "No, I don't feel better."

"It was worth a try," Ben said with a small laugh. "Pretty good driving and twirling at the same time. I'm gonna have to try that."

"Your attempt at making me feel better isn't working. I'm worried, okay? She's worried, and well, that can't be good for the baby. We need to solve this. We're running out of banks to check. This damn key could belong to anything. Carly didn't recognize it. Young didn't either. It fit nothing in their house or his office. Not even Mills's house. If we can't find this flash drive...when do you think this person will make a move on Zoe?"

Ben shrugged. "You can't think about it, man. It'll only drive you nuts. Which it's clearly doing. We'll find it because we're tenacious. I have faith. Dee or Rina call with any news?"

"You mean, did Rina call?"

"I meant what I asked. I know they decided to sleuth a little harder into the company for us and I was wondering if they found anything. I do feel better knowing there's a guard at the office now. Young was quick to agree on hiring a private security company during working hours until we figure this shit out. And we know the guard, so that's a plus. Three dead employees doesn't look good for Young or the company. Just wondering if they called."

"Because I would deviously hold that information until we were in the car driving down the road simply to annoy you. You're hoping Rina called. You wanted her to call you, didn't ya?" Zeke said with a boisterous laugh as he slapped his leg.

"I'm going to let you get your digs in just because you're feeling a bit down. Enjoy it while it lasts," Ben said, glancing out the window. His attention didn't last long looking at the scenery. "Does that mean she called you?"

Zeke busted out laughing, slapping the wheel with gusto. "Thanks, Ben. I think I truly feel better. I needed that."

"Where did the damn pencil fall so I can throw it at you?" Ben muttered as he leaned down to search the floor when he didn't see it on his lap.

"Settle down, Romeo. She didn't call and neither did Dee."

Ben sat back up. "Why didn't you just say that? Why you gotta keep a man in misery?" Ben shook his head. "So you think she'll call me or you, if something pops up?"

"Well, I don't know. Zoe told me I have this honey-smooth voice. She might call me to hear it. I have that affect on women."

"Ouch," Zeke yelled as the pencil hit him in the neck. "Really? Not much space here, man. You could've poked my eye out."

"You have a woman. Don't go honey-smooth talking other women. Especially Rina," Ben said with a scowl.

"Finally, the man admits to liking her."

"That wasn't an admission of shit. I don't like her. I was

only wondering who she would call. I helped her last time, so I thought she'd be more comfortable talking to me, that's all," Ben said, glancing out the window again.

"De-nial...don't confuse that word with the river," Zeke said with a laugh.

"I'm gonna throw you in a damn river is what I'm gonna do. If you're feeling better, then this conversation is over. Have we made it to the bank yet?" Ben asked.

"Not quite. Five more minutes of me getting to rub it in that you like her," Zeke said with a snicker.

"Where'd that pencil go?" Ben said, looking around Zeke's lap. "Better drive faster before I find it."

"You and your pencil don't scare me."

"It should. I'll really show you my pencil."

"I don't want to see your pencil. Don't say shit like that to me."

"What sort of pencil are you talking about?" Ben asked, laughing.

"What pencil are you?" Zeke countered.

"This one, you idiot," Ben said as he found the pencil near the gearshift and threw it at Zeke one more time.

"Knock it off. Quit throwing it and talking about your pencil," Zeke said, grabbing the pencil from his lap where it landed after hitting him in the arm. He threw it down on the floor by his feet. "About Rina, do you think—"

"Ouch." Zeke rubbed his head after Ben smacked him.

"Quit talking about Rina. I don't like her. I don't need a pencil to attack you."

"Let me repeat. De-nial. You wouldn't be smacking me if you didn't. It's so obvious. Just admit it like a man," Zeke said, rubbing his head one more time. "And you're welcome."

"Do I even wanna know why?"

"For meeting Zoe, falling in love, and finding a woman who has a friend you happen to like," Zeke said with a wide grin.

"Oh, look. We made it to the bank. I can't wait."

Zeke pulled into a parking space, laughing softly. Before he could put the car in park, Ben opened his door and stepped outside. That made Zeke laugh even harder.

"Quit laughing. Act like a professional," Ben muttered as they made their way to the bank entrance.

"Thanks for making me feel better, buddy. That's what friends are for," Zeke said, clapping him on the back.

"I'm reconsidering being your friend." Ben opened the door.

"No, you're not." Zeke almost bumped into Ben as he stopped abruptly.

He turned his head around slowly with a devious grin. "Am, too."

"Can I help you, gentlemen?" a brunette wearing a bright-green blouse and a black pencil skirt asked as she walked up to them with a friendly, yet concerned expression on her face.

"Yes. I'm Detective Chance, and this is my partner, Detective Stoyer. We need to speak with the bank manager, please," Zeke said, holding up his badge.

"Yes, of course. Wait right here," she said, walking away quickly to the left.

"You're scaring the bank people. Ask her out already," Zeke whispered to Ben.

"I'm not afraid to find a pencil while standing in this bank," Ben whispered back, smiling at a bank teller, who gave them a curious glance.

"Detectives, how may I help you? I'm Jerry Smith, the bank manager," Jerry said, holding out his hand to shake.

Zeke shook it. "Detective Chance, sir. My partner, Detective Stoyer." Zeke gestured at Ben. "We have a key, evidence in a murder investigation that we think might belong to a lockbox. We were wondering if it's from this bank. We think it belongs to George Murphy. Perhaps you can check and see if he has an account here."

"Well, without a warrant, I can't divulge a customer's privacy if this Mr. Murphy has a lockbox here. I can look at the key and tell you if it's one of ours," Jerry said, stone-faced.

"You can't do a little tap, tap, tap on the keyboard to tell us if Mr. Murphy has an account here," Zeke said as nicely as possible.

"No, detective. Show me a warrant," Jerry replied with no change in his expression.

"Well, can you tell us if you recognize this key?" Ben said, taking it out of his pocket, holding it up.

Jerry leaned closer to Ben, eyeing the key through the plastic evidence bag.

"May I?" Jerry asked, holding his hand out.

"Yeah, but don't take it out of the bag," Zeke said.

Jerry glanced at him. "Of course not, detective." He grabbed the bag from Ben, looking at it closely, turning it around a few times. "It's not one of ours."

"Are you sure, Mr. Smith?" Ben asked, accepting the bag back.

"I'm positive, detective. It's not ours."

"And you can't go check to make sure if Mr. Murphy has an account here," Zeke said, trying one more time.

"Show me a warrant. That key doesn't belong to us. Obviously, because it doesn't take a genius, you want to know what's in his lockbox. That key isn't ours. Therefore, does it matter if he has an account here," Jerry said sardonically.

"Gee golly whiz, I guess not," Zeke said, irritated.

"What my partner means is, are you sure?" Ben stated.

"I'm one hundred percent positive. Every bank, at least, I assume so, has an identifying mark on their lockbox keys. It's to differentiate them from each bank and stop people from duplicating them. It's been known to happen. Our identifying mark isn't on that key, thus making it not our key," Jerry said matter-of-factly.

"Hmm. You'd be the first to point that out. No other bank told us that. Can you tell what bank this key is from?" Zeke asked.

"To be honest, it doesn't look like a bank key," Jerry said, taking it back from Ben. He didn't give Jerry an option as he held it practically under his nose until he grabbed it.

Jerry inspected it one more time, sighing in annoyance. Zeke and Ben shared a look, wondering why this case couldn't go right for once.

"I don't think it's from any bank. It has a number...52...I think it says on the one side. No bank would just have a number like that. It might not be, but this funny curved shape on the bottom, the way the key is designed. It sort of looks like a key from the lockers at the gym I go to," Jerry said, handing the key back.

"What gym?" Zeke asked. They needed something to work with if this key didn't belong to a lockbox.

"The new one off Division Street, Pump It Up Fitness. I've only been a member for about a month, but I've rented a locker a few times and it looks like that key," Jerry said.

"Well, we thank you for your time, Mr. Smith. And the helpful information," Ben said with a smile.

"Of course, detective. Have a nice day," Jerry said, finally offering a smile.

Zeke walked away first, holding the door open for Ben, and walked out behind him.

"A gym key. Carly never mentioned Murphy was a member of a gym, did she?" Zeke asked as he opened the car door and slid into his seat.

"No, but she fails to mention a lot of stuff. Cheaters...never can trust 'em," Ben said, pulling his phone out of his pocket. "Let's see where Pump It Up Fitness is located. Division is a long street."

"I think they put it by the mall. Sounds kinda familiar, and I remember thinking it was an eyesore," Zeke said, taking a left out of the parking lot.

"An eyesore? Sore on your eyes 'cause you don't see yourself ever working out," Ben said, chuckling.

"I don't need to work out at a gym. I'm fit as a fiddle, and Zoe has never complained," Zeke said proudly, sucking in his stomach a little.

"Women don't tell their man that. They'll simply think it and eventually deny you sex 'cause it's gross to be with you," Ben said, barely lifting his eyes from his phone as he searched the internet. "And I saw you suck it in."

"Did not," Zeke said, letting it out, glancing at his stomach. Flat. That's all he saw. Perfectly fine. "Are you trying to mess with me again? Zoe's going to deny me sex now because she thinks my body's getting disgusting. No more shit about the pregnancy?"

"Oh, she'll deny you for that reason, too."

"Maybe that's why you're afraid to ask Rina out. You don't work out that much either," Zeke countered.

"I don't want to ask her out because I don't like her like that," Ben said as he shifted in his seat.

"Ha! I saw you. You thought about it. You tried to suck it in," Zeke said, pointing an accusing finger at him.

"Ignoring you," Ben said in a singsong voice. "Damn, you're right. I hate it when you're right sometimes. It's across from the mall."

"Oh, I love it when I'm right. Which is, oh, all the time," Zeke said, as he took a right.

Ben rolled his eyes and put his phone away. His silence made Zeke laugh.

They made it to the gym fifteen minutes later. Zeke parked the car. Ben took his time to exit the vehicle this time. "You're right. It's kind of an eyesore."

"Told ya."

"Did you have to throw that in?"

"Yep," Zeke said with a smirk as he held open the door for Ben. "After you."

Ben rolled his eyes again, walked inside, and went straight to the counter. A young kid, about eighteen, sat looking at a magazine, his feet propped up on the counter. When he saw them approach, he dropped his feet, stood up, and pasted a smile on his face.

"Welcome to Pump It Up Fitness where we will pump. You. Up. How can I help you?"

Zeke walked up by Ben with a slightly alarmed expression on his face. "Not here for any pumping up. Can we speak to the manager on duty?"

"Yeah, sure, bro. Let me go get Dickens. He'll change your mind. He always does," the kid said with an arrogant attitude, yet smiling as he did. He walked away, arms swinging wide, as if he were trying to show his muscles when there were clearly none to be found.

"We will pump you up. Catchy phrase. Makes me wanna join," Ben said sarcastically.

Zeke laughed. "You should."

"What does that mean?" Ben asked with a frown.

"Means nothing. Or does it mean something?" Zeke said, leaning an arm on the counter.

"Oh, it's on now. You must not have gotten any this morning. You're normally not this squirrely," Ben said, leaning his arm on the counter as well as he glared at Zeke.

"I don't talk about my sex life with you, Ben. Especially concerning Zoe. But since it's on... As a matter of fact, I did get some. A whole lotta some. It's too bad you're not getting any. You could, if you just manned up and asked Rina out," Zeke said, leaning a bit closer.

"Oh, it's like that, is it?" Ben said, shaking his head, his lips pressed into a thin line. "Damn, I got nothing."

"Is that an admission you like Rina?" Zeke asked curiously with a grin.

"Nope. I can't argue when I'm not getting any. You lean any further and I might duel you in an arm wrestling contest."

"Now who's being unprofessional? Arm wrestling. Yeah, I can already hear the captain hollering at us about that one," Zeke said, straightening up when the biggest guy he'd ever seen in his life walked up to them. His neck was the size of his head, his shoulders broad, stuck out in the air, and his arms circled wide of his body, they were so large. Not one inch of the man's body was devoid of muscles. Zeke figured he took pumping it up to the extreme.

"Gentlemen, Tommy here said you were looking to join. I'm Dickens, the manager, the owner, and the best personal trainer you'll ever have," he said, reaching out to shake their hands.

Zeke wanted to step back, suddenly afraid to defy the man. Maybe that's what the kid meant by he would change their minds. He cleared his throat and shook hands with Dickens. "Well, Tommy there, misunderstood. We're not here to join. Detective Chance, and this is my partner, Detective Stoyer. We're investigating a murder and we found a key. We were wondering if it belonged to one of your lockers. Do you mind taking a look at it?"

"Sure. Don't see why you have to make a trip just for that. Doesn't take much to sign up," Dickens said with a friendly smile.

"It's tempting, Dickens, but we'll pass," Ben said, handing the evidence bag to him.

He barely glanced at it. "Yep. That's ours. Who was murdered? I have a great memory of every member. I keep a tight ship. I don't want anyone to waver from their goal."

Zeke cringed inside, picturing this man yelling down his neck to do one more set. He was definitely not joining. "George Murphy, from Mills, Murphy, and Young Accountants."

"Ah, yes, George. Marital problems. Wanted to boost his image a bit and get the wife back in his arms. That is sad to hear. Although, the past few weeks he did fail to show. I called him a few times and he always sounded distracted. He promised me he was working on the exercises I insisted he do at home."

"He was killed about two weeks ago. When's the last time you saw him?" Ben asked.

"I would say about a month ago. He was fine the last time I saw him and then he failed to show up for his next appointment. I called him and he was very distracted. I figured more marital problems occurred and I didn't want to make the guy feel even worse. I insisted he continue his regime at home and make the next appointment," Dickens said, inhaling, making him look more massive than he should to Zeke.

"Did his wife know he joined a gym? We looked through his financial records and never saw your gym pop up," Zeke asked.

"No idea if she knew. I'm going to gander a guess and say no. He seemed pretty determined to win her back. He had suspicions she was cheating, but he didn't care. He said he loved his wife. And about the financial statements, he always paid in cash. I would guess he was trying to keep it from his wife," Dickens said.

"Do you mind if we have a look at the locker with this key?" Ben asked.

"Of course not. When you're done, you two mosey on down to my office and we'll get you signed up lickety split," Dickens said with a smile. "Tommy, show these detectives to the locker room, and I'll get the process started."

"Ah, no thanks...never mind," Zeke muttered as Dickens walked away without hearing a word. He turned to Tommy. "Lead the way."

Tommy nodded with a pumped-up grin and started walking to the left. He hopped down a set of stairs with intense energy, turned left again at the bottom, and pointed to the door at the end of the hallway. "Men's locker room. You don't need me at this point, do ya, bro?"

"Na, bro, we're good," Zeke said, holding his hand out for a fist bump.

Tommy nodded in awe. "Right on, bro. Holla, holla if ya need me." Tommy turned around with zealous energy and rushed up the stairs.

"If I have a boy, please, do not allow him to speak like that if I'm not around," Zeke said, shaking his head in alarm.

"Don't worry, I won't. Let's make this quick. Hell, let's try to sneak out. I do not want to become a member. I can actually see Dickens showing up at my door, saying, "Let's pump it up." It's terrifying to think about," Ben said, shivering from the imagery.

Zeke laughed, agreeing. They would be quick. He opened the locker room door and started searching for locker 52. When he found it, he held his hand out to Ben. "Moment of truth."

Ben gave him the bag. Zeke ripped it open, grabbed the key, and tried putting it in the hole. It wouldn't fit. "What the hell?"

"Are you doing it right?"

"It's a key. How hard can it be?" Zeke said as he tried again.

The bottom portion of the key was curved so funny it refused to go in properly. He fiddled and fiddled until he heard Ben say, "Apparently, very hard. You need some help? You need a real man to do it?"

Zeke gave him a hard glare. "Back it up, Ben, before I pump a little fist into you. I got this." Zeke lifted the key at an angle, then pushed down, finally inserting it into the hole correctly. He turned the key and heard the click. The moment was upon them.

"I think they make it difficult so you have no choice but to stay and continue pumping it up," Ben said with a flash of fear in his eyes. "We need to get outta here."

"You're probably right. Scary-ass place."

Zeke blew a hard breath and opened the door. He started laughing when he saw gym clothes, a pair of sneakers, and toiletries for the showers scattered in the locker. "Wow, and here I thought it would be empty with the flash drive sitting perfectly in the middle. Now we have to touch Murphy's disgusting gym clothes."

Ben pulled a pair of gloves from his pocket. "Hey, try not to let the place rub off on you when you touch his stuff. I'm not joining."

Zeke chuckled as he pulled on a pair of gloves as well. Together, they took turns taking things out and searching through everything.

"I think I got something," Ben said, pulling his hand out of the pocket of the gym shorts. Displayed brightly in his hand was a blue-and-white flash drive.

"I take every mean thing I ever said to you back. I love you, man," Zeke said, taking the flash drive from his hand. "Now to find out what's so damn important to kill three people."

"Ah...you always know the right words to say," Ben said sarcastically. "I'm dying to know what's on that flash drive. I know you are, too."

"We have to escape Alcatraz first. I'll bag and tag the flash drive. You wrap up everything with Dickens," Zeke said with a smile.

"Why do I gotta wrap it up with him? I'll bag and tag the flash drive. Give it back," Ben said, reaching for it.

"Paws off, man. Too late. I'll even let you call Rina, to be fair," Zeke replied, trying to hold in his laughter.

"Why would I call Rina?"

"Well, now that we have the flash drive, I think it's best every damn person in that office knows that we have this thing. I need whoever's trying to harm Zoe to stop. She doesn't have it, and they need to know we have it," Zeke said, squeezing the flash drive tighter.

"Good call. That's a good idea," Ben said a little hesitantly. "But you know, I don't really want to let this person know that Rina spilled the beans. They might think she helped us in locating it. I don't want her in danger either."

"Good point. Okay, we'll tell Young, who can spread the word. That better?" Zeke asked.

"Much better," Ben said, throwing Murphy's stuff back in the locker.

"You can still call Rina," Zeke said, backing up as he spoke.

"Well, there's no point in it now...except she might like an update." He saw Zeke's stupid grin and grimaced. "I'm not calling her. You tell Zoe and she can call her."

Ben threw the last thing in the locker and slammed the door shut. He grabbed the key out of the locker with ease and threw his hand in Zeke's face. "Lead the way."

"How in the hell did you get the key out so easily? It was a bitch to get in," Zeke asked with his jaw hanging down.

"I guess my skills are better than yours. I know how to handle a key." He walked around Zeke when he made no effort to move.

"Is this the same kind of conversation we had with the pencil? You're saying you're better with a key than me?"

Ben groaned. "You try my patience sometimes, Zeke."

"And yet, I'm your best friend."

"I said I was reconsidering it," Ben replied, pulling open the locker room door. He made his way to the stairs and turned the corner. He barely managed to hide the wince from seeing Dickens walk toward them.

"You gents done? I got all the papers ready to be signed," Dickens said with a smile.

Ben opened his mouth to reply when Zeke clapped him on the back and said, "Yeah, Ben here is ready. He likes this woman. A lot. He wants to improve his image to catch her attention. You know what I mean, Dickens."

"Heck, yeah. That's what I'm talking about. Come on, Ben," Dickens said, waving a hand for him to follow.

"I'm gonna kill you very slowly," Ben muttered as Zeke walked by him on the stairs.

ZOE PLOPPED down on the couch, grabbed her blanket that fell to the floor, and tried zoning in on the program on TV. She'd already been to the bathroom a billion times today and it was starting to annoy her. Nine long months of this seemed like pure torture. Why couldn't pregnancy be simple? She even opened the book Dee considered disgusting and immediately agreed with her. Having a baby didn't seem simple, or painless. Why did a woman have to endure so much pain? It wasn't fair.

"Long thoughts over there. Are you doing okay, Zoe?" Richard asked, coming into the living room with two glasses of lemonade.

"I hope one of those isn't for me. I suddenly hate the bathroom. That's all I've been doing today."

Richard lightly laughed, setting the lemonade within reaching distance. "We have to keep that baby hydrated. I've seen the worry on your face all day. I know it's hard not to, but you have to let it all go. You have to be as stress free for the baby as possible. Everything will work out. Zeke's a damn fine detective, as is Ben. My son loves you. That makes his determination a little more fierce."

Zoe smiled at those words. "Yes, I know he does. You raised a good man. He irritates me sometimes, but he has a heart of gold that is slowly melting mine."

"So you're not fully committed to him yet? What about this baby? What's going to happen when the baby comes?" Richard asked.

A slight frightened look appeared on her face. She

pulled the blankets closer to her chest to shield herself. "Are you talking about marriage, Mr. Chance?"

"It's Rick, Richard, Dad, or Hey You, remember?" Richard said with a wink. "Of course, that's what I'm talking about. I even had the talk with my son. He knows you're apprehensive and won't rush you. I've never seen him with a woman like I have with you. He does love you. Remember that."

"It's hard to forget when he says it all the time," Zoe replied a bit wistfully.

"I had my say. I won't bring it up again. I hope I didn't drive you nuts all day," Richard said, taking a sip of his lemonade.

"I don't think that's possible. Next time I'll beat you at Scrabble. I refuse to lose again."

"It's a date. I'll take you in a game of Scrabble anytime," he replied, giving her another wink.

"Should I start something for supper? Do you think he'll be home soon?"

"You can. Although, I can't say when he'll get here. He's determined right now. I would offer to make supper, but I have this feeling you want to get some nervous energy out."

"Smart man. I guess Zeke gets it from you," Zoe said, smiling as she stood up. "Any requests?"

"I'm not picky. I eat what a beautiful woman puts in front of me. I learned that early on with Deborah. She doesn't tolerate nonsense," Richard said with a smile.

"Well, let me see what the kitchen holds," she said, walking out of the living room.

RICHARD KEPT his smile until she left his view. She tried to hide her worry, but it was nearly impossible not to see it. He worried about her. He worried about Zeke. Deep down, he suddenly worried about them making it. What was he missing?

He sat there quietly in the living room, ignoring the TV, pondering those thoughts when he heard the lock turn in the front door. He stood up, slightly on alert, but had a strong feeling no threat would walk through. He nearly made it to the door when it opened.

"Hey, Dad. How's Zoe?" Zeke asked, the tiredness evident in his eyes.

"Making supper. You know, working the worry out. It hasn't disappeared since you left this morning. Not sure it's going to until this case is wrapped up," Richard replied. "Is everything okay between you two? Anything I should know?"

"Yeah, of course. Why do you ask? Did she say something?" Zeke asked, sudden concern on his face like he did something wrong.

"No, she didn't say anything. I feel like I'm missing something in this relationship. Something you're not telling me," Richard said with a stern look. The same look he always delivered when Zeke was growing up and he managed to land himself in a boatload of trouble.

"Zoe and I are fine, Dad. If you're back on the marriage kick, let it rest. I'm not going to rush her. There's nothing you need to know. We're good."

He thought he saw a flicker of guilt pass through Zeke's eyes, wondering what that could possibly mean. But what good would it do to argue with him? Zeke never divulged his secrets when he was a child, and he certainly didn't expect him to as a man.

"What progress have you made? Did the crime lab check out the flash drive yet?" Richard asked, rubbing a hand over his face in frustration. He knew when Zeke lied to him. It really bothered him about what he didn't know.

"Yeah, a bunch of numbers that made no sense. Initials next to them. We think it's some sort of payoff list. You know, like bookies keep or whatever. Now we're trying to figure out if one of them had a gambling problem or something."

"No money was missing from the company?" Richard asked.

"Not that forensics found, or that Dee or Rina could find. They dug deep for us today. Dee's tenacious. She would've found something if there was something. For whatever reason, I think Murphy was involved in something shady and kept it on his computer at work. Perhaps Mills found out about it and that's where the tension started between them. We have to figure out what the numbers and initials mean and hopefully we'll find our killer," Zeke said, mimicking his dad's actions from earlier by rubbing a hand over his face in frustration.

"Sounds dumb to leave that sort of information at work if it's not work involved," Richard said.

"Yeah, well, he wasn't exactly honest with his wife about certain things. He probably didn't want her to know. She's not the best at honesty either. Maybe she would've promised to keep it a secret but would've ended up blabbing anyway. Who knows? This whole damn case is messed up."

"Did you talk to her about it?" Richard asked.

"Not yet, but we talked to Young and he had no clue. He also spread the word throughout the office that the flash drive was found. Zoe should be safe from now on. I'm worried about what to do tomorrow. I don't want to leave her alone," Zeke said with a sigh.

"But you think you can now?"

"I don't know. I don't want to, but we still have a lot to do. I need to find this bastard."

"I'll be fine. I need the rest anyway and some time to read those pregnancy books. It's a lot to read, you know," Zoe said, walking up to him and sliding an arm around his waist.

Zeke smiled, grabbed her tighter, and kissed the top of her head. "Doesn't mean I want to leave you alone."

"But you can. You found the flash drive and the word is out. Why would they need to keep bothering me? I don't have it," Zoe said.

"I worry about you. How much did you worry today?" Zeke asked.

"Not much."

Richard cleared his throat and raised his brows at her.

"Okay, maybe a tiny bit. It can't be helped. I'll worry whether I'm with someone or not. I'll keep the door locked, check it before I answer it, and call you immediately if something goes wrong. Okay?" Zoe said, gazing into his eyes with a sweet smile.

Richard saw the hesitation to agree on Zeke's face. He wanted to interject in the conversation, but didn't think it would be appropriate. Whatever issue between them had nothing to do with the murder cases. That much he knew. Zeke's hesitation was nothing but fear for her safety. And knowing his son, he would never know what he was hiding.

"I don't like it, but I can't argue with it. Carry your cell with you around the house, just in case," Zeke said, planting a tender kiss on her lips. "I love you."

Zoe smiled, then rested her head on his shoulder. "Supper's cooking. I'm glad you're home."

"Whatever it is, it smells delicious. I missed you. Ben was off the hook with his annoyance today."

"What kind of bickering occurred between you two?" Richard asked.

Zoe chuckled. "I'm sure you were just as bad."

"Hey, I was the epitome of innocence," Zeke said with a smirk.

"Somehow I find that hard to believe," Richard said, raising his eyebrows in disbelief.

"What are we having, Zoe? It smells delicious," Zeke said, as he kissed her head.

Zoe smiled, shivering a little. "Chicken, salad, and baked potatoes. That's all I had the energy for."

"It sounds like a feast. I'm sure we'll love it," Richard said.

"Yep. I agree. I love everything about you," Zeke said, squeezing her tightly to his body.

Maybe he didn't have to worry about them. He smiled tenderly as he watched Zeke walk to the kitchen holding Zoe's hand. The energy of happiness that surrounded them was obvious. Perhaps he was creating a problem in his head. This was a new relationship. A delicate one with a baby on the way.

No more worrying.

He followed them into the kitchen, laughing joyfully at Zeke's story about Ben being forced to sign up for a membership at a gym. And he no doubt figured it was forced—by Zeke—in some sort of mischievous way.

Those two. Best partners at the precinct. They'd solve this case soon. He knew it.

12

THE ALARM RANG with piercing annoyance. Zeke didn't want to get up or leave the bed where he held the treasure that kept him going each day. He would've never thought he'd fall this hard or fast for a woman. Knowing the ringing wouldn't stop until he moved, he reluctantly let go of Zoe and silenced the alarm. Because he couldn't help it, he rolled back to his spot and pulled her closer.

"You'll be late if you don't get up. You set the alarm with barely any time to snuggle," Zoe mumbled sleepily.

Zeke nuzzled her neck, kissing lightly. "I don't care. I don't want to get out of bed. Which is why I set the alarm so late. I want as much time with you as I can."

Zoe lazily opened her eyes. "Well, you have no choice. You have some murders to solve. I need some peace of mind. I need you all to myself for a few days. I can't have that when you have these murders to take care of."

Zeke rubbed his hand down her arm in a light caress, slowly making his way to her breast where he cupped it gently. "What do you want to do with me?"

She turned her body toward him and smiled. "Stuff."

"Can you describe what sort of stuff?" Zeke asked as he caressed her nipple, wondering why he didn't just toss her nightgown off. Clothes were such a nasty barrier.

"Ouch. Careful," Zoe exclaimed as she grabbed his chest, only grazing his skin.

"I didn't even pinch. That's never hurt before," Zeke said, leaning down and kissing her breast through her shirt.

"Well, mister, in case you forgot, I'm pregnant. I guess it's a little sensitive."

He frowned slightly, almost a painful expression thwarting his features. "I'm sorry, Zoe. I didn't mean to make it hurt."

"Don't get like that. All moody. I know you didn't. Maybe you should read those pregnancy books with me. They have a wealth of information."

He grinned slightly. "Maybe I should. I hope it's not like that the entire pregnancy. I like playing with your breasts. I might go insane if I can't."

"You poor man. You'll live," Zoe said with a light snicker.

"I might die of starvation." He kissed her deeply, then sighed heavily. His stomach twisted at the thought of walking out the door. "I'll be late if I don't get out of bed."

He slowly rolled, not making it very far. She grabbed his boxers, reached inside, gently grabbing his heat, and stroked once. He stopped moving and sucked in a harsh breath. "Oh, Zoe, honey. What are you doing?"

She smiled, stroking him again. Another harsh breath escaped. "Making you late for work."

He closed his eyes as he let her play. And play she did. Stroking him up and down, circling his tip, squeezing him hard and then lightly. His mind lost all thought. She knew exactly how to touch him, to find the spot that made his body tingle with delight.

He should stop her. He should be the one pleasuring her, especially since he unintentionally hurt her.

Sensitive.

Why did her body have to be overly sensitive? He wanted to touch her in every delectable spot, but not if he had to worry it would hurt.

His hand clenched the bedsheets as he moved his hips with her delicious strokes. He loosened his hand to reach over to stop her so he could finish this sweet torture deep inside her when she increased the pace. Tighter, faster, hotter than he ever imagined. Before he could stop her, his body exploded into fire, the building sensation igniting into flames of pure bliss. His body shook as the waves of pleasure poured out of him with quiet delight.

"Did that feel good?" she whispered into his ear, lightly nibbling before she backed away.

He turned his head to her, still trying to control the ecstasy that ran rampant through his veins. "Oh, I think you know it felt good. I've never gone off like that so fast in my life. Did I tell you I love you this morning yet? Because I love you."

"I'm glad you enjoyed it," she said, rolling out of bed to wash her hands of the pleasure she held.

She was wiping her hands dry on the towel when Zeke walked into the bathroom gloriously naked. He nodded toward the shower. "Join me?"

"I think I already made you late enough." Zoe took her time drying her hands as she perused his body.

"Yeah, but—"

"You can have me tonight. It's okay, Zeke. You're gonna be late," she said with a laugh.

"I don't care," he said with a pout as he stepped inside the shower. "You're sure?"

She nodded. He reluctantly closed the curtain and turned on the water. He found the right temperature and stepped under the spray, letting the warm water relax his body even further. He almost had a hard time standing with the tingling flow of pleasure still running through his body.

He wanted to argue with her more, but didn't.

Sensitive.

He'd never hurt her like that. How could he touch her if it would hurt every time? Maybe that's why she didn't want any sex right now.

No. It couldn't be true.

Damn Ben and his annoying pregnancy advice.

He slapped a hand to the wall as he bent his head in dismay.

No sex. For nine long months.

Had he been right? He groaned at that horrifying possibility. He enjoyed her pleasuring him, but there was no way he'd survive nine months of no sex. He needed her body, too.

He let the water fall over his body, the warmth soothing his rattled nerves. Once he stepped outside the shower, who knew how horrible his nerves would be. Probably ramped up again.

A pair of hands suddenly snaked around his chest, and a soft, delicious body cradled him from behind. A happy sigh floated out.

"You're already late, I guess," Zoe whispered as she moved her hands around his chest.

He turned around, backing her up against the wall and pressed into her. "So you're not denying me sex?"

"What gave you that crazy idea? I don't want you to be late," she said, rubbing a hand over his cheek in a gentle manner. "You were stewing in the shower thinking about that, weren't you?"

"No...maybe...yes." He kissed her, relishing in her sweet taste. "I don't want to hurt you...being sensitive and whatnot."

"My body might be overly sensitive, but I can't go without having you. Nine months is a long time," she said with a laugh. Her smile dimmed a bit. "You love me. You say it all the time."

"Of course I do. I wouldn't say it if I didn't mean it."

"It's not just sex or—"

He brushed a finger over her lips to stop whatever nonsense she was about to say. "Is the sex we have amazing? Damn right it is. But I love you for who you are. Not just your body. Which is delectably sinful, I might add," he said with a devious grin. "There's something between us and it's not just sex. Maybe that's what brought us together, but the moment I laid eyes on you, I knew you were something special. I didn't know you'd be the love of my life, but I know now. I love you. And I always will."

"My track record with men is nothing to brag about. I guess I worry."

"You have enough to worry about. Don't worry over something that needs no worry," he said firmly, pressing his lips in a tight line. Suddenly, his lips curled into a bright smile. "Now, we might as well make me really late for work."

He lifted her up and slowly lowered her down onto his hard erection as she wrapped her legs around him. He sighed in true satisfaction. "I will always gladly be late for work if I get to do this every morning."

He smiled as he rocked her up and down, holding her tightly against the wall, pushing as deep as he could go. She moved her mouth to his neck and kissed him as his thrusts became faster, harder. Her kisses turned into sucking on his neck, the pleasure euphoric. He never had a woman cling to him in such a way, latching on as if she would slip away. Pain and a mixture of pleasure erupted as she bit down lightly.

A painful moan escaped, but he didn't stop until the desire was so intense they came together into a beautiful harmony. Her lips lingered, then faintly moved away from his neck. He waited until she leaned her head against the wall and glanced into his bright-blue eyes.

"You bit me, you little minx," he said with a laugh.

Her eyes went wide with shock. "I did?"

His laugh got louder. "Yeah, you did. I kinda liked it."

She shyly chuckled, clearly embarrassed. She glanced at his neck, her lips turning into a stunned expression. "You might not when you look in the mirror."

His brows pinched in contemplation. "Why?"

"Do you own any turtlenecks?"

"Turtlenecks? Hell, no. Do I look like a turtleneck kind of guy?"

"Maybe you should own some. I might've left a small mark," she said softly, giving him a hopeful smile.

"You left a small mark like a...a hickey?" he asked, surprised.

"Umm...yeah."

He stared at her stone-faced, then curled his mouth into a grin. "Sort of like branding me. You can mark me up all you want. Like I said, I kinda liked it."

She laughed, pressing her face back into his neck and lightly kissing where she bruised him. "You should get ready for work now. How about you let me down and I'll make you some coffee?"

He sighed, still hating the thought of leaving her. "If I have to."

He gently lowered her down, making sure she was steady on her feet, considering he felt a little unstable himself. Those pleasuring tingles still coursed through his body, making him think he'd feel them all day. That's how great he felt. "You wanna shower with me?"

She patted him on the ass, quickly pulled the curtain open, and stepped outside of the shower before he could argue. "I think not. You'll never make it to work if I do."

She left without waiting for a response. He closed the curtain, quickly showered, and hopped out to tackle shaving as fast as he could. He wiped the mirror clear of the steam and almost grimaced in horror at the large hickey displayed on his neck. There was absolutely no way he could hide that.

Damn it. He did need a turtleneck.

Although, he didn't care how many hickeys she gave him. He would never wear a turtleneck.

His grimace turned into a smirk. The way she held onto him, gripping him tighter, and then biting down. The elation that coursed through him could never be forgotten. He would do it again. In fact, he couldn't wait for her to do it again. The only thing that had him grimacing once more was the thought of Ben's witty remarks he would dish out. He'd endure anything for his Zoe.

He quickly shaved, brushed his teeth, got dressed, and met Zoe in the kitchen ten minutes later. She held out a coffee mug for him and a bagel slathered with cream cheese.

"Your to-go breakfast is ready."

"You're spoiling me this morning. I might expect it every morning from now on," he said, grabbing the coffee, bagel, and a quick kiss.

"I find that I enjoy spoiling you," she said, ushering him to the front door. "I hate that you're going to be late and that you have that mark on your neck. Now everyone will know why you're late." She opened the door.

"I like my love mark. You should place a few more in other unseen areas," he said with a wink.

She giggled. "You'd like that, huh?"

"Oh, how I'm gonna spoil you tonight," he said, grabbing another kiss. He gave her another sweet, honey-filled wink and walked out the door.

He set his coffee mug on top of the car and opened the door. Grabbing for the mug, he turned to her with a smile and climbed in. He set his mug and bagel down on the center console and leaned his head out of the car, holding onto the door. "I love you, Zoe."

A slow smile crept on her face as she started to close the door. "I love you, Zeke."

The door firmly closed after those words slipped from her lips. He lost his grip on the car door and slightly fell down. Heart pounding like a jackhammer, he straightened back into his seat.

Shit.

Did she just say what he thought she said? She loved him. She finally said it back—and shied away from him by closing the door.

It didn't matter. She said it and he'd hear it again tonight. He'd love her body up and down until she uttered those beautiful words again.

He grabbed the door handle with a shaky hand and tried to close it. He didn't get a good swing and had to open and close it one more time before he heard it close securely.

Complete numbness. Combined with pleasure. How in the hell would he make it through the day?

Surprised that he got the key in the ignition the first time, his hands still shook like crazy as he backed out of the driveway. He couldn't believe she threw that bomb-shell on him. Especially as he was climbing into his car to leave.

He couldn't even enjoy the way the words flowed through him. Or how he couldn't show his love for her back. He could if he really wanted to be late. He could shut this car off, walk back inside, and take her again. But it would take all day to get over hearing her say that. He'd never make it to work if he walked back inside.

He took a deep breath as he drove past the house. His nerves were so wired from their lovemaking and her sweet rendering of love, he had no idea how he made it to work. A deep wince escaped as he parked next to Ben's car.

He knew he was in for it. There was no escaping Ben's wrath or shrewd teasing. He quickly hopped out of his car and made his way inside, dreading each step. Oh, how he wished he could be with Zoe.

He slid into his chair, barely glancing at Ben.

"You're late."

"Yeah, sorry about that. Traffic was a bitch," Zeke replied smoothly, grabbing a report from the side of his desk.

"You're edgy. Your hand shook grabbing that folder. You won't make eye contact. And you're late. You're never late."

Zeke met Ben's leveled gaze and gave him a grin. "Don't dig. You won't find anything."

Ben cocked his head to the side. "Is that a hickey on your neck?"

Zeke almost raised his hand to cover it, but stopped himself. "It's nothing."

"You're late. You have a hickey. But why is your hand shaking? I can figure the first two questions out myself," Ben said, biting the bottom of his lip as if he were trying to figure out the puzzle sitting in front of him.

"Where are we at on this case?" Zeke said, opening the folder.

"What happened this morning besides hot sex?" Ben asked.

"Oh, man, you got that right. It was hot sex. I almost didn't make it into work," Zeke said with a grin.

"You admit to the hot sex, something you never do, especially since you hate talking about your sex life concerning Zoe. So what else could've happened?" Ben said, tapping his fingers on the desk.

"She loves me," Zeke blurted.

Ben stared at him, confusion written all over. "Clearly she showed you some lovin' this morning."

"No, Ben. She said it." Zeke blew out a huge breath. "She watched me walk to my car and I said I love you as I got into the car. Right before she closed the door she knocks me off my damn feet and says it back. Then closes the door on my face."

Ben still looked confused. "Isn't this a good thing?"

"Yeah, of course. But now I gotta wait all day to hear it again and worry that it was nothing but a fluke. A momentary lapse of judgment on her part. Why'd she wait until I was in my car? I was already running late. If I would've walked back inside that house, I wouldn't be sitting at this desk right now. My ass would've never even made it into work."

"Love's scary, Zeke. You've never been in love, and look how you're freaking out about stuff all the time. She's probably freaking out herself. She said it. That means she means it. Don't over analyze it, man. You'll drive yourself nuts today. I need you clear and levelheaded. If you can't be, you might as well go back home and talk to her about it."

"I expected teasing and a whole lotta jesting from you. Why are you being all...serious?"

"Because I can see how freaked out you are. I can see how much you love her, and I want everything to work out. Once you calm down and realize she meant what she said, then I will tease you up and down the block about that damn hickey on your neck," Ben said, pointing at it with a laugh. "It's huge. What the hell did you two do this morning?"

"I am not going into detail about what we did. It was a surprise to me as well. But it felt so good," Zeke said, closing his eyes as he remembered the exhilarating feeling when she nibbled on his neck.

He opened his eyes to stare at the pencil that bounced off his chest. "Did you seriously throw a pencil at me?"

"I don't wanna see you relive a sex moment that you had with Zoe. Do it somewhere else," Ben said dryly.

"Fine. And thank you. I needed that pencil thrown at me. I feel more grounded. You're right. She was probably nervous to say it, but now she said it. Everything is good. We're good. I feel a little better she won't leave me. You know, I still have that insane fear she'll leave me," Zeke said, picking up the pencil to twirl it.

"Well, get over it. She's not gonna leave you. You two were made for each other. Sometimes it's so obvious it makes me sick."

Ben picked up a stack of papers and handed it to Zeke. "See those numbers and initials I highlighted. Notice anything?"

Zeke looked at the papers, flipping through them with a critical eye. "They all have the same initials. MTJ. Different set of numbers, though."

"Well, you were late today—"

Zeke looked up at the clock, interrupting Ben. "By twenty minutes. That's it. I wasn't that late."

"Late enough. I was looking over Mark's financial statements and he was withdrawing a lot of cash the last few months. Sometimes a hundred to a couple hundred every so many days. Kinda odd, don't you think?" Ben said.

"MTJ? What's his middle name?"

"Thomas. Mark Thomas Johnson." Ben handed Zeke the financial statements as well. "If you look at the withdrawal dates, they match up perfectly with the numbers on that list."

Zeke looked at the financial statements, then back at the list they printed off from the flash drive. MTJ followed by random numbers directly across from the initials, usually 100/1, displayed frequently throughout the list. His withdrawals from his bank always matched the list.

"If you refer back to the autopsy report, he had high levels of cocaine in his system. He had a drug problem. That list isn't from a bookie dealing with gambling. It's a drug dealer's buy list. They mark down their buyer's initials, how much they paid, and how many grams of cocaine given," Ben said, leaning back in his chair.

"You figured all this out within the twenty minutes I was absent?"

"Well, I am smarter than you," Ben said with a smirk. "But no, I couldn't sleep. I came in an hour early. I don't have a warm body to keep me company while I sleep like you do."

"You could if you—"

"I love interrupting you. I'm gonna interrupt you every time I think something ridiculous and crazy is gonna leave your mouth," Ben said with an aggravated smile.

Zeke raised his brows and smiled. "Okay, buddy. Whatever you say."

"Murphy doesn't strike me as the type to be into drugs, especially dealing them. Neither Murphy nor Mills had any drugs in their system when they died. How in the hell do they fit into all of this?" Zeke said, looking at the list of initials a little more closely.

"If you're looking for their initials, I didn't see them. But feel free to double check. I have no idea how they tie into it. Mark had a drug problem. Somehow, Murphy got his hands on the drug dealer's buy list. Maybe they knew Mark had a problem. Did they try blackmailing him?" Ben said with a shrug.

"None of the financial statements that we looked over suggested they were receiving any amounts of money that couldn't be explained. Unless they created an account under another name. Murphy didn't seem to trust his wife much, and they were having marital problems. If he was involved with the drug business somehow, he probably would've made up a pseudo name."

"Do you want to head over to narcotics and see if they have any insight? Maybe they'll recognize the list or even some of the initials," Ben suggested.

"Worth a try." Zeke pushed back his chair to stand up when Tray walked up to his desk. He barely managed to stifle a groan. "If you're here to ask for help again, the answer is no."

Tray laughed. "Na, man. I'm not. We finally had luck last night. Bagged one of Ray-Ray's prostitutes. Problem is...she ain't talking. Tight-lipped as can be. We need her to talk because another dead John popped up a few days ago. These drugs are getting serious. You got a way with interrogation, Zeke. Just wondering if you'd take a crack at her."

"Funny you mention drugs. The murders we've been working on popped up drugs as well," Zeke said, handing

Tray the list of initials and numbers. "Does this list mean anything to you? We can place our last victim, Mark Johnson, on that list. Buying cocaine every couple of days."

"Looking at it at a glance, no. But I wonder if I could match the names of the dead Johns that I have. They just might. Ray-Ray's name is the only name I've been hearing when it comes to cocaine. You can even ask the guys in narcotics. He's involved. I guarantee it," Tray said, handing the papers back. "Do you want to interview his girl now?"

Zeke stood up. "I think I do."

"You go do that and I'll go with Tray to match up more names on that list. Whadya say, Tray?" Ben asked, standing up as well.

"Hell, yes. I feel like I'm finally getting closer to the end," Tray replied, a smile forming.

"Me, too. I need these cases closed," Zeke said, thinking of Zoe, her beautiful face, her sweet words she uttered this morning, and her fierceness. He needed this to end with a passion. He wanted her all to himself until he was fully sated with pleasure. Which would probably be never. He'd never get enough of her.

13

ZOE POURED herself another glass of lemonade and walked to the living room where her blanket and book waited patiently for her. She hadn't done much all day but sit, read, relax, and worry.

Why in the world did she blurt out what she had? The moment he woke up and pulled her closer, she had wanted to utter those words. But nerves took over, making her scared. She tried to show him as best she could, but they always connected physically. She knew he wouldn't understand with her simple touch.

Then he looked at her with his gorgeous blue eyes shining with love as he got into his car and said those three little words he always said. The words spilled from her lips before she could stop herself. She continued the motion of closing the door, the shock overwhelming her to do anything else. Now she wasn't even sure she had said it loud enough. She expected him to walk back into the house to hear it again. But he didn't.

She tried not to over analyze it, but it was difficult when she had nothing else to occupy her mind. Rina had called her briefly to see how she was feeling and to tell her how things were at the office. Whispers were running rampant about the mysterious flash drive and what it held, but no one admitted to knowing anything. She didn't have the nerve to tell her she simply didn't care about the flash drive.

She had almost blurted to Rina what she said to Zeke but clamped her mouth shut at the last minute. It wasn't a big deal. She didn't know why she was making it into a big deal. He loved her and she loved him. End of story.

She had made lunch, barely tasting the salad. Over the last few days, she found it was one of the few meals she could keep down. None of her favorite foods tasted delicious anymore. She needed more nutrition than salad, but she was afraid to try anything else. She hated throwing up.

After lunch, she had napped, snuggling closer to Zeke's side. She had imagined him lying there and it instantly conjured images of the morning, making her miss him like crazy. She had napped a long time, practically the entire afternoon, just to feel closer to him. She tortured herself by doing that. It was the longest day of her life.

She put her book down, since she couldn't register any of the words anyway. Frazzled nerves. Worry. Numbness. All over saying three little words.

She glanced at the TV to the clock below.

Ugh. Still another hour or so until Zeke would be home. He had called earlier to check on her. He said he'd be home around suppertime and if something popped up that he wouldn't be, he'd call again. He never once mentioned what she had said that morning, making her believe he hadn't heard her.

Her eyes zoned out as she stared at the clock. How would she ever manage to utter those words again? Why was it still terrifying to say those three little words? It shouldn't be. They rolled off his tongue with ease. Why couldn't she do the same thing?

She picked her book back up. Forget about it. Quit worrying. That's what she needed to do.

She threw the book back down again. She should make supper. What was she thinking? He would be home soon.

She stood up, adjusting her sweats. She needed to go to her house and grab more clothes. When Zeke originally packed her suitcase, he threw in only a few lounging clothes, the majority of them work outfits. She wouldn't be going to work for at least a week, and she'd never survive with what she had.

She wrapped her cardigan closer to her body. Her phone smacked against her side. A small smile formed as she thought about dressing in his clothes. She imagined he would get excited seeing that. Although, it didn't take much to excite him.

Excitement or not, she needed more of her own clothes. Perhaps if he called on his way home, she'd mention getting more items from her house.

Except he didn't have a house key.

Okay. They could go together after they had supper.

Moving back into her house didn't seem necessary anymore. It didn't seem plausible that he would want her to go back to her house. She had already walked into the spare room several times imagining how they would decorate it for the baby.

She pulled open the pantry to find something for supper when the doorbell went off. The pantry door slid closed with a soft click as she slowly moved toward the front door. Worry lingered in each step.

Who could be at the door?

Maybe it was the mailperson. Or a solicitor.

Breathing a soft sigh, she figured it had to be Richard or someone Zeke knew.

With measured movements, she glanced in the peephole. An eyebrow lifted as surprise swept through her.

Tori Black, the office manager, stood on the other side.

Figures. She couldn't take a week off work without some issue popping up. She unlocked the door and pulled it open. "Ms. Black, how are you?"

"Fine, Zoe. May I come in a moment? I need to speak with you about an issue I have," Ms. Black said with a friendly smile.

Zoe couldn't remember a time when Ms. Black didn't have a smile on her face. Friendly, gregarious, easy-going. They were very blessed to have such a great office manager.

Unless you screwed up. Watch out. Ms. Black could produce talons without blinking. Not that Zoe ever did anything wrong to see that happen. And with the smile she had now, she figured it wasn't a mistake she did. Most likely, Ms. Black needed her to fix someone else's mistake.

Zoe held the door open farther. "I hope it's nothing too serious. I know I've taken a bit of time off work lately and it hasn't exactly been the best around the office. If you need me to come in earlier, I could probably work it out."

Ms. Black stepped inside and took a few steps into the living room as Zoe closed the door. "Yeah, the office has been in such an upheaval. It's horrible about Mr. Mills and Mr. Murphy. And now Mark."

Zoe sighed at those words. Upheaval did not begin to describe the horror of the past few weeks.

Ms. Black glanced around the room, then swiveled her eyes back to Zoe with a sweet smile. "I didn't know you were pregnant."

Zoe glanced at the couch where the pregnancy book lay.

"Umm...yeah. I was waiting to tell everyone. Can you keep it a secret for a while? You know, they say it's best to wait until the three-month mark to tell people. So many things can go wrong."

Ms. Black's lips went from sweet to frightening as her hand dipped into her purse. "Yeah, so many things can go wrong."

Zoe backed up a step when the gun emerged. "I don't understand."

"Of course not. You've been too busy screwing me over. Screwing that detective. Getting pregnant, obviously," Ms. Black said, waving the gun. "Move. Get away from the door. Have a seat."

Ms. Black stepped back from the couch, the gun never wavering in her hand as Zoe walked past her to sit. She tried not to let her nerves show, but it was impossible to walk without a slight tremble.

With the powers of stealth, she slid her hand into her pocket, unlocking her phone as best she could. She never thought she'd have to do it, but she did. She had set her phone to Zeke's number in case she had to dial him quickly. Moving her hand around as if she could see perfectly, she hoped she hit the right buttons. There was no way of knowing unless she looked down, which she couldn't do.

"Relax. Sit back. Hands out of your pockets," Ms. Black said with the patience of a teacher watching twenty kids all alone as they rushed around like bats out of hell. "Why didn't you just hand over the flash drive when we asked for it?"

"Oh, God. You killed them. You killed Mr. Mills and Mr. Murphy. Did you kill Mark, too?" Zoe said as she leaned forward, a hand clinging to her chest in horror.

Why didn't she realize that when the gun emerged? That should've been the first clue that Ms. Black killed them.

"Zoe, Zoe, Zoe. Are you that slow? Are you really that dumb? Answer my question."

She sank back into the couch. No amount of distance would remove the sight of the gun in her hands. She'd probably see it in her dreams. If she made it out of here alive.

Why did she open the door?

Ms. Black should've never known where to find her. How had she known she was at Zeke's?

"I'm losing my patience. Why didn't you hand over the damn flash drive?"

"I never had it to begin with. How did you know I was here?" Zoe said as confidently as she could.

"I know a lot of things. It's my job to know things. And I know you had the flash drive. I saw Mills that night in the office. I followed him. I saw him stop at your desk. When I went to his house later that night, he didn't have the flash drive. He gave it to you," Ms. Black said, moving to her right, standing more in front of Zoe instead of at an angle.

"He was just as surprised when I pulled a gun out. He didn't know he was going to die until I pulled this out." She reached inside of her purse, pulled out a silencer, and proceeded to twist it onto the end of the gun as horror filled Zoe's eyes.

"When he didn't have it, I thought maybe he gave it to Murphy before I got to the house. So I paid Murphy a visit. He begged for his life right up until I pulled the trigger. He claimed he didn't have it either. I thought it might raise a few flags with both of them dead, so I disposed of his body. Obviously, not well enough. But neither of those idiots had it, which means Mills handed it to you when he stopped at your desk. I didn't think so at the time. Otherwise, I would've taken care of you then. You made me look like a fool."

"Please, Tori, I never had it. He never gave it to me. Murphy hid it in his locker at the gym. That's where the police found it. I don't even know what's on it. I swear. Please."

"The police..." Ms. Black cackled, reminding Zoe of a wicked witch.

This was a nightmare. The witch was waiting to feast on her.

"The same police you're sleeping with. Yeah, I don't believe you. You had it all along, and instead of handing it over to us, you handed it to the police. I don't like being made a fool of. Mark made me look like one, too. If Mark would've gotten it back from you without being an idiot, I wouldn't have had to kill him."

She waved the gun around. Zoe tried to sink farther into the couch. Of course, that wouldn't make a difference. Ms. Black had already killed three people. Clearly, she knew what the hell she was doing.

Suddenly, Zoe wanted to cry. She wouldn't be walking out of this living room alive.

"It's his fault to begin with. He got greedy. He stole that information, thinking he could extort more drugs and money from us. The idiot let Murphy find it. Then Mills found out about it, and suddenly it spiraled into a damn cluster."

"Please...think of my baby. I swear I never knew anything. I didn't. I still don't. I never heard a word. I swear," Zoe said, knowing her words weren't even reaching Ms. Black's ears.

"Ray-Ray told me to get the flash drive back, and quite frankly, you pissed me off. If you would've handed it over from the beginning, I wouldn't have to do this. Now the whole operation may crumble and it's your fault."

"Ray-Ray?" Zoe asked, then shook her head in a terrified frenzy. "Never mind. I know nothing. I'll say—"

"Nothing. I know."

Zoe clutched her chest as a deep pain radiated throughout her body.

"Silencers. They're the best. You never even saw it coming."

Zoe dropped sideways onto the couch. The pain slowly numbed as darkness wanted to take over. Her eyes fluttered close. She could survive this.

How?

She tried to blink. To move. To do anything to save herself, but nothing but the deep abyss called her name.

Play dead. Just play dead. Don't actually die. Perhaps Ms. Black would leave and then she could call Zeke.

Zeke.

Yeah, she just needed to call him.

A loud noise, a popping of some sort echoed throughout. She told herself to open her eyes, to check it out, to see if Ms. Black left.

Instead, she dropped her hand from her chest, losing all feeling. She felt her hand rising again and a heavy aching pain in her chest. So painful, she moaned out loud and then let the darkness take over.

"Oh, God, Zoe. Stay with me. Do you hear me? Talk to me, honey," Zeke said as he pushed hard into her wound. "Ben, we need an ambulance. Where's the ambulance?"

"It's coming, man. It's coming," Ben said as he stood up after checking for a pulse from Ms. Black. "She's dead."

"I want to shoot her all over again." Zeke pressed harder onto Zoe's wound.

A second sooner. One second, and they could've prevented Zoe from getting shot.

Her blood slowly seeped out between his fingers. That one second would cost him the love of his life. She was losing way too much blood.

"Please, honey, please don't leave me. I'm here now. I got your call. I'm so sorry it took so long. Yell at me, fight with me about it. Please, say something," he said, lowering his head and kissing her forehead. "Zoe."

Before Zeke could say any more, or plead for her to speak one word, in walked the paramedics. They swiftly moved him out of the way and started working on her, laying her onto the stretcher.

They started to wheel the stretcher out when Zeke hollered at them, "She's pregnant. She has to be all right. You have to help her."

They didn't stop, but as they walked out, one turned to Zeke. "We'll do everything we can."

"Come on, Zeke. I'll drive. We'll be no more than a foot away," Ben said, laying a hand on his shoulder and ushered him out of the house.

Tray met them in the driveway. Ben gestured with his head to the house. "Ms. Black, the office manager, is dead inside. Zoe's shot. We need to go to the hospital."

"I got it covered here. We found Ray-Ray. He's in custody as we speak," Tray replied and started toward the house with long purposeful strides.

Ben jumped inside the car and backed out of the driveway as fast as possible. Less than thirty seconds later, he caught up with the ambulance that had gotten a huge start on them.

"She'll be fine. She's a fighter. I mean, you guys fight all the time and she wins most of the fights. Right? That makes her a fighter."

"Your attempt at making the situation better is useless. She was shot in the chest. Most of her blood is on my hands," Zeke said, barely above a whisper.

"I'm just saying, think positive. That's all."

"I broke that prostitute. She revealed all of Ray-Ray's operations. How he made a list of all his drug deals, how Mark stole it, how Tori Black was Ray-Ray's girlfriend. Why couldn't I have broken her sooner? Why couldn't I have done it before she ever stepped foot at my door? Why weren't we a few seconds quicker? Why?" Zeke said with a strangled sob. "I can't lose her, Ben. I just can't."

"You won't. I told you. She's a fighter."

14

"WHAT DO you think about this one? This one is freaking adorable," Dee said, holding up a blue dress, a flower adorning the top right corner and a big bow in the center.

"I like that one. But they're all adorable, Dee," Rina said from across the room where she sat in a chair next to the bed.

Zeke glanced over at her, eyed the dress, then brought his attention back to Zoe, who lay quietly in the hospital bed. "I think...you'd better not dress my little girl up in slinky, provocative dresses when she turns eighteen. I'll destroy you, Dee."

"So you don't like this dress?" Dee asked.

He looked back over at her. A tender smile lingered on her face. A very rare occurrence. He'd never seen Dee look like that. "It's cute. We're having a boy, though."

He glanced at Rina when he heard a small chuckle leave her lips. He shrugged, giving her a weak grin.

"There you go. Argue with me. It's better than your annoying grim face and sulkiness. You're driving me nuts." Dee tossed the dress onto a chair near the window.

"No one said you have to be here, Dee. I can't say you've been the best companion to have here either. You're driving me nuts right back," Zeke said as he squeezed Zoe's hand and started to rub the top of it.

"Not be here? I've known her longer than you, buddy boy. My beautiful face will be the first thing she sees when she wakes up. Count your blessings I haven't kicked you out of that chair yet," Dee said, raising an eyebrow at him that she might do it right then.

"As much as I'd love to see you try, I'm going to pass. I don't have the energy to spar with you right now. I didn't have the energy when Ben was here a while ago, and I won't down the road either. The only energy I have is to hold Zoe's hand until she wakes up. Go grab a coffee or something. You are seriously driving me nuts," Zeke said without sympathy.

He jerked slightly when a hand landed on his shoulder.

"I know you love her. It wasn't your fault she got hurt. Nobody's perfect. I guess you're not a douche or an SOB anymore. But I'm still gonna drive you nuts as much as possible. Because I enjoy it," Dee said with a smirk.

She walked around the bed and stopped by Rina, who gave her a tender smile. "Let's grab a cup of coffee and let lover boy have a moment by himself. Do you want a coffee, too, Zeke? I'll give you a moment's peace for about...uhh...five minutes. That good with you?"

Despite how he felt, he gave her a grin. "Make it ten and I'll let you talk my ear off without complaint. I don't need any coffee."

Dee winked at him and started for the door. Rina stood up and laid a gentle hand on the bed near Zoe's leg.

"She'll be fine. She'll wake up soon. Dee's right. Try not to be so hard on yourself. You did everything you could,"

Rina said, glancing over at him as she pulled her hand away and wrapped her arms around her stomach.

"I should've been there. She never should've gotten hurt like this." Zeke brushed a hand over Zoe's forehead and back across her hair, reveling in her beauty. She may lay silent, sick, and slightly pale, but her beauty would never waver.

Rina leaned over the bed. "I'll try to make it fifteen minutes for you."

"You're a good friend, Rina," he said appreciatively, his lip curling into a warm smile.

He watched Rina leave the room, Dee's loud voice trailing down the hallway. He pulled Zoe's hand to his mouth, giving her a small kiss, and lowered it back to the bed. He thought about letting her hand go and leaning back in the chair for a rest, but he couldn't. He wanted her to know he was here, to feel his strength and absorb some of that. He wanted their little monster to feel his strength.

He couldn't describe the feeling the moment the doctor had come out and said she would be fine. That they removed the bullet and put her back together like it was as simple as sewing a hole in a shirt. One more inch to the left and the bullet would've torn her heart apart. To his extreme relief, and her luck, it hit more near her shoulder. She had been lucky, according to the doctor.

Once the shock cleared that she would survive, he mumbled, just barely, if the baby had survived the injuries. To his shock again, the baby was okay. Both would be fine after they had plenty of rest, the doctor had uttered in response.

He stared at her hand as he traced small circles. The blue dress caught the corner of his eye, and he gave it a full-on glance. He hoped for a boy, deep down, always wanting a boy first. He'd love a little girl as well. She certainly wouldn't have a shortage of dresses if Dee had anything to say about it.

He smiled. The dress was pretty cute.

"I love your smile. Although it was your eyes that held me mesmerized when I first saw you."

Zeke whipped his head to Zoe's beautiful face, the relief plain in his eyes. He lifted her hand to his mouth, giving her another kiss. "I believe the first thing that mesmerized me was your legs and the way you sat perched on that stool. I was dying to feel them from your dainty toes right up to your creamy breasts."

"I don't believe my legs go all the way to my chest," Zoe said with a chuckle.

"I think you know what I mean. Everything about you screamed at me. I had to refrain from adjusting myself in a crowded bar. You had me hard so fast. You always do." He squeezed her hand lightly, then reached over with his other hand to caress her cheek. "Don't ever scare me like that again. I don't ever want to see you lying in a hospital bed again. Until you have the baby, of course. That's the only time it's okay. Do you understand me?"

She reached up, covering his hand that held her cheek. "The baby's fine?"

"You're both fine. I had my worries when I saw you on that couch, bleeding like you were. Please, Zoe. Don't scare me like that. My heart can't handle it."

"I...I didn't know what to do. I should've never opened the door. I never thought she would be involved," Zoe whispered.

"I know, honey. I know," he said, rubbing her hand gently, soothing her as best he could. He wanted her to know it all. To understand it all. He didn't forget this time he was a cop and shouldn't, not like those other times he'd lost himself in her beauty and did things he shouldn't. No. This time he knew she needed to hear it.

"Mark had a drug problem, so much so that he managed to get his hands on his drug dealer's buyer list. This list contained who bought drugs and how much cocaine they received in return. It only spelled out people's initials, but it could've done damage in the right hands. Murphy saw him looking at it at work and demanded he hand it over. Suddenly, Mills found out and they argued about what to do. Little did Mark know that Ms. Black happened to be involved with Ray-Ray, the drug dealer. Nobody knew that. She figured it out and knew that Murphy had the information."

"How did you figure this all out? Did Ms. Black tell you?"

The distress in her voice tore his heart to shreds. God, the images she was probably experiencing. The last thing he wanted was for her to relive the brutal horror of getting shot. Squeezing her hand, he tried to give her his best comforting smile.

"She's dead. A few seconds sooner and you wouldn't be lying here. Just a few seconds. We busted through that door and I didn't stop to ask her any questions. I will never hesitate to shoot someone who is putting you in danger," Zeke said as the fierceness of his words vibrated throughout the room.

"We interrogated one of Ray-Ray's prostitutes, Merriwell. She spilled most of his operation. If I could've cracked her sooner, Ms. Black would've been arrested before she even knocked on our door. But I didn't."

"Don't beat yourself up, please. I don't like it when your blue eyes shine with sadness." She looked behind him at the flowers, the cards, and the bags of baby clothes all perfectly situated on the ledge of the window. "I see Dee has been here. Only those baby clothes could've come from her."

She sighed, glancing away from him. "I should've never opened the door to Ms. Black. It never occurred to me until a gun was in my face how in the world she knew I was at your house."

"She was a cunning woman, honey. Her criminal record indicated about fifteen years ago, when she was eighteen, she was arrested for prostitution. If I look hard, I bet Ray-Ray was her pimp then. She managed to craft her way from a prostitute into his arms as his girlfriend and right-hand...woman, so to speak. She got a respectable job, working with respectable businessmen. Ray-Ray isn't dumb. He utilizes every weapon he has to create a booming business. They were rolling in the dough with prostitution earnings, but that obviously wasn't enough for him. He had to get into drugs as well." Zeke sighed, holding her hand tightly as he spoke. He could feel her tremble, but he also saw the yearning in her eyes for the information.

"Merriwell told us all about her. She could be even more ruthless than Ray-Ray sometimes. She had a sharp eye and took notice of everything. Maybe she found out you were at my house simply by hearing you, Dee, and Rina talk about it at work. Or maybe she figured it out some other way. It doesn't matter. You're safe. We arrested Ray-Ray as well. He cried lawyer immediately, of course. And who? None other than Mark's dad, Lawrence Johnson, best criminal defense attorney in town."

Zoe's hand shook harder at that, but Zeke squeezed her hand. He didn't want her to worry about anything ever again.

"Listen, Zoe, honey. You have nothing to worry about. Remember? I got the dad who is the best judge in town. Not to mention, if I really dig, and I'm going to, I think Lawrence is on that list we found. LPJ is listed several times. His full name happens to be Lawrence Peter Johnson. Coincidence...not a fan of that. We'll link him to the list and then I'll bury them both. The best part, because I want you to be free of this mess, is I don't need you to tell me anything she said to you. I got your call. I heard everything. My heart nearly fell out when I heard you and I could hear Ms. Black in the background. I love you, Zoe."

She yanked her hand that he held to his chest, making him lean closer to her. "I love you, Zeke. I said that already. Did you hear me then?"

He smiled tenderly. "I did. I nearly fell out of the car. I wanted to walk back in the house and hear it again. I wanted to have my wicked way with you in every damn spot of the house. But I left for work. Because if I would've stepped inside the house, I would've never made it to work. Maybe I should've walked back inside. Maybe you wouldn't be—"

"I love you."

"I love when you interrupt me to say that," he said, leaning even closer to kiss her lips. "But do you have to interrupt me?"

"Well, I love interrupting you. You get this annoyed look that gets me all hot," Zoe said with a sly grin. "It's over. There's no going back to what-ifs or maybes. So if you keep it up, I'll just keep interrupting you."

"Are you arguing with me?" he asked with a glimmer in his eyes.

"Do you wanna argue?" she asked with the same glimmer shining back.

"Maybe. It gets me all hot when you're fired up. I don't think I can climb on this bed and have my way with you here."

"Why not?" she asked with a smile that held a slight come-hither look to it.

"Do I need to lock the door? Don't tempt me, Zoe. I will not hesitate to take you. Especially when you talk to me that way," he said, almost moaning in anticipation.

"I think you should lock the door. When you look at me like that... What can I say? Those eyes just undress me with little effort," she said, biting her lip as she tried to hide her smile.

He stood up without thought, bringing his lips to hers before she could utter any more tempting words. He dug his tongue in, meeting her tongue with ease. She playfully matched his fervor, giving him a small moan that had him leaning farther onto the bed. As he kissed her deeply, he tried his hardest to resist the temptation to join her on the bed. He could take her right here, right now, the pleasure zinging to life. He knew he couldn't. The reason had nothing to do with being in a hospital. He couldn't care less where they were. He would indulge in pure bliss with her anytime, anywhere.

The one and only thing to stop him was the mere fact she had been shot. She needed to heal. He didn't think she would admit it, but she had to be hurting. She just woke up from an injury that could have killed her. That simple thought had him slowing down the kiss. He mingled his tongue one more time with hers, lightly bit her bottom lip, and pulled away. "Don't tempt me, Zoe. You need to rest."

He sat back down, clasping hands with her again. "I love you. So much that I might give in to you. Please, don't make me."

"I love you. So much that I'll listen," she said, closing her eyes.

"Or it could be that you finally feel you need to heal.

Rest, honey. I won't be leaving your side until you're released from this hospital."

"Promise?" she asked as her eyes opened once more.

The love poured from her eyes as he held her gaze. He knew from the beginning he wouldn't have to worry about her falling in love with him. Even if she wouldn't have been able to say the words, he would've still seen it in her eyes.

"I promise. Close your eyes. Rest up. You're in for it when we get home. I have some serious, serious plans for you."

"What kind of plans? How serious?" she whispered as she closed her eyes one more time. "I think I'd like to hear a taste of what's in store."

"Well, the first thing I'm going to do...it sort of involves a red dress that fits like a glove to every delicious curve on your body. I will slide my hands down your back, slowly, making sure I feel every part of you. Then, once I reach the end of the dress, I'm going to caress my hands up underneath to your soft, luscious ass and squeeze. 'Cause that's one of my favorite parts. And then, with slow, hungry steps, I will back you up against the wall and love you as you wear that delicious red dress," he said with a gentleness in each word so he didn't fire up his own body too much by the erotic images he'd just painted.

"Mmm...I can taste that already," she whispered, her eyes still closed.

He leaned closer, holding her hand tightly. "Next, after we're both quivering with pleasure, I'm going to carry you to the bed, still deep inside you, and gently lay you down. I'm going to peel that dress off, taking my sweet time, kissing every inch of your body as I do. When it's fully off, I'm going to ravish each breast, taking my time to show you how much I truly love them. And when you're begging me to stop and to move my hips just a little, I'm going to start real slow.

When I can't take it anymore, I'll lean down for you to take over and give me one of your love marks. Because they make me feel so good. That, my sweet Zoe, is a little taste of what's in store for you."

He stared at her beautiful face. Her eyes were closed. Her lips in a tender smile. But she had fallen asleep.

He wondered how much she had heard. He'd have no problem describing that again. Speaking those enchanting words had him wanting her with a passion. No matter how much he tried to control himself, he had foolishly made himself ache even more for her. He scooted on the chair trying to adjust himself when he heard a snicker across the room. He glanced over to the doorway to see Ben standing there.

"I only heard the ending. But damn, man. You had me hot and bothered by those words. I'm always a blubbering idiot when it comes to women. Can you teach me?" Ben said, walking farther into the room and standing at the foot of the bed.

"If I didn't want to let go of her hand, I'd kick your ass right now," Zeke said, rolling his eyes. "But hey, if you want some pointers to help you with Rina, then I'm game."

Ben jerked as he shuffled on his feet. "Forget I said anything. How is she doing? Has she woken up yet? Your sweet words penetrating through?"

"As a matter of fact, she heard the first part. She woke up a little bit ago. It was heaven to hear her speak. She's tired, though. I almost lost her, Ben. I still can't get over it."

"It'll take some time. But you have each other to get through it." Ben walked over to the chair next to Zeke, picked up the blue dress, and sat down. "Dee's been here I see."

"Yeah, I begged her to get a coffee. Her and Rina walked

out a while ago. She was driving me nuts. She's a good friend."

"Yeah, you're in for it when your little girl gets older. Auntie Dee is...whew...let's not think about it actually," Ben said, setting the dress on the ledge behind him.

"I agree. I don't want to think about it. We can think of ways of how you'll ask out Rina. I'm down with that," Zeke said, glancing at him with a smirk.

"Glad to see you're feeling better. Your moodiness was starting to annoy me and worry me. But if I gotta walk around this hospital to find a pencil, I will."

"You and your pencil," Zeke said, shaking his head.

"Is that what men do? Talk about their dicks? That's disgusting," Dee said, walking up to the bed, surprising them both, as they hadn't heard the door open.

"We were talking about pencils. Real ones...that you write with," Ben said.

"Ooookay. If you say so," Dee said.

"She woke up. She's resting again. Where's Rina?" Zeke said, noticing the way Dee looked at Zoe.

"What? And you made me go get a stinking coffee. Now that pisses me off. Rina's father called. She's still talking to him," Dee said with a piercing stare.

"Are you going to hurt me? Is that what that look means? I didn't know," Zeke said with a shrug. "Don't make Ben find a pencil. He likes to throw them at people. He'll defend me. Right, Ben?"

"Yeah, right after I throw the pencil at you first," Ben said, nodding in agreement.

"Why at him first?" Dee asked.

"Oh, you know—"

"Because he's a douche. You said so many times," Ben interrupted him.

"He's managed to reduce himself from that status. Unless I see something that warrants it to rise up a level," Dee said with a pointed glare at Zeke.

"You do scare me. I won't lie," Zeke said.

Ben laughed, hitting his knee in amusement. Zeke looked at him, grinning like an idiot. "That one over there is now on your douche list."

Ben glowered at him as Dee turned her head slowly to Ben. "And why is that?" she asked, her tone implying that they better quit messing with her.

"Didn't I tell you, Dee? I thought I did," Zoe said, opening her eyes slowly.

Dee looked at Zoe, a smile replacing her death glare she had been giving Ben. "Girl, don't scare us like that. I hate seeing you like this."

"I already got that speech. It won't happen again," Zoe said, gently grasping Zeke's hand tighter.

"Good. Now, what did you tell me that I forgot?" Dee asked as she gave Ben a slide glare. That simple look, barely touching him, made him squirm in his seat.

"He likes Rina," Zoe said with a gentle smile.

"Oh, does he now? He finally admitted to liking her," Dee said, now giving him her full attention.

"I never admitted to shit. Rina's nice, she's beautiful, she has this voice that...I don't like her like that," Ben said, shaking his head in denial.

"Hmm... You have now entered the list of douches. I won't tolerate just anyone dating her," Dee said firmly.

"I don't want to date her," Ben exclaimed.

"She's nice, she's beautiful, she has this voice that... What was all that?" Zeke asked.

"De-nial. Don't confuse it with the river," Zoe said with a laugh.

"Did Zeke tell you that? Did you two have a laugh about that at home together? I hate you all," Ben said.

"No. I just came up with that. Why?" Zoe asked, confused.

Zeke kissed her hand as he leaned closer to her luscious lips. "Because I said the same exact thing to him before. Only the woman who speaks to my heart would think to say the same beautiful words."

Zoe tenderly smiled. "You did, huh?" She pulled him closer, so close he stood a breath away from her lips. "Can you speak a little more about that delicious red dress? Tell me again how you're going to peel it off me."

"I can whisper those words to you all day. Even better for you. Wait until I actually peel it off. Slowly, carefully, deliciously, with a kiss each inch it rises," he whispered against her lips.

"Take me home, Zeke. I want to wear that dress."

"Soon. Oh, my beautiful Zoe, soon. For now, listen to the words I whisper in your ear. I love that red dress. But mostly, I just love peeling it off you," he said, right before he kissed her senseless.

EPILOGUE

7 1/2 MONTHS LATER

THE PAIN ZOE saw in Zeke's face was almost laughable. He didn't know the meaning of pain. She didn't think any man could know the true meaning of pain. But she would help him experience a little bit with her. It was only fair. She squeezed his hand harder as she watched him grit his teeth and try to smile to hide his pain.

"Zoe, honey. You're doing great. One more push. That's it, honey."

Glaring at him out of the corner of her eye, she decided she wasn't squeezing his hand hard enough. "If you say that one more time, I'm going to break your hand." She tried to crush his hand even tighter to get her point across.

He wasn't able to hide his wince that time, but he smiled anyway. "I'm only trying to give you encouragement."

"Encouragement? Encouragement?" she exclaimed as another contraction made its way to the surface. "Why isn't the damn epidural doing its job? I can still feel the pain."

"You're doing great, Zoe. You dilated very fast. It's almost

over. Just like your husband said, only one more push. I see the baby's head. Push for me," the doctor said in a soothing manner.

Zoe clamped her hand harder around Zeke's as she gave another push. She dilated fast. Who cared? She'd been pushing for a good two hours with every single person in the room stating, "One more push." Lies. Why didn't the baby emerge already? She couldn't take it anymore.

"You did good. The baby's head is right there. We need another good push when the next contraction comes," the doctor said.

Zoe lay her head back a moment to gather some patience and blew out a few breaths, trying to calm down. It didn't work. "We're never having sex again. Never. I can't take this pain."

Zeke's eyes got wide, making him squeeze her hand back this time. "Don't say things like that, Zoe. Please. Go ahead and break my hand. Do what you gotta do to get through this. But don't you ever deny me like that."

Zoe glanced at him, almost smiling, until another contraction made its way. She sat up, pushing, gripping his hand with as much fierceness as her body would allow. Zeke held on tight, gritting his teeth again at the pain, but said nothing. She could already picture Zeke's muttering about the annoying way Ben had been right. He had told her all about the teasing Ben dished out, including the dreaded words he never wanted to hear from her.

No sex again.

She couldn't help but laugh, catching Zeke's confused look. She had said it on purpose to help him experience some pain. Breaking his hand would never work. Denying sex would have to do the job.

Of course, he didn't have to know she was only kidding

right now. She would never be able to deny him sex. She enjoyed it way too much. He could pleasure her body in so many different ways it would be impossible to lose that.

"Yes, there you go, Zoe. I think one more push will do it. I truly mean it this time," the doctor said softly.

"You're doing great, honey. Just think of our beautiful baby boy and how great it will be to hold him in your arms finally," Zeke said, kissing her hand.

"A boy? We're having a girl," she said with a smirk.

"Are you arguing with me, Zoe?" he asked as a sly grin formed.

"Do you want to argue? I can argue."

"You know what happens when we argue. And sadly, I have to wait until you fully heal until I can show you what happens when we argue," Zeke said, kissing her hand again.

The doctor chuckled at their happy squabbling. "You wouldn't need to argue if you found out what the sex of the baby was a few months ago."

"Oh, but we enjoy arguing, Doc. If you know what I mean," Zeke said with a sexy grin and wink to go with it.

"Oh, I think I know, Mr. Chance. Here we go, Zoe. One good push," the doctor said in a soothing manner.

Zeke kissed her hand as she prepared herself for the oncoming pain. She gripped his hand firmly and pushed for the last time. As soon as she felt it was all over, she crashed her head to the pillow and turned to see Zeke's beautiful blue eyes shining at her.

"You did it, honey. You did great," he said, kissing her hand several times before glancing at the doctor. "What's the verdict, Doc?"

"Come over here and cut the umbilical cord and see for yourself," the doctor said, a soft smile on her face.

Zeke reluctantly let go of Zoe's hand, stood up with wobbly feet, and stepped near the doctor. With shaky hands, he cut the cord and then turned his eyes to Zoe. "We made a beautiful baby girl, Zoe. She looks just like you, honey. So beautiful."

A nurse whisked the baby away to clean her, check her vitals, and weigh her while the doctor finished her job with Zoe. Zeke sat back down by Zoe, grabbing her hand again as she lay there with tired eyes. "You okay, honey?"

"I'm fine, Zeke. I'm tired, happy, and dying to hold her." A few minutes later, the nurse walked over with the beautiful miracle they created.

"She's beautiful. Do you have a name picked out yet?" the nurse asked, gently handing her the baby.

"Zabrina," Zoe whispered, as she stared at the beauty in her arms.

"Lovely name." The nurse stepped away as Zeke leaned closer to Zoe.

"A baby girl. Gosh, won't Dee be ecstatic," Zoe said with a smile.

A small cringe emerged on Zeke's face. "If she even tries to bring any more dresses over I'm gonna...gonna...do something."

"Something, huh? She scares you," Zoe said with a laugh.

"Damn right she scares me. But I'll put my foot down on any red dresses."

He stood up and leaned down to kiss her, glancing at their little girl. She saw the love shining out of his crystal-blue eyes and wanted to bottle that look for eternity.

In a delicate whisper, barely touching her lips, he said, "Only you are allowed to wear red dresses. Just one red dress that I love. It always makes me ache for more than one taste of you."

———

DON'T MISS THE NEXT BOOK IN THIS EXCITING ROMANTIC SUSPENSE SERIES! DOOMED LOVE

For Ben & Rina's Story
Doomed Love
A Slaying Love Novel, #2

A protective detective. A woman with dangerous secrets. A killer who will stop at nothing to have his way.

Detective Ben Stoyer has wanted Rina Chastain for far too long, but she keeps turning him down with sweet excuses he's tired of hearing. When the victim in his latest murder case looks exactly like her, Ben's protective instincts kick into overdrive—and this time, he won't take no for an answer.

Rina wants to give in to Ben's relentless charm, but her controlling father has destroyed every relationship she's ever tried to have. Now, with a serial killer targeting women who look like her, she's caught between the detective who's determined to protect her and the man who's determined to control her.

As the body count rises and Ben's investigation intensifies, they'll discover that some dangers come from within, and the deadliest enemy might be the one you trust most.

Get ready for pulse-pounding suspense, sizzling chemistry, and a detective who'll defy everyone—including the woman he loves— to keep her safe.

FOR SAUER & DEE'S STORY
DEADLY CRAZY
A SLAYING LOVE NOVEL, #3

A sassy woman who doesn't believe in love. A shy detective who'll die to protect her. A killer who picked the wrong target.

Dee O'Malley has learned the hard way that men don't stick around, so she's not about to risk her heart on sweet, shy Detective Sauer—even if his kisses make her believe in impossible things. When she's brutally attacked, Dee's determined to find the bastard herself, even if it drives her would-be protector crazy. After all, he's adorable when he's worried.

Detective Sauer might be tongue-tied around most women, but loud, fearless Dee O'Malley turns him into a stammering mess for all the right reasons. The moment she's hurt, his shyness vanishes and his protective instincts take over. But when the attack connects to one of his murder cases, Sauer realizes keeping Dee safe means keeping her close—and his biggest obstacle might be Dee herself.

As the threat escalates and Dee refuses to back down, they'll learn that sometimes the most dangerous thing you can do is fall in love with someone who's willing to die for you.

Get ready for sharp-tongued banter, explosive chemistry, and a shy detective who transforms into a fierce protector when the woman he loves is threatened.

For Stitch & Susan's Story
Evidence of Sin
A Slaying Love Novel, #4

A tattooed bad boy with a record. A police department analyst who should know better. A killer who's making it personal.

One night of scorching passion with straight-laced Susan left tattoo artist Stitch running scared—straight out of her life. But now he's back, and everything about the woman he can't forget terrifies him in the best possible way. She's law enforcement, he's got a record—they'll never work, but when she's in his arms, none of it matters.

Susan knew getting involved with Stitch wouldn't end well, but she can't resist the way he makes her feel alive with just one heated look. She should be focusing on the latest string of brutal murders—no evidence, no leads, no time to waste —but Stitch keeps dragging her into dangerous territory, and she has no idea how close the killer is to making her his final victim.

As the killer's obsession with Susan escalates, Stitch realizes his criminal past might be exactly what she needs to survive. Because sometimes the only way to protect what you love is to embrace the darkness inside.

Get ready for sizzling chemistry, heart-stopping suspense, and a bad boy who'll risk everything—including his freedom—to save the woman who owns his soul.

For Newman & Amelia's Story
Finding Redemption
A Slaying Love Novel, #5

A disgraced ex-detective. A woman who won't give up. A case that could save them both.

Ex-Detective Newman wants to be left alone to wallow in the wreckage of his ruined career and shattered life. When a gorgeous woman with vibrant pink hair and a stubborn streak shows up at his door, he wants nothing to do with her case—or the way she makes him feel like he might be worth saving.

Amelia Benedict doesn't take no for an answer, especially when her younger brother's life hangs in the balance. The police think he ran away, but she knows something terrible has happened. A disgraced ex-cop with nothing left to lose and everything to prove, Newman definitely isn't the right guy for the case—but he's her last hope. But as they dig deeper into her brother's disappearance, they uncover a web of danger that threatens to destroy what's left of Newman's soul and put Amelia in the crosshairs of a killer.

In a race against time to save an innocent boy, Newman must decide if redemption is worth the risk—because this time, failure doesn't just mean losing his last chance at salvation. It means losing the woman who believed in him when no one else would.

Get ready for second-chance redemption, heart-stopping suspense, & a broken hero who'll risk everything to prove he's worth loving.

For Rory & Brooke's story
Obsessed Hope
A Slaying Love Novel, #6

A detective with lethal instincts. A woman who attracts danger. An obsession that could destroy them both.

Detective Rory Walker's latest murder case should be simple —kinky sex gone wrong. Until he meets his prime suspect. Sweet, adorable Brooke Duncan with her terrifying cat and hidden depths is everything he never knew he needed. One look, one touch, and he's a goner. But as he digs deeper into the case, he realizes the dead man had enemies everywhere, and Brooke might be next on someone's list.

Brooke knows she should stay away from the intense detective who looks at her like she's both his salvation and his downfall. But when the investigation takes a deadly turn, Rory becomes her only protection against a killer who's growing more obsessed by the day. Now she must decide whether to trust the man whose obsession matches the killer's intensity...or face a predator alone.

As the case spirals out of control and the killer closes in, Rory will discover that sometimes love and obsession are separated by the thinnest of lines—and crossing it might be the only way to keep them both alive.

Get ready for possessive passion, heart-stopping suspense, and a detective whose protective instincts know no boundaries when the woman he loves is threatened.

ABOUT THE AUTHOR

I'm a *USA Today* Bestselling Author that loves to write contemporary romance and romantic suspense novels, although I am partial to romantic suspense. I even dabble in paranormal. Honestly, I love anything that has to do with romance. As long as there's a happy ending, I'm a happy camper. And insta-love...yes, please! I love baseball (Go Twins!) and creating awesome crafts. I graduated with a Bachelor's Degree in Criminal Justice, working in that field for several years before I became a stay-at-home mom. I have a few more amazing stories in the works. If you would like to learn more about me and my books, head to my website by scanning the QR code. Thanks for reading!

Scan me